MURDER IN THE GROVE

A *Willie Mitchell Banks* Novel

MICHAEL HENRY

Michael Henry

Author Photography: T.G.McCary
Cover Design & Formatting: Laura Shinn Designs
http://laurashinn.yolasite.com

Other books by this author:
Three Bad Years (2010)
At Random (2010)
The Ride Along (with William Henry – 2011)
D.O.G.s: *The Secret History* (with William Henry – 2011)
Atmosphere of Violence (with William Henry – 2012)
The Election (2013)
Finding Ishmael (2014)

For more on the author, visit http://henryandhenrybooks.com

REVIEWS

"An exciting page-turner set in Oxford and the Delta; it's Mike's best novel. I highly recommend."
—Archie Manning, Quarterback, Ole Miss and N.O. Saints

"Michael Henry draws on the drama of the Ole Miss riot in 1962 to create an intriguing new mystery with his latest novel, 'Murder in the Grove'."
—Curtis Wilkie, author of *"Dixie"* and *"The Fall of the House of Zeus"*

"Michael Henry delivers another compelling southern noir story with twists and turns you won't see coming."
—Neil White, author of *"In the Sanctuary of Outcasts"*

DEDICATION

This novel is dedicated to Oxford, Mississippi—
a very cool town.

CHAPTER ONE

I was the elected District Attorney for twenty-four years in Yaloquena County, deep in the heart of the Mississippi Delta. You might think murders would be rare in my rural county, but you would be wrong. I tried murders of passion, contract murders, arson murders, kidnap murders, vehicular murders, overdose murders, domestic murders, race-based murders, religious murders, random murders, and misdemeanor murders. I tried white, black, brown, and yellow murderers.

I won some of these murder trials with eyewitness testimony. I've asked many a man or woman in the witness chair to point to "the person you saw pull the trigger that night," and the witness always points to the defendant. The twelve jurors follow the witness's finger to the defense table. But defense attorneys and psychologists will tell you how unreliable eyewitness testimony is. I'm going to let you in on a secret: they are right. Violent crimes take place in a few seconds. The action is a blur. You're shocked by what you see.

I convicted most of the murderers with circumstantial evidence. You hear defense lawyers on television procedurals tell jurors that the evidence against their client is *only circumstantial,* as if that somehow makes it less reliable than direct evidence. I say this: give me compelling circumstantial evidence in a jury trial. Fingerprints on the murder weapon or at the crime scene, DNA analyses, and ballistics comparisons are all considered *circumstantial* evidence. I'll take this kind of forensic evidence any day over direct evidence.

Circumstantial evidence is objective. Direct evidence, especially eyewitness testimony, is subjective. The event seeps through the witness's emotions, expectations, and prejudices—it becomes altered. When the trial takes place two years after the murder, sometimes the facts are hardly recognizable.

And if the murder occurred many, many years ago, the odds of getting to the truth are almost insurmountable. When the truth is finally revealed after being buried for decades, it may do more harm than good. It may reopen old wounds rather than heal them. Purists say the truth must prevail no matter what. I don't always agree with purists, but when it comes to murder, I believe they are right.

In all my years dealing with homicides as District Attorney, I never pursued a murder that occurred over five decades earlier. Now, that is no longer true. I want to tell you about my part in helping solve a murder that happened fifty-three years ago on the campus of Ole Miss.

I was drinking a Tin Roof draft in the bar at the Country Club of Oxford after a round of golf on a warm afternoon this past April. I had been living in Oxford, Mississippi just over a year. Two foursomes and one threesome made up the Geezer Group that day. I was in the middle group, and the seven of us in the first and second group were sitting around tables talking about the day's round. We couldn't figure the bet until the last group came in.

I left my seat and asked the bartender to draw me another Tin Roof. The Baton Rouge-brewed beer was new to the club, and my current favorite. I was watching the pour when I felt a pat on my shoulder. I turned to see Francis Fratelli, or what was left of him.

"I need a favor, Willie Mitchell."

"Anything for you, François," I said.

"Would you meet me for coffee in the morning at High Point? Just the two of us."

"What time?"

"Earlier the better for me. I don't sleep much these days."

"How 'bout nine?"

"Okay," he said and turned to the bartender. "Put that LSU beer on my tab, but don't tell anyone."

I thanked François and watched him trudge back to his chair. A round of golf wore him out these days, and if François were on your team, you could only expect good play from him on the first nine and half of the back. Once fatigue set in around fourteen, he struggled to make double bogey.

I took my seat and sipped my Tin Roof, glancing over at François at the next table. His head was down and his eyes remained closed even as the final group stormed loudly into the room led by my lifelong friend from Sunshine, Jimmy Gray, whose 312-pound frame bumped chairs and tables on his way to the bar.

"What'd your group have on the front?" Jimmy Gray demanded, shaking his scorecard at me, "and don't tell me your scrawny ass can beat four under."

CHAPTER TWO

I started running at seven, although "running" is a generous description of what I do these days. Four miles at an embarrassingly slow pace, three days a week, and walking for an hour and fifteen minutes three other days. Sundays I rest. After the run I showered, dressed, and worked in my home office until 8:45. Made it to the coffee shop right at nine.

I scanned the tables and chairs. No François. I ordered a freshly brewed dark blend and spoke briefly to the young lady with lovely metallic blue hair at the register, Morgan Pennington, a talented singer/songwriter who played at a couple of local events I attended. I spotted a small table across the room with two empty wooden chairs. I checked out the usual suspects, an eclectic collection of students, professors, businessmen and retirees, some chatting and laughing, others working on laptops or tapping in text messages.

I didn't know a soul.

It was one of the small pleasures of living in a new place. A year ago, Susan and I joined the growing exodus of Delta residents to Oxford. Oxford is considered a small town, but not by my standards. I grew up two hours away in Sunshine, Mississippi in the heart of the Delta, and lived most of my life there. Still have my family home, the farm, and much of my heart in Yaloquena County. I know almost all the people who live there. When I ate at cafes and restaurants in Sunshine, I generally knew everyone in the place. When out in Oxford, I might see one or two people I recognize, even though I spent seven years here in undergraduate and law school over three decades ago.

François dragged his aching body through the North Lamar Street door and slowly glanced around. He held up one finger when he spotted me, then pointed at the serving line. He limped to the end of the line and waited his turn, keeping his head down. When the line progressed he shambled forward without raising his eyes or his feet. I had played many rounds of golf with François in the past year. I knew exertion was painful for him because of aches in every joint in his body. He was always tired.

Non-Hodgkins lymphoma will do that to you.

François weaved through the patrons and took the seat across from me, exhaling loudly. I watched his crooked, arthritic fingers work the lid off his black coffee. He took a sip, looking over the rim of the cup at me.

"You stiff this morning, François?" I asked.

"Every place but one," he said without a smile, taking another sip. "Let me ask you something, Willie Mitchell. When you began playing with our Geezer Group, why did you start calling me François?"

"Wish I could tell you, but the French version just popped in my head. It just rolls off the tongue. You don't like it?"

"I do. Everybody in the group calls me François now. I like it. My first nickname ever."

François looked older than his seventy-two years. He inherited smooth olive skin from his parents, but was currently growing things on his face, neck, ears, and the backs of his hands—moles, wiry gray hairs, liver spots, a wart or two—all things I had to look forward to if I lived long enough. I made a mental note to get Susan to put a close eye on me the next time we're together in the shower—check my nose, ears, eyebrows, neck, back—any place I can't inspect myself. I want to put off looking like an old booger as long as possible.

That morning at High Point, François had the unkempt appearance common to widowers—unshaven, hair too long, bad clothes. He wore a faded ancient sweatshirt celebrating the upcoming third annual Double Decker Arts Festival, which by my incredibly fast and always accurate calculation occurred seventeen years earlier.

"You playing today?" I asked.

"If I'm alive I'll be there. You?"

"Nah. Twice a week is plenty for me. I'll play Saturday. How are your treatments going?"

"I'm in between now, so I'm feeling all right."

He started to say something else, but hesitated. I could tell he was trying to come up with just the right words.

"Thing is, Willie Mitchell, I don't know how much longer I have. It's been seven years since my diagnosis, and what I read and what the doctor tells me is the older I get, the more likely it is that the disease will progress to where treatments don't do that much good any more. And they make me feel so bad." He paused. "I've just about gotten to the point of throwing in the towel. Not there yet, but it's getting to be a tougher struggle every week."

"I feel for you, François. Everyone in the group admires you for sticking it out. We all know it's painful for you to play sometimes."

"All the time. But thank God for the group. I'd have given up a long time ago if it weren't for golf. You guys are really all I have left."

I watched François sip his coffee. He wasn't being maudlin, just matter-of-fact. He told me one day when I rode in his cart that his parents were Sicilians, descended from the immigrants brought in to the Mississippi Delta via the port of New Orleans in the late 19th century to work on the river levees and pick cotton. His parents, Giorgio and Louisa Fratelli, lived their entire lives in Clarksdale, running a small neighborhood grocery store and raising their two sons, Russell and Francis, in their frame home behind the store. Neither of François' parents went to college, but Giorgio was determined that his boys would. He sent them both to Ole Miss, The University of Mississippi in Oxford, demanding that they make good grades and behave themselves. That day in the golf cart François told me his big brother Russell died in 1962, at the beginning of his senior year. He did not tell me how, and I didn't ask.

"You never knew Maria, my wife. Her people were farmers from central Italy, came over in the early nineteen-hundreds. They looked down on Sicilians," he said with a low chuckle. "And in those days in Clarksdale, the sixties, plenty of Protestant parents would not let their daughters date Italians. Or Catholics. I was both, so it narrowed down the number of girls I could ask out. Maria's folks were Umbrian and didn't think much of me at first. I went with them to the Catholic Church on Sundays until I gradually won them over. I guess they forgave me for being Sicilian. Then I went to work on Maria. It wasn't easy, but I finally convinced her to marry me. She was a good wife. We never had kids. She had some sort of problem that caused her to miscarry a half-dozen times. They finally took out her ovaries."

"It was just you and your brother growing up?"

"That's right. And my big brother Russell was the apple of my mother's eye. Handsome, good athlete, charming—he had it all. He was an altar boy all through school, and was a devout Catholic until the day he died. He was a regular at the Catholic Student Center while he went to college up here.

"When he died the spark went out of Mama's eyes. She was never the same. She still worked with Papa in the store every day, never missed Mass on Sunday or holy days of obligation. As far as I know Mama and Papa never travelled outside of Coahoma County except to the hospital in Memphis when my mother got diagnosed. She died in 1992. Then Papa in 1996. Maria five years ago."

"You never told me how your brother died."

François put down his coffee and looked at me, his eyes finally alive.

"That's what I want to talk to you about."

Chapter Three

"I was beginning my freshman year in the fall of 1962. I came up to Oxford early with Russell before school started. I was going to stay with him on a couch in his apartment until the freshman dormitory opened. Russell had a good job at the drug store on the Square, where Square Books is now, and made enough money to have a car. That was a big deal in those days. It was his senior year and he was going to schedule his classes both semesters so he could put in a forty-hour week at the drug store."

"Sounds like he was a go-getter."

"He was. Not a lazy bone in his body. A natural when it came to business. I guess Russell learned it growing up in my parent's grocery store, working every day after school and Saturdays. He was a business and finance major and planned on starting his own business as soon as he finished school. He used to ride me around Oxford and point out different stores, telling me how they made money or why he didn't think they were well-managed."

"Car wreck?" I asked.

"No. That's how a lot of kids died around Oxford those days—lots of them on the highway coming back from drinking beer in wet counties. Russell drank beer on occasion, but never had more than one or two. He said it made him sluggish, slowed him down. And he wanted to be hitting on all cylinders all the time. You know about the Meredith riots that year?"

"A little. At the time it happened I was about seven years old so I wasn't paying much attention to things like that. My father didn't talk a lot. I guess when I came to school up here I began to learn about it, how people wanted to block James Meredith from integrating Ole Miss. I know the Mississippi National Guard was called out, and the governor at that time, Ross Barnett, tried to block his admission. There was a standoff and demonstrations."

"It was more than that. It was a full-blown war zone, with Molotov cocktails and bullets flying everywhere. Two thousand people or more in front of the Lyceum building among the trees. It was in the part of the Grove west of the Confederate Monument that some people call the Circle now. Back then, they just called it the Grove. Guns were everywhere; lots of guns. Those who didn't have guns threw bricks. They were building a new science building right there at the Grove, providing plenty of bricks and construction stuff all over the place for the people to throw."

I shook my head. "So Russell was one of the people killed in the riot?"

"Not officially. The riot was a Sunday night. Tuesday, after the dust settled, they put out the death total. By some miracle, only two people were killed, a reporter for a French newspaper, and a young fellow from Abbeville just over for a look-see. Russell was killed that night but wasn't found until the following Thursday morning. The officials were trying to put a lid on the publicity about the riot and all, and the local cops and Highway Patrol convinced the FBI that Russell's murder didn't have anything to do with the riot. It didn't take much. Today they'd call it a cover up. The Justice Department was in cahoots with everyone else on suppressing how serious the riot was. Bobby Kennedy was Attorney General. He and JFK were right in the middle of the whole thing, negotiating with Governor Barnett, sending in federal troops. They didn't want to lose votes over it."

"You think Russell was hit by a stray bullet?"

"I guess it's possible, but not likely, unless that bullet had eyes. He was shot at the base of his skull, right at the top of his cervical spine." François pointed to a spot on the back of his neck. "The coroner said the bullet had an upward trajectory and stayed in his head. And they found him a good ways from the Lyceum, where all the shooting was."

"Hold that thought," I said and left the table to get another half-cup.

While I waited in line I turned to glance at François. His elbow was on the table supporting his upturned palm, which cradled his chin and face. I walked back to the table with my coffee. François's eyes were closed. I sat down quietly. He took a deep breath, leaned back in his chair, and looked at me.

"Sorry about your brother," I said.

"I'm long past sorrow. I grieved for Russell for a long time. Went back to Clarksdale to help in the store while my mother mourned. The college administrators were nice to me, accommodating my schedule any way they could. Took me five-and-a-half years but I eventually graduated with an Ole Miss degree. It was kind of a waste, though, 'cause I went right back to working in the store in Clarksdale. But it had a bright side. I started dating Maria and married her."

"When did you move up here?"

"1993. Right after Mama died. I had been buying rental property on the side in Clarksdale since 1970, doing the work myself to fix them up. Eventually I had about thirty properties. Just about ran out of places to buy in Clarksdale."

"You know the mayor up there now?"

"Bill Luckett? Hardest working man in the Delta. Doing his best to save the town."

"I've played golf with him a few times. He'd be good if he ever played. When did you start buying properties up here?"

"I started scouting for properties in Oxford in the late eighties. Things were really cheap back then. I wasn't all that smart, but I figured if I concentrated on places around the campus, I'd always have tenants. I used Charles Walker to do the legal work. He was the best real estate lawyer in town and put me on to probably a third of the houses I ended up buying.

"Starting out, I picked up a half-dozen small houses and did the rehab work myself like I did in Clarksdale. Students were hard on the houses, but their parents always made good on past due rent and they paid for any damage done to the place. No one ever made a fuss about their damage deposit, which I ended up keeping just about every time to make repairs. Maria and I would go up to Oxford on weekends, stay in a little cottage I fixed up for us to have a getaway place. She liked it up here so much, we didn't see any reason to stay in Clarksdale after Mama passed away. Papa closed the store in 1994, and a young, up-and-coming black businessman wanted to buy me out of my rental properties. He had financing from some government program, and we came to terms. Maria and I spent every nickel of that money buying houses and duplexes within walking distance to campus. We plowed our rental income back into the properties. Kept buying until we had a hundred units, mostly single family homes, tiny little houses."

"No telling how much they're worth now," I said, "with all the people moving or retiring to Oxford. Second homes and condos are scarce."

"I'm told the value is somewhere north of twelve million or so all together. That's according to my insurance man."

"Mr. Potato Head?"

"The one and only," François said with a smile. "He insured my first one in the late eighties and I been with him ever since. He makes so much money off me you'd think he'd let me win at golf every once in a while."

"He's ruthless on the course," I said. "Didn't take me long in the Geezer Group to figure out I always wanted Potato Head on my team."

"You and everyone else."

"They ever find out what happened to your brother? How he got killed?"

"No. That's why I need your help."

"To do what, François?"

"Find out who murdered my brother."

Chapter Four

On the way home from the coffee shop I walked into Square Books just as the owner, Richard Howorth, was talking to a young clerk about how he wanted her to rearrange the books in the front window. I waited at a discreet distance until Richard was through, then asked him if he had something I could read about the Meredith riots in 1962. He took me to the Mississippi History shelf and pulled out two books, explaining the difference in the authors' approaches. I asked him if he remembered the riot. He said he was a kid in Memphis when it took place, but visited Ole Miss with his parents a few days after the riot. He saw roadblocks, the scorched places in the Grove where vehicles had been burned, and soldiers and jeeps all around the school. He was about to go into more detail when the clerk at the register announced that the publisher from New York Richard had been trying to reach was on the line. He mumbled his apologies and bounded up the steps to his office.

I paid for the books and walked the remaining three blocks to our condo, technically Susan's condo. I thumbed through the picture sections of the books on the way. I returned a couple of calls in my home office then started flipping through the books, studying the photographs and reading a passage or two to get a feel. I decided to read William Doyle's *An American Insurrection* first because it was a slimmer volume with fewer footnotes.

Late that afternoon, I stood at my office window to watch the drizzling rain. I had read 150 pages of Doyle's book. For the first time I realized the enormity of what had happened in the Grove in 1962—a violent confrontation between enraged Southerners, U.S. Marshals, and federal troops over the desegregation of the University of Mississippi through the forced enrollment of James Meredith. I was embarrassed that I knew so little about it before moving to Oxford. And several times while reading, I felt guilty about telling François I couldn't help him find out what happened to Russell.

"I don't see why you can't look into it a little," Susan said over dinner that evening. "You've been complaining about not having enough to do."

"But it's impossible. Russell Fratelli died fifty-three years ago."

"They're still doing TV shows investigating who Jack the Ripper was."

"And my trying to solve a murder that happened in 1962 is just about as ridiculous with the same likelihood of success."

"You're going to do what you want to do no matter what I say, but I think you ought to humor Francis a little, talk to some law enforcement people who were around then."

"If they're still alive, which is not likely." I paused. "This pasta is good."

We cleaned the kitchen, and by that I mean I helped Susan clear the table and put a couple of plates in the dishwasher. In my easy chair, I flipped back and forth between *Ancient Aliens* and *Alaska Gold.* I could not get François off my mind.

Susan was right. I hadn't hit a lick at a snake since I won re-election. I had served as the elected District Attorney for Yaloquena County for twenty-four years, got talked into running again, and was about to lose big time to Eleanor Bernstein until some salacious photographs of Eleanor *in flagrante delicto* with her long-time Asian girlfriend got circulated by an enemy of her campaign manager. When I found out the photos had been distributed, I met with Eleanor to assure her I had nothing to do with it, which was the truth, and to offer to go public with an ad telling the voters to disregard the pictures as irrelevant. I offered to assure the voters of Eleanor's ability and integrity. She thanked me but said there was no need. And she was right, the damage was irreversible. The race was over.

I won re-election but was never sworn in. I talked to Governor Jim Bob Bailey and explained that I declined to serve and asked him to appoint my assistant district attorney, Walton Donaldson, to serve as acting District Attorney for Yaloquena County until a special election could be held. I told Jim Bob that the two strongest politicians in the county, Sunshine Mayor Everett Johnson and Sheriff Lee Jones were in full support of Walton, and would help him when the special election was held. Congresswoman Rose Jackson, who represented all the Delta counties, was on board with Walton, too. She generally went along with Sheriff Jones and Mayor Johnson. I reminded Lee as often as I could that the Congresswoman always did anything he asked because she had a powerful, unrequited crush on him.

My political career was over, thank God, and I wasn't sure what I wanted to do. I turned down an offer from Patrick Dunwoody IV, the second-highest ranking official at the Justice Department, to become a roving Assistant U.S. Attorney. Dunwoody said I would handle high-profile federal criminal prosecutions in different districts. I thanked Patrick but declined the offer. I was like the dog having sex with a skunk. I had had about all that fun I wanted. I was tired of prosecuting. I had sent enough people to the penitentiary, tried enough jury trials for now, and played the Avenger of Blood in the cause of too many victims.

White collar criminal defense lawyers in Memphis and Jackson contacted me about associating with them, but I wanted no part of criminal defense work yet, having been on the opposite side for so long. The lawyers in Memphis and Jackson who reached out were honorable men, first rate lawyers, and conducted their criminal defense practices with dignity and integrity. But a lot of sleazeball lawyers worked the criminal defense bar, and their frequent malefactions left a bad taste in my mouth. Truth be told, I did not want to have anything to do with the state or federal criminal justice system, either as a prosecutor or a defense lawyer.

So, I treaded water our first year in Oxford, being fairly worthless, getting under Susan's feet in the condo when we weren't traveling. The place was the right size for us, plenty big enough to accommodate our two sons on the rare occasions when they came home. Our oldest, Jacob

Pinckney "Jake" Banks, worked as an Assistant U.S. Attorney for a couple of years but now worked in a federal quasi-law enforcement capacity. His mother and I did not know exactly what he did or where he did it, except when Jake felt we needed to know. We were aware Jake had undergone special operations training and had successfully completed some dangerous missions. He was now more soldier than lawyer. Our youngest, Scott, worked for Jimmy Gray's good friend, Mississippi Senator Skeeter Sumrall in D.C. Scott had recently married Donna Piersall of South Carolina, who also worked as a staffer in D.C., giving us some hope for a grandchild eventually.

Sitting in my easy chair, I watched Alaskan gold miners work their claims with excavators, bulldozers, and complex mechanical sluice boxes. After my favorite miner team collected a prodigious quantity of gold flakes in their final cleanout, I hit LAST on the remote. I then spent fifteen minutes considering the learned comments of the *Ancient Alien* experts concerning the stone monuments at Puma Punku near Tiwanaku, Bolivia. Even though the commentators ranked high on the goofy scale, I agreed the hundred-ton stones could not have been cut and stacked with such precision by Incan artisans circa 600 A.D. without the aid of extraterrestrial sub-contractors.

I turned off the TV and decided Susan was right. I needed to get off my behind and do something constructive. I thought about calling François, but decided to wait until morning. I was about to go upstairs when the phone rang.

"Judge Williams granted Buddy Richardson a change of venue," Yaloquena District Attorney Walton Donaldson said. "She granted Helmet Head's motion and ordered the trial moved to Oxford."

Chapter Five

I met François at the Beacon on North Lamar for breakfast at seven the next morning. He ordered eggs, grits, bacon and biscuits. My better instincts were telling me to order plain oatmeal, but I managed to fight them off. I ordered the same thing as François. You only go around once.

"I don't mind paying you, Willie Mitchell," he said, "I know your time is valuable."

"My time's not valuable to anyone but me anymore, François. I'm willing to look into your brother's death as long as you understand up front the likelihood of uncovering anything after all these years is very remote."

"I know that."

"And I'm sure there have been a lot of investigators and journalists, both at the time it happened and in recent years, who have looked at the evidence and concluded there wasn't enough to go on."

"You'd think so, wouldn't you? But the truth is, Willie Mitchell, Russell's murder was hushed up. I told you they didn't include him in the death toll of the riot because his body wasn't found for three days. The feds, the State, and the locals wanted to downplay the violence that took place that Sunday and Monday. They wanted to keep the death toll at two, period. And let me tell you something else, they call it the Ole Miss riots, but the people I've talked to over the years tell me ninety-five percent of the people in the Grove that night when the violence happened were outsiders. Almost all the students left when it got dark. The few college kids in the night-time crowd were mostly there out of curiosity."

"That's what I read. Have you ever asked anyone else to look into the case? Including law enforcement?"

"I told the investigators everything I knew the day they found Russell's body, which wasn't much. I stayed on the authorities to do something for a year after the murder, but I was just a little Italian kid from Clarksdale and nobody paid much attention to me. I talked to the Sheriff and the Chief of Police here, even the Chancellor of the University. I didn't get anywhere. And my parents were no help. Mama didn't want to talk about it anymore. All she knew was Russell was dead, and finding out who did it would not bring him back, so she didn't care. Papa was a timid man and didn't want to be around the authorities, much less confront them. He just shrugged his shoulders and went on minding his store. Far as I know, you'll be the first one asking questions about it since 1962."

"There had to have been an autopsy."

"I never saw the coroner's official report, but I talked to him after he examined Russell. He told me it was a bullet to the back of the head that killed him. Said it went in about at his hairline and went up into his brain."

"Is the doctor still alive?"

"No. Died years ago."

"Who is still alive in Oxford who might talk to me about it?"

François thought a moment. He looked better than he had the day before at the coffee shop, but that wasn't saying much.

"You might go see Cissy Summers."

"Who is that?"

"She dated Russell a few times I think. She was upset for a good while about his death. She was a state senator from over around Chickawamba County. Retired back here from Jackson about five years ago."

"You mean Cissy Breedlove? Senator Chad Breedlove's mother? I remember reading about her when she was in the Senate in Jackson, but I never met her back then. In the past year I've been introduced to her at functions around town. She's still a beautiful woman."

"Breedlove. That's right. Summers was her maiden name. After the riot and everything settled down she went on to run for Miss America. I think maybe she got it, but I'm not sure. Chief of Police from back then is dead, and so is the Sheriff. There's a retired U.S. Marshal by the name of Boyland Burr I think is still around. He was one of the four or five hundred Marshals ringing the Lyceum the night all the shooting happened. He might be a good man to talk to. He'll probably know who's still living from the Oxford Police and the State Police. If there's any Sheriff's deputies surviving he'll know who they are."

"Do you have a photograph of your brother from his time here at Ole Miss or any newspaper articles about the riot or his death?"

"I have his 1961-1962 yearbook. The picture was taken in the spring of 1962. It's what he looked like when he died. I don't have any articles. I imagine the *Oxford Eagle* has them all from back then. For weeks the school newspaper, *The Mississippian*, ran a bunch of stories in each issue."

"Where was Russell buried?"

"Clarksdale."

The waitress placed our breakfast plates in front of us and asked if she could get us anything else, calling each of us "hon" in turn. Conversation faded as I concentrated on salting, buttering, and situating the eggs, the biscuits, the bacon, and the fabulous Beacon grits exactly the way I liked to see them on the plate. François did the same. I took a bite of everything in front of me and tried to think of anything else I needed to ask.

"I want you to know something," he said. "I don't have any family, so I'm leaving half of everything I own to Ole Miss, and the other half to the local Catholic Church. I've already got my will done. Signed and notarized at the lawyer's office. I have plenty of money just sitting in savings accounts in the local banks not earning anything. I know you said you're not going to charge me, but I'll be glad to pay you whatever you ask. I'd be happy to. I'm not going to use it for anything."

I noticed tears in his eyes. His hand, deformed and scarred with age and dark spots, began to tremble resting on the table between us.

"I'm doing this for you as a friend," I said patting his hand.

He cleared his throat and began to work on opening the small, white plastic tub containing strawberry jelly. I picked up another strawberry from the bowl, peeled off its cover and gave it to François in exchange for the one he was struggling with.

"I read in the paper this morning that they're moving the Buddy Richardson trial from Sunshine to Oxford," he said.

"That's right. The D.A. Walton Donaldson is my former assistant. He called me yesterday to talk about it. He's got his hands full with that old gangster. Do you know Richardson?"

"Know of him. Well enough to stay away from him."

"Yep," I said. "That's Buddy Richardson."

"I want to tell you something about the riot that Sunday night. I told the police and a deputy sheriff at the time. I don't know if they followed up on it or not. No one ever told me." François said, looking around to make sure no one could hear him. "I was with Russell that evening at his apartment. He wasn't going anywhere near the Lyceum. Fact of business was Russell thought they ought to let Meredith in school. He didn't think they ought to make a big deal about it. He told me that a bunch of times."

"He was right. But why did he end up in the Grove?"

"He got a phone call at the apartment right after dark. I was sitting close to the phone but I couldn't hear who it was and he didn't say. Which was kind of unusual, because he told me just about everything. He picked up the phone and listened and broke into a grin. I can see him clear as day right now. He said, 'that's wonderful,' and listened some more. Then he said 'I'll be there,' and hung up the phone. Whoever it was, whatever they said made him real happy. Just about happier than I'd ever seen him, grinning from ear to ear. He changed out of his work shirt and told me to stay put in the apartment, that it was dangerous that night on the campus for someone who didn't know their way around."

"Where did he go?"

"I don't know; he didn't say. But he didn't take his car. He left walking. I went on to sleep and the next morning when I got up he wasn't there. His bed hadn't been slept in. I looked out the window and his car hadn't moved from the night before. I figured he must have spent the night somewhere else. But he didn't show up for work. They called the apartment from the drug store wanting to know where Russell was, because he never missed work. I started looking for him then, reported him missing to the police, told them about the phone call. Then three days later some student came across his body in that ravine leading down to the Hilgard Cut, you know, the railroad tracks going under the bridge."

"Is his apartment still there?"

"Yes. It's a little frame house over on North Eleventh. I don't know the number but I can show you the place if you want."

François grabbed my ticket from the waitress and said he was paying for my breakfast, no matter what. I left him at the Beacon sitting at a table of men his age by the door, drinking coffee and swapping tales. On the drive back to the condo, I called Walton with an offer to help him, too.

"Anything I can do to assist you up here, Walton, just let me know."

"How about trying it for me?"

"You can handle it. No doubt in my mind. I've told you what I know about Buddy Richardson, but when you get here I'll talk to Jimmy Gray and the three of us'll get together. Jimmy had business dealings with him and may have something to add that might give you some insight."

"I know he's a mean-looking old dude. Some of the jurors we questioned wouldn't look at him. Especially the black prospects."

"Yeah. There's good reason for that."

I ended the call and thought about the rumors that swirled through Yaloquena County years before I became District Attorney—rumors of Buddy Richardson killing black farm hands on his place and burying them in Dundee County. Stories about bags of cash being delivered to High Hope at all hours of the night. The crown jewel of his land holdings, High Hope Plantation, straddled Yaloquena and Dundee counties, with Buddy's house being in Dundee County, the Wild West of Mississippi counties. The west half of Dundee county was Delta flatland. Hills covered the eastern half toward I-55. The families that lived in those hills, the Brewers, the Derrys, the McDonalds, descended from the Scots-Irish that made their way down the

Appalachians into the hills of northern Mississippi, By birthright, they were some of the toughest people in the world, just as soon fight you as look at you.

Buddy knew how to play the split jurisdictions, and I suspected that he tried to restrict his felony activities to Dundee County, where law enforcement was almost non-existent. He rarely came to Sunshine, but when he did it was to transact business. My late father, Monroe Banks, co-founder of Sunshine Bank with Jimmy Gray's father, told me several times he wouldn't put anything past Buddy Richardson. He said Buddy "was the meanest man he ever knew."

CHAPTER SIX

In a couple of days, between Wednesday afternoon and noon Friday, I had gone from having nothing to do to undertaking two *pro bono* cases. It sounds like a bigger deal than it was, because I knew I wouldn't be able to do much to help François. And Walton was fully capable of trying the murder-for-hire case against Buddy Richardson. I watched Walton try his first jury trial in Sunshine, and knew right then he was capable of being a good trial lawyer. He's diligent; follows through. That's what it takes, more than brilliant cross examination or argument. Pre-trial preparation is the key to being a good lawyer. If you're not prepared, you're not going to notice those openings the defense lawyer or his witnesses give you. When you know the case backwards and forwards before you make your opening argument, you can seize every chance to score points to make your case. If you're not prepared, you won't even know when those opportunities arise.

I knew there was a good possibility that Judge Zelda Williams might have to move Walton's murder-for-hire case out of Yaloquena County. Buddy Richardson was hated and feared in the black community because of the rumors of what he did on his place and because of his involvement with the Citizens' Councils in Yaloquena and Dundee counties. Walton said Judge Williams did what she always did—deferred ruling on the Motion To Change Venue until *voir dire*. She liked to hear the prospective jurors talk about their perception of the defendant and the crime before she ruled that the defendant could not get a fair trial in Sunshine. She did the same thing when I tried to pick a jury in Sunshine in the murder trial of Adolfo Galvan Zagara, a.k.a. El Moro, when the defense wanted a change of venue.

Walton said they questioned about twenty prospective jurors in jury selection in the Richardson trial at the

Yaloquena Courthouse, and hadn't seated a single juror. Fourteen of those prospects were black. A couple of them said they had heard that Buddy Richardson had lynched people out at High Hope and nothing was ever done. Walton told me everyone in the courtroom heard the prospects' comments, including about thirty prospective jurors waiting to be questioned. Murmurs and whispers got louder and louder until Zelda banged her gavel, something she rarely did. Another prospect said Buddy Richardson was part of the Yaloquena Citizens' Council group that kept her daddy from getting a job at the chicken plant, threatening to burn it down if "they hired a single nigger."

Walton said Zelda banged her gavel again, but the die was cast. After three grueling days of provocative *voir dire* answers by black prospective jurors, and outbursts and reaction by those watching in the courtroom, Zelda granted J.D. Silver's motion and ordered the trial moved to Oxford. She said she had already talked to the Lafayette County Circuit Judge and made arrangements to preside over the case in Oxford. The judge in Oxford said he had jurors reporting a week from Monday for a jury trial that had settled. He said Judge Williams was welcome to have her case tried to that Lafayette County panel.

Walton said defense lawyer J.D. Silver, being the professional he was, had a muted reaction to Judge Williams's ruling. We called Silver "Helmet Head," the nickname I came up with during the Ross Bullard murder trial. He sported a perfectly coiffed head of thick white hair combed straight back and stiffened with spray. In contrast to Helmet Head, Walton said Buddy preened and strutted when Judge Williams left the courtroom, then sneered at the blacks in the gallery, grinning at their catcalls.

I recounted all of this to Jimmy Gray when we started our walk from the condo Saturday morning at eight and headed east on University to Lamar. He said he wasn't surprised by what happened during jury selection. He agreed that Buddy Richardson was the most hated man in Yaloquena and Dundee counties. As CEO of Sunshine Bank, Jimmy had dealings with Buddy on occasion. Jimmy kept their relationship strictly professional. Buddy didn't bank in either Yaloquena or Dundee counties, but loaned money at times to Yaloquena County farmers. Some of them came to see Jimmy later to ask if Jimmy could bail them out of their loan arrangement with Richardson. Jimmy said the personal loans Buddy made were legal on their face, but borrowers told of Buddy keeping a portion of the stated principal as "prepaid interest" and having the borrowers sign documents verifying they had received the full amount of the principal. Jimmy couldn't help some of the folks. Buddy foreclosed on a slew of mortgages and deeds of trust, picking up farmland at bargain basement prices.

"There's plenty of white people in Yaloquena County hate Richardson's guts, too," Jimmy said, huffing and puffing as we turned north at Abner's to head to the Square.

"Walton's coming up next week to meet with us about Buddy. I told him you might be able to add to what I've told him."

"Be glad to."

"What'd you and Martha do last night?"

"We met a big wad of the Geezer Group for dinner at The Oxford Grillehouse on the Square. They all came by the house for a drink or two before we went out. I had the ribeye, and it was delicious, as usual."

"Who all showed?"

"Potato Head, Tiger Woody, Blackie, Terry Lee, Tush, Brainer, Duck, EO, Fload, Otis, and Cap'n Kenny Wayne. Plus the wives. I tried to get François to come with us but he said he wasn't up to it. I talked to him after the match yesterday. He told me you were going to help him look into his brother's death."

"I am."

"That pissant Tiger Woody made an eagle on three yesterday."

Tiger Woody was skinny as a rail, with a disappearing *derriere* that made us all wonder how he could sit comfortably. One day Jimmy was giving him grief about it on the golf course. Tiger Woody said he'd rather have a skinny butt than one like Jimmy Gray, whose "ass was so big it could be seen from space." Jimmy fired back. He said when looking at Tiger Woody from behind, "he looked like a frog standing up."

"I'm going to try to help François," I said to Jimmy Gray. "Not sure what I can do about something that happened in 1962. I'm on my second book about the riot. *Price of Defiance* by Charles Eagles. I don't know how I could be so ignorant about such a historical event."

"You and me both."

"How far can you walk today?"

"Not feeling all that chipper, Boudreaux. I'll make it to the coffee shop and wait on you. The scenery's always pretty good there."

"Better at Bottle Tree. Younger crowd. How much to drink last night?"

"Not much. Four or five beers at the club. Four Maker's Mark and water at home. Then a couple of bottles of wine at the Grillehouse."

"You really have cut back, haven't you?"

"Martha wants me to stop drinking altogether, but I told her I just couldn't live knowing when I wake up in the morning that's the best I'm going to feel all day. That's just depressing."

"This is a social town. I tell people since I moved here a year ago I've put on five pounds and become an alcoholic."

"You go to meetings?"

"No."

"Then you ain't an alcoholic. And speaking of drunks, old man Fite told me the other day at the bank his hands have gone to shakin' so bad from the whiskey that he has to mix it with Jello to keep it from spilling."

"I didn't know Mr. Fite had a drinking problem," I said, "until the first time I saw him sober."

Though we had used these same lines on each other many times through the years, we both laughed out loud at as we walked in front of Bouré on the Square. Jimmy Gray is the funniest man I've ever known, and I've known him all his life. He's a banking genius, but talking to him, you would never suspect it. He should be on Comedy Central. We grew up together in Sunshine; hunted, fished, played sports, went to Ole Miss together, then wound up back in Sunshine. Jimmy ran the bank our fathers started, and I practiced law and became the elected District Attorney for twenty-four years. In the twenty years Jimmy had been CEO, he had quadrupled the bank's assets. Jimmy was the largest stockholder in Sunshine Bank and I was second, both of us getting our stock the old fashioned way, inheriting the shares from our fathers.

"When's Buddy's trial start?" he asked.

"Jury selection begins a week from Monday. Walton may be coming up sometime this week to talk to you."

"I'll call him and get him to come by the bank in Sunshine."

"You up to brainstorming with me on François's deal if I manage to come up with anything?"

"You bet. I'll dust off my private eye badge."

Jimmy stopped at High Point Coffee and I kept walking, calling out over my shoulder for him to avoid the pastries and giant muffins in the place. He patted his big belly, winked and gave me a thumbs up. I walked north on Lamar planning to turn west on Price Street at the old fire station, thinking about the times Jimmy Gray walked with me in Sunshine wearing a bright red tee shirt with big white letters stretched across his expansive back reading: I BEAT ANOREXIA.

CHAPTER SEVEN

When I finished my walk I looked for Cissy Breedlove's number in the slender Oxford phone book. Not a single Breedlove listed. I thought a moment about the times I had said hello to Cissy at functions, trying to recall anyone who might have been with her. I called Linda Spargo, an administrator at the University, who knew how to get in touch with just about anyone in Oxford. She said she would make a call or two and get back with me. Within fifteen minutes she called me back with Cissy's cell number. I punched in the number and saved it to my contacts list. I checked the time. If I wanted to see Cissy today, it had to be soon if I wanted to make my one o'clock tee time.

Cissy Breedlove answered on the third ring and was very pleasantly professional. I could tell she preferred to meet next week but I was pushy. The sooner I got started on François' mission the sooner I could tell him I wasn't able to uncover anything. Spargo had told me where Cissy's townhouse was, and warned me that Cissy's husband Gavin could be somewhat off-putting. She urged me not to take it personally; he was like that with everyone. She said it was a good thing their son Chad, Mississippi's junior United States Senator, took after Cissy and not Gavin.

I cleaned up and made the five-minute drive to Cissy's townhome in a quiet neighborhood northeast of the Square. A half-dozen handsome structures lined the west side of the narrow street, each one with distinctive architecture. I parked my silver Ford F-150 pickup in front of her home and rang the doorbell. She ushered me in to a sitting area in the back part of her home. While she poured me a half cup of coffee, I glanced around. Part of the back room was den-like, with comfortable stuffed furniture facing a wall of books and a large television screen. The north half of the room was Cissy's office, with a grand antique partner's

Michael Henry

desk and photographs on shelves and the wall behind the desk tracking her career as a beauty queen and politician. The most prominent was a recent shot of Cissy standing with son Chad, the U.S. Capitol dome in the background.

She emerged from the kitchen adjoining her office and joined me in the sitting area. I took a sip and placed the mug on a coaster on her coffee table. It was Saturday morning, but Cissy looked like a million dollars in black slacks and a beige linen top. I had spent fifteen minutes online the night before trying to learn something about her. She was seventy-four, but looking at her that morning, I found that hard to believe. Cissy was still a beautiful, elegant woman, and looked much younger. She kept her hair a dark brunette, the same color in the photos I had seen online. According to the biography I found, she was Miss Mississippi in the Spring of 1963, her senior year at Ole Miss, then third runner-up Miss America later the same year. Sitting in her den, it was easy to believe.

"Thank you for seeing me," I said. "I hope it's not too inconvenient."

"Not at all, Willie Mitchell. My schedule these days is quite flexible."

We chatted a moment about the last time we had spoken. It was a very successful fund raiser for St. Jude's Children's Hospital at The Library, Jon Desler's expansive night club on Van Buren just off the Square. Oxford's *glitterati* were out in force that night, but Susan commented that Cissy was the best-dressed woman there in a slinky beaded black full-length evening gown, a beautiful pearl necklace and sparkling diamond earrings. She would have looked right at home at an exclusive dinner party in Georgetown or Manhattan. Cissy was tall, at least 5'8", and had kept her figure. Sitting across from me that morning, her posture was perfect without appearing stiff. I firmly believe the most beautiful women in America attend Ole Miss, and Cissy was no exception.

"Russell Fratelli was a wonderful young man," Cissy said after I explained the reason for my visit. "He had his whole life in front of him. Out of all the people in the Grove that horrible night, why that bullet had to hit Russell I will never understand. What a tragedy."

"It was a stray bullet?"

"That's what everyone said. It was just bad luck."

"How well did you know him?"

"We dated a few times. We were both in summer school the year he died."

"Do you remember if he was upset about Meredith being...?"

"Just the opposite," Cissy said. "That's the irony. Russell told me he thought they should let Meredith in school and any other blacks who qualified to get in. He said he knew a little bit about discrimination."

"Growing up Italian in the Delta?"

"Yes. Have you ever heard of anything so ridiculous?"

"It was a long time ago, Cissy. Do you know Francis very well?"

"I used to see him out and about, but not lately. With his illness I think he's become reclusive. He has lymphoma, you know, and the treatments take a lot out of him I'm sure."

"Were there a lot of students at Russell's funeral?"

"I'm not sure. It was in Clarksdale and I just couldn't bring myself to go. Things were still in an uproar on campus. It was such a tragedy. So sad."

"Do you know anyone local I might talk to about the facts surrounding Russell's death? Someone who was there at the riot and the investigation?"

"Let me think. It's been so long ago," she said and paused a moment. "I just...oh, you know who you should talk to? James Butler. He worked on the student paper at the time of the riot and later became editor of *The Oxford Eagle*. He's very smart and knows more about the history of this town and the University than anyone I know. He was a year behind me in school. I'll bet he can help you."

Out of the window I saw the wooden gate open and a man walk in carrying a plastic bag of fertilizer on his shoulder. He dropped it off his shoulder onto the grass in the small courtyard behind the townhome.

"That's Gavin, my husband. He's trying to get our flower beds in shape. I don't think you two have met. Let me introduce you."

"No, Cissy, he's busy and I have to run. I'll meet him another time."

I stood up and watched Gavin a moment. He was wiry and slightly stooped, not a big man, with a narrow, hooked nose. I walked my coffee mug back to the kitchen counter and Cissy accompanied me to the front door. We shook hands. I was impressed with her grip, a woman politician's practiced handshake, firm but not aggressive.

"Thanks again for seeing me on such short notice," I said.

"I hope you find out something for Francis's sake," she said. "It was such a terrible time for all of us. It's hard to believe people could have been so stupid. It was just a kind of mass hysteria I guess."

I hopped in my truck and headed to the golf course. I was shocked at the things I was reading in my books on the riot. Cissy was right. We Mississippians were very short-sighted and inhumane to do what we did in 1962 to James Meredith. Our response to Meredith was ignorant and hateful, and from what I had been reading the past few days, Mississippi Governor Ross Barnett's behavior was the unkindest of all.

CHAPTER EIGHT

I played well that Saturday afternoon, but lost money. The other three geezers in my group didn't help much, and I missed an easy five-foot putt on seventeen that turned out to be the margin of victory for Jimmy's team. Susan and I took a leisurely walk to town and sauntered around the Square, one of my favorite things to do on soft spring and summer evenings. Invariably we run into acquaintances and grab a drink on one of the upstairs balconies. That night was no exception. We enjoyed two drinks luxuriating in the warm southwesterly breeze on the Old Venice balcony on the south side of the courthouse. We walked home and called it a night.

The following day it rained off and on, so I spent most of the day reading. I finished Charles Eagles's book and read two chapters in Curtis Wilkie's *Dixie* that dealt with the riot and unrest surrounding Meredith's admission. Wilkie's eyewitness account made it clear the situation that night did not get really dangerous until after the Marshals lobbed their first tear gas volleys. Wilkie recounted how after that opening salvo, rednecks from all over the South began infiltrating the Grove in the darkness. Most of the students had left.

By nine-thirty my eyes were worn out from reading all day, so I got into bed. Not surprisingly, I dreamed I was in the Grove with bullets whizzing past me. No matter how hard I tried to run, my legs wouldn't move. Instead of crouching behind a tree, I stood out in the open while retired General Edwin Walker walked past in slow motion, leading a noisy civilian phalanx toward the Lyceum. He gestured for me to follow, and I tried to explain about my legs but for some reason I was also unable to talk.

With my first cup of coffee Monday morning, I read the *Wall Street Journal* online, but my mind kept coming back to the first mystery I had encountered: what was Russell

Fratelli doing in the Grove around the Lyceum that Sunday night? He wasn't against Meredith enrolling, and he knew it was dangerous, based on what he told François. The phone call was obviously the catalyst for his leaving the apartment. I made a note to find out if the investigators had checked out who made the call to get Russell out that night.

I opened a Word file on my computer and called it RUSSELL FRATELLI—NOTES. Opened another entitled FRATELLI: QUESTIONS. I called James Butler and asked if I could come by his house at eleven. We hadn't met but he said he knew who I was, and would be glad to help me any way he could. I finished my coffee and got some exercise.

At eleven o'clock I parked on Washington Street where it begins to go down a steep hill towards Price Street. Looking at its architecture, I guessed Butler's house had been built in the seventies. The exterior and the front yard were attractive and well-landscaped. He invited me in to have a seat at the kitchen table, and introduced me to his wife Naomi. Without asking, she placed a cup of coffee on the table before me.

"Cream or sugar?" she asked.

"No, thanks."

"Then I'll excuse myself and let you gentlemen have your discussion."

I could not take my eyes off the hyper-realistic oil painting on the wall above James's head. It was a painting of the Italianate bell tower of First Presbyterian Church viewed from Van Buren Street. The bell tower had been depicted in many photographs and works by local artists, but I had never seen it rendered so realistically. I knew it was oil, but it could have passed for a photograph.

"Where did you get this painting?" I asked.

"I painted it," he said after glancing over his shoulder.

"That's incredible work. I've never seen anything so realistic."

"Naomi says my paintings look too real, too stark."

"I disagree. Do you show your work?"

"Never sold a one. But I'm going to have to do something. I'm running out of walls in this place to hang them. Before you go I'll give you a tour to see the rest of them if you want."

Butler was a nice-looking man in his early seventies. He looked fit with neatly combed gray hair, bushy gray eyebrows, and intelligent eyes. I took a sip of coffee and explained in greater detail the reason for my visit. I told him what I had learned about the riot and Russell Fratelli's death. I leaned back and listened as he described the days leading up to September 30 and October 1, 1962.

"I was there in the trees east of the Lyceum on Sunday afternoon, watching the crowd collect and feeling the tension rise. Hundreds of Marshals ringed the Lyceum. The Highway Patrol was there too, but all they did was watch. They didn't help the Marshals a bit, sometimes even taking the side of the people throwing the bricks. I say people because after dark the crowd changed. In the afternoon it was almost all students in the Grove, hanging around treating it like a pep rally or something. When it got dark and the tear gas came out, students realized how dangerous it was and most of them went back to their dorms or apartments. That's when the rednecks started streaming into the Grove. They were from all over North Mississippi, Alabama, and Louisiana. Some drove here from Texas and Arkansas.

"I was covering it for *The Mississippian*, and had to conceal my camera, because people were grabbing reporters' cameras and smashing them on the concrete. A couple of them threatened me with a brick if I took their picture. Once I saw the fire truck heading toward the building, I started putting some distance between me and the Lyceum. I was west of the bridge on University near the campus entrance when they brought out the body of that reporter who was a stringer for some French news service. He was assassinated, you know, shot in the back at close range. That wasn't a stray bullet. He was a big, Scottish-looking fellow with a reddish beard by the name of Paul Leslie Guihard. There's a bench with a plaque in his honor next to the Grove.

"The boy from Abbeville who got a .38 slug in the middle of his forehead, Walter Ray Gunter, that was just pure bad luck. He was a jukebox repairman in the Grove for the entertainment. He was a long way from the Lyceum when he got shot standing on a wall to see the cars burning on the street. His friend said they were about to leave and the Gunter boy wanted one last look."

"When did you find out about Russell Fratelli?"

"Same time as everyone else. Thursday morning, more than three days later. He fell into a ravine that was grown up with privet and briars."

"Did you know him?"

"I had seen him around campus a good bit that summer. I knew his name but we weren't friends."

"Could you show me where his body was found?"

"Be glad to, Willie Mitchell, but there's a building there now. You know where the Alumni House is? A deep gulley between there and the bridge ran down to the railroad tracks in the Hilgard Cut. Gertrude Ford Street is now where the tracks ran in those days. The ravine where the body was found is all filled in with buildings on top of where it was. I can show you which building."

"That's all right. That location is a long way from the Lyceum. I'd say a good three or four hundred yards or so."

"Maybe. Everyone at school figured the Fratelli boy caught a stray bullet to the head Sunday night and just wandered off and fell into that ravine."

"You're sure he was shot Sunday night"

"I am. I was going to write a story on Fratelli's death and talked to the coroner, who at that time was just a general practitioner who had a practice in town. He was young and plenty smart, and told me the body had begun decomposing. He said certain bugs were working on it, you know, like they explain now on CSI, to help determine time of death. First three days of October the nights were still plenty warm. The doc did some research, talked to a few people and told me based on the condition of the body and the bugs in it he was sure the Fratelli boy was killed Sunday night or early Monday morning."

"So you wrote an article on Russell's death for *The Mississippian*?"

"I wrote one and submitted it, but the administration put pressure on the editor and wouldn't let us publish it. They were bound and determined to keep the official death count at two. It was embarrassing, you know, to those of us who had any sense, to see what these outsiders did on our campus to oppose integration. They made it their fight, did the burning and the killing, then slithered out of town back to the holes they came out of leaving Ole Miss and the State of Mississippi to deal with the mess they made."

"Mississippians did plenty on their own," I said.

"Oh yeah, I agree. I didn't mean to minimize what the state legislature and Governor Barnett did. They brought on the confrontation, but if the protestors had all been local, I guarantee you it wouldn't have turned into a riot that killed two, three counting Russell Fratelli, and injured hundreds more. Most of the injured were the U.S. Marshals, who had to stand there and take all that abuse without fighting back. I read afterwards that twenty-nine of the Marshals were hit with bullets, birdshot, or buckshot. Another two hundred or so had other kinds of injuries. Eventually the Kennedys sent in the National Guard and regular army MPs and troops, I think upwards of 30,000 were mobilized, and all the redneck troublemakers skedaddled out of town."

"You don't by any chance have a copy of that article you wrote, do you?"

"No. That was back in the day when copy machines were just about non-existent anywhere except big cities. The University had one in its library, but students didn't have access to it. We had carbon paper at *The Mississippian*, but I hated using it and rarely did, especially on a longer article. I handed in my original story to the editor and never saw it again. I guess I should have insisted on getting it back, but to tell you the truth, everyone just wanted to get things back to normal. Go to class, football games, you know. Regular life."

"Do you know where *The Eagle* keeps its old papers? I'd like to look at the original coverage at the time. And photographs, too, if they're available."

"It's all there, I believe, in the archives. I'm still on good terms with the staff and I'll make a call or two for you."

"That would be great. Like I said on the phone, I talked to Cissy Breedlove this past Saturday. She said she had some dates with Russell Fratelli that summer before the trouble."

"Now that you mention it, I do remember that. Cissy's a fine lady. Smart as a whip. Could have gone further in politics, in my opinion, if she had a husband that was worth a damn. Her son Chad wouldn't be U.S. Senator if it weren't for her. You know, Ole Miss Chi O chapter had two Miss Americas in a row, Mary Ann Mobley in 1959 and Lynda Lee Mead in 1960, and I think Cissy was prettier than they were. But she came in third place the year after the riot. I don't know if one thing had to do with the other."

"I remember when she was in the state senate," I said, "but I never knew much about her political career. I haven't met her husband."

"You haven't missed much. He was in school that summer, fresh out of the military. I remember seeing him around. They're both from Tupelo originally. I cannot imagine what she ever saw in Gavin Breedlove. He's a low-life drunk, if you ask me. Never would have had a job if it weren't for her connections. Always lived off her coattails."

"My mother used to say you never know what's cooking in someone else's pot. Maybe he's got some good qualities."

"Maybe so, but I doubt it. I always wanted her to be Mississippi's first woman governor. I guess I blame him for holding her back."

"He ever get into any trouble or anything?"

"No, nothing like that. No public scandal. He's just, I don't know, too much of a leech. Doesn't have many friends around here, far as I know. They've been here five or six years. Moved up from Jackson. Now, she has a lot of friends. You see her all over the place. He pretty much keeps to himself."

"Maybe that's why he drinks." I paused. "Who else could I talk to that was there that night and may know something about Russell's death?"

"No one knows a thing about Fratelli's death. Take my word for it. You could talk to Boyland Burr, lives over on South 11th. He was one of the Marshals who worked that night. I really don't know anyone else who's still living that could help you out. And let me warn you. Townspeople who were kids or teenagers or even students at Ole Miss at the time, they'll tell you this or that for a fact, and it's all a bunch of baloney. I have this one friend who swears he talked to a witness who saw a dozen or more dead Marshals that night stacked up like cordwood in the Lyceum hallway. That's hogwash. Two people died as a result of the riot, three counting Russell Fratelli. And that is all, believe me."

Butler gave me a private showing of his paintings before I left, and I was blown away by what I saw. I told him I'd like to own one and would be willing to pay whatever he thought was fair. He told me he'd think about it. As I was about to leave, Butler confirmed what François had told me about the minimal investigation done by the Mississippi Highway Patrol into Russell's death. The MHP claimed jurisdiction over the crimes committed that Sunday and Monday. Butler said if reports or records regarding the case existed, the Highway Patrol investigative division would have them.

He said he would also call his friends at *The Oxford Eagle* about my accessing their archives and then call me with the names of whom to talk to. I thanked him and drove away, placing a call to the Colonel who headed up all the divisions of the Highway Patrol to see about getting access to the state investigative files. Then I called Robbie Cedars, Director of the State Crime Lab. If any physical evidence from the murder scene still existed, Robbie would be able to tell me more about it than anyone else in Mississippi.

CHAPTER NINE

I spent Tuesday in *The Oxford Eagle* archives reading the contemporaneous reporting on the riot. When I first arrived that morning, I spoke to Tim Phillips, the genial publisher whose family had been involved with *The Eagle* for decades. Tim introduced me to the woman who looked after the archives. She could not have been more accommodating. She pulled all of *The Eagle* editions published in September and October of 1962 for me, and placed a box of original photographs on the table. All she asked was that I be careful, that the papers were easy to tear. I went through the photos quickly.

I had studied the photographs in the Doyle and Eagles books on the riot, so the newspaper's prints of the burned out station wagons and sedans near the Lyceum were no surprise. The bulk of the photographs in the box showed the National Guard and U.S. Army troops arriving in Oxford and marching on campus. Only a few photographs captured the actual riot, and they were of poor quality, shot at night from a distance. The box contained a good number of images of students in a festive atmosphere gathered in the Grove in front of the Lyceum on Sunday afternoon. The male students in white socks, short-sleeved shirts, and crew cuts were smiling, even laughing. Many of them puffed on cigarettes. The women wore full skirts and stood back from the young men at the front of the crowd. An aerial shot showed white-helmeted U.S. Marshals ringing the building.

I was struck by the fact that none of the faces of the students I studied showed any fear or anticipation of danger. The State Police in front of the students appeared relaxed as well; a few smiled at the young men laughing behind them. It seemed that no one expected the deadly violence that was to arrive with the darkness.

I leaned back in the wooden chair a moment. The photographs of the Marshals, the Highway Patrol, and the students gathering that Sunday afternoon were easy to capture. The photographers were in no danger. It was still daylight. Same for the pictures of the National Guardsmen and regular Army MPs and troops arriving in the days following the Sunday night riot. But the atmosphere for the photographers changed when it grew dark on Sunday. The students receded, and in their place came the violent segregationists from all over the South determined to protect what they thought was their way of life. They welcomed the cover of night, and used it to conceal their identities, grabbing and smashing cameras, threatening reporters or anyone else wanting to witness their lawlessness or take their photograph.

When the guns came out in the crowd and Molotov cocktails rained on the Marshals and their vehicles around the Lyceum, the photographers must have retreated to safety. Protecting themselves with bullets flying around the Grove undoubtedly became more important than covering and photographing the events. That's just human nature— the reason why so few photographs were taken of the riot as it occurred. And the equipment available to reporters in 1962 was primitive compared to the high-tech devices used today.

I put all the photos back in the box and read *The Oxford Eagle* articles published in the week leading up to the riot, some of which recapped the political posturing by the Governor and state legislators, who demagogued the issue of Meredith's enrollment to show off for their constituents. I was struck by the Ole Miss Chancellor J.D. Williams's consistent call for reason and conciliation in contrast to the bombast coming out of the State Capitol complex in Jackson. In the pre-riot articles no hints of the detailed negotiations between Attorney General Bobby Kennedy and Governor Barnett were mentioned. Those discussions were exposed in great detail by Charles Eagles in *The Price of Defiance.* Barnett wanted to orchestrate his blocking Meredith from entering the Lyceum door for the cameras, yielding reluctantly in the face of overwhelming federal military might. Attorney General Kennedy was willing to play along with the Governor's theatrics, but the violence that came Sunday night eliminated Barnett's planned *kabuki* theater.

I was disappointed in the paper's coverage of Russell Fratelli's death. A small article ran on page two in Friday's paper, the day after his body was found, but no photograph of the Ole Miss senior or the ravine. The story said the cause of death was unclear and an investigation was underway. There was no suggestion in the paper that his death had anything to do with the previous Sunday night's riot. I went through editions for three weeks after the discovery of the body, but no follow-up about Russell Fratelli's death appeared. James Butler was right. The powers-that-be in Oxford, Jackson, Ole Miss, and Washington, D.C. wanted to suppress anything that reminded the public of the violent battle on the Oxford campus.

By four o'clock I had gone through everything. My nose was stopped up from the dust and decay of old newsprint. I thanked the archivist for her hospitality and told her I might be back again for another look. Walking outside, I was struck by the beauty of the warm spring day. I remember thinking I should have spent the afternoon on the golf course instead of in a dusty vault. I headed home, walking through the alley running from Jackson to Van Buren Street. As I stopped on the corner by The Library, a black Escalade with dark tinted glass came to a halt in the crosswalk. I watched as the driver lowered his window.

"What do you say, Willie Mitchell?" the white-haired, bearded driver said to me. "How's that pretty wife of yours?"

Buddy Richardson had arrived in Oxford.

CHAPTER TEN

I raised my hand slightly to acknowledge Buddy Richardson's greeting. I refused to smile, but held his dark eyes with mine. In a couple of seconds, the driver of the car behind Buddy tapped his horn politely. Buddy continued to stare until his dark-tinted driver's window closed. His black Escalade moved ominously up Van Buren to the Square.

I want to explain to you my lack of hospitality. It's true that all defendants in our system are presumed innocent. But this presumption does not mean Buddy was *actually* innocent. He was not. One of my few regrets in abandoning the District Attorney's office in Yaloquena County after being re-elected over a year ago is that Walton Donaldson, not I, had the pleasure of presenting the murder-for-hire charge against Buddy Richardson in connection with the shooting death of his grandson-in-law Carl Sanders in Yaloquena County. This is the first time Buddy has been charged with a crime, but it's not the first time he's had someone killed.

I probably owe you an apology for being circumspect in my description of Buddy Richardson thus far in this story. I have understated his malevolence because *this is a story about my investigation into Russell Fratelli's death.*

I've mentioned Buddy several times and given you some background, but not nearly enough for you to appreciate how sociopathic the man is. You might think a rogue like Buddy would mellow at his age, maybe tone down his illegal activities in the netherworld of crime in rural Mississippi.

I've got news for you—he hasn't.

If anything, Buddy's age seems to have emboldened him, as if he's got nothing to lose. He's lived to be eighty-five, and I guess he figures what's the worst the law can do to him? I'll give you an example. Over a year ago, one month before my final election day, I was in my office in the courthouse, certain my campaign for re-election was doomed. My gatekeeper in the office, Louise Kelly, asked me to speak with a young woman from Dundee County who had come to us for help. I asked Louise to bring her in. Out of privacy concerns, I'm not going to tell you her name. I will say I know there are many other young women with similar stories.

I studied her across the desk. I guessed her age to be around twenty-five. She was attractive enough, with long, ash blonde hair parted in the middle. Her pale skin was somewhat rough, her eyes sad, but vibrantly green. She dressed like most young women her age from Dundee County—torn jeans, a faded football jersey, and flip-flops. She told me she and her boyfriend had one child, a two-year-old son. She said she was the child's sole caretaker, and she was afraid of Buddy Richardson.

Her boyfriend was one of the hundred or so crystal meth cooks in the dense hardwood hills of Dundee County. Buddy Richardson loaned him money to buy some first-rate equipment for his lab deep in the woods south of Brewer Hill. At first, things were fine. Then after a few months, Buddy told him his monthly payments would be double what they had agreed. In addition he wanted to be paid in kind with ten per cent of each new batch.

I listened with equanimity to her tale of redneck venture capital gone awry, fighting the urge to shake my finger at the stupidity of the young mother and her boyfriend. She continued.

The boyfriend balked at Buddy's retroactive restatement of the deal, so Buddy sent two of his associates to talk some sense into the boyfriend. After a broken nose and fractured eye socket, the boyfriend understood the fairness of Buddy's proposal and even agreed to an additional term occasioned by the boyfriend's initial intransigence. Buddy decreed that the next payment of money and crank was to be delivered in person by the young man's girlfriend to High Hope Plantation. Buddy added that she was to be prepared to spend some quality time relaxing with Buddy as his guest in the big house. The young woman explained she did not want to be part of the deal, but the boyfriend begged her to comply to save his hide. He promised her he would get the money to pay off Buddy somehow, and this one time would be her last.

The young lady described in graphic language the events of the one night she spent with Buddy at High Hope Plantation. I'm going to spare you the details and just say her time with the crystal meth-crazed, Viagra-fueled, violently abusive eighty-five-year-old was a triple X-rated night from hell. She went on to tell me she knew from talking to others she wasn't the only woman to endure it.

After asking enough questions to make sure none of the events she described took place in Yaloquena County, I asked her if she had talked to Sheriff Cheatwood in Kilbride.

"He ain't no better than Buddy Richardson, if you ask me," she said. "I complained to Sheriff Cheatwood and he started asking me about my boyfriend and where his place in the hills was, and I saw real quick-like where it was going. I know old man Richardson's got Cheatwood on the take and ain't a thing going to be done in Dundee County about what he done to me that night. I don't mind taking a little beatin' if I deserve it, but he gave me a black eye and three broken ribs even though I was doing exactly what he told me to do."

I explained I had no jurisdiction over what happened in Dundee, and asked her if I contacted the State Attorney General, the State Police, and the FBI to investigate would she cooperate. She shook her head no, saying her boyfriend told her, "If they couldn't get nothing done local to just let it go." She said her boyfriend had finally paid Buddy off and ended their business deal.

She stood to leave and without a trace of embarrassment or reticence, told me, "I'll give Buddy Richardson one thing, Mr. Banks, he is the fuckingest old man I have ever seen. I mean he went on for hours and hours. Seemed like forever to me."

Buddy Richardson would have been successful playing by the rules. He was a shrewd businessman and had made plenty of money buying and selling farms and ranches in north Mississippi. It was said he ran a first-rate farming operation on his many places in the Delta, and had accumulated over ten thousand acres of loamy cotton land,

and another five thousand acres suitable for soybeans, milo, pine timber, or cattle. And, the story continued, Buddy didn't owe a nickel to anyone.

I learned in my career as a prosecutor that there are some men, and some women, too, who welcome the thrill of living on the edge. They enjoy associating with criminals, even if they don't have to. Buddy was one of those people. His first taste of crime, according to my father, was placing illegal slot machines in the late nineteen-fifties and early sixties in small juke joints hidden away on back roads across the Delta, providing a gambling venue for people who could least afford to waste their money. Each joint owner and Buddy split the profits from the machine. Buddy kept his joint owners honest by personally administering, with the help of his associates, an occasional beating.

My father and Jimmy Gray's dad told us Buddy enjoyed hanging out in the bars and strip clubs in Biloxi on the Mississippi Gulf Coast, and made connections in the hierarchy of the Dixie Mafia, a loose collection of non-ethnic mobsters who operated across the South, providing arsonists, hit men, and gangsters for hire. The Dixie Mafia headquartered in Biloxi, and it was there that Buddy became associated with the criminals who ran the lonely hearts club scam out of Angola Prison in Louisiana, conning lonely homosexuals into sending large amounts of cash to a post office box on the coast in exchange for the promise of love after the prisoner was out of Angola. Buddy Richardson's involvement in the Dixie Mafia murder of Judge Sherry and his wife in Biloxi was rumored in the Delta, but his name never appeared in the newspaper or the official investigation.

Buddy learned through his Louisiana Dixie Mafia associates of the likely passage in the 1991 Louisiana Legislature of a video poker bill that would legalize the addictive gambling machines at "truck stops" throughout the state. The video poker bill was supported by one-term "reform" Governor, Charles "Buddy" Roemer II. Acting on the information, Richardson bought a soybean farm adjacent to the first exit off I-20 in Louisiana directly across the Mississippi River from Vicksburg. He built his "truck stop" and installed a hundred video poker machines as soon as legally permissible. His was one of the first such facilities to open, and Buddy made a fortune, even after paying off the gangsters in Biloxi and the shady middle-men/lobbyists in Baton Rouge who helped him secure the license.

Jimmy Gray's father had banking friends in Louisiana who told him about Buddy making a fortune in his video poker venture. Mr. Gray in turn told Jimmy and me about Buddy's "truck stop," saying video poker was the probable source of the rumors of bags full of cash being delivered at night to Buddy at High Hope.

About thirteen years ago, I was at the end of my third term as Yaloquena District Attorney. A Dundee County man who had worked for Buddy for a decade died in a boating accident in an oxbow lake in an adjoining county. The driver of the fishing boat survived and was subpoenaed to testify in the grand jury impanelled to look into the mysterious death. The day before he was to testify, the boat driver was abducted from the parking lot of a convenience store in Yazoo City. He was never seen again.

No law enforcement agency found any proof that Buddy had his former employee and the boat driver both killed to keep them from testifying about Buddy's various criminal enterprises, but several FBI Special Agents whose word I trust told me Buddy was behind it. They also said they could never prove it.

In all my years living in Sunshine, I saw Buddy in town no more than three or four times, and it was always at a distance. He did not socialize, rarely came to Sunshine and spent little time there when he did. So, it seemed more than odd when I saw him in his Escalade that particular Tuesday in April on Van Buren Street that he made a point to inquire about my wife Susan. I knew Buddy had never met her and wasn't interested in her health. He was sending me a message—Buddy Richardson was in Oxford, and he was running wide open.

Chapter Eleven

At nine o'clock Wednesday morning I parked on Hayes Street and walked toward Boyland Burr's house on South 11th. His house was near the intersection of the two streets. Because both streets were too narrow for parking, the curbs in front of Boyland's house were painted gold. I admired the old cedar trees lining the streets in front of the small, frame house, walked up the steps onto the porch, and knocked. I heard movement inside the house and felt the porch shake as someone made their way to the door. When it opened, a big man stood there, filling the frame.

"Mr. Burr?" I said and extended my hand. "I'm Willie Mitchell Banks."

"Come in. Come in."

He backed away from the entrance in a straight line, and when I followed him in I understood why. The front room of the house was filled with newspapers and magazines stacked five feet high, leaving only a narrow passage through the front room. I had to wait for him to step away from the entrance before I could walk inside.

We stood a moment in the next room, a dining room converted to a den of sorts off the kitchen. It appeared Boyland Burr spent most of his time in this room. An overstuffed La-Z-Boy faced a big screen television on the wall. TV trays on either side of the recliner were stacked with dirty plates on top of issues of the Jackson *Clarion-Ledger*, the Memphis *Commercial Appeal*, and the *Oxford Eagle*.

"Have a seat," he said, pointing to a small aluminum dinette by the door to the kitchen.

Boyland Burr plopped down and pushed against the back of the La-Z-Boy in one motion, causing the foot rest to shoot out with a grating, metallic screech. I made sure I wouldn't be sitting on leftover food and took a seat. Hardened SpaghettiOs dotted my side of the aluminum table, so I clutched my legal pad in front of me. The house smelled as bad as it looked, and I hoped he wouldn't offer me anything.

"I can make some coffee if you'd like some," he said. "And I just opened some Sugar Wafers."

"No thanks, Mr. Burr. I just had breakfast and my limit of coffee."

"You call me Boyland. I'm pleased to finally meet you. Followed your career as a District Attorney, especially the case you were trying in Jackson when you and your son got hit by that car on the Reservoir road. You're lucky to be alive."

His voice cracked several times, reminding me of the actor I watched in cowboy movies as a kid, Andy Devine. Boyland was as big as Andy Devine, too, maybe bigger. He was well over six feet and must have weighed two-seventy. He wore a dirty white tee shirt, old khaki pants, and government-issued black brogans that were at least thirty years old. His hair was a dirty gray and long.

"We were lucky that evening for sure. How long have you been retired from the Marshal's office?"

"Had to leave the service when I reached seventy, thirteen years ago. I spent my whole career just about, here in the Northern District of Mississippi. Forty-three years. The last five I did bailiff duty around the courthouse."

"I bet you saw a lot in those years."

"You can say that again. I wish'd I could have kept on working. I don't do anything now but sit around watching TV and reading the papers. The wife died five years ago. She had a cancer."

Boyland and the Mrs. must have been hoarding newspapers and magazines together, because at least thirty years' worth was stacked in the front room. A lovely pastime for a married couple, I thought, something they could enjoy together in their golden years.

"You said on the phone you wanted to ask me about the riot."

"That's right," I said. "Some folks I've talked to said you were there."

"Yep. I'm about the only law enforcement still alive around here that was at the Lyceum the night all hell broke loose."

"You must have been young."

"I was thirty, only three years on the job when the order came down from D.C. that we were to keep the peace when Meredith presented himself at the Lyceum to be enrolled. Marshals from all over the country came to Oxford, probably over four hundred total. Well over half of them got hurt, some of them bad, taking birdshot and buckshot after being ordered not to fight back."

"You?"

"Nope. I was mighty lucky. Bullets were flying all over the Grove that night. Bricks, too. And Molotov cocktails."

"I've been reading up on it. Must have been something."

"It was."

"What did you think about it? Meredith coming to Ole Miss?"

"Weren't none of my business, the way I looked at it. I was just doing my job like I was told by my supervisor and the big shots from Washington."

"Did you see the reporter from the French paper get shot?"

"Naw. No one did. It was in the dark over in the bushes by the street to the girls' dorms. And the other boy that died, the one from Abbeville, it was just his time. He was way on the other side of the Grove, south of the Confederate monument. That was a sad thing, him catching that stray bullet."

"Did you know the student who was found dead in the ravine the following Thursday, Russell Fratelli?"

"Not personally. I heard about them finding the body and went over there to look around. The State Police and the local boys were at the scene. The body had already been taken away by the time I got there."

"Why did you go?"

"Just curious, I guess. Never been involved in something like that riot, before or since. And you got to remember it was 1962. It was the Stone Age compared to now. Not much was going on in this little town and shooting deaths were unheard of. I was just wanting to see the investigators work the crime scene, but I didn't see much."

"What do you mean?"

"I mean they didn't really do anything except do a search of the ravine for an hour or two after they took the boy's body out. Nothing like they do nowadays. Didn't find anything."

"What do you think happened to the Fratelli boy? A stray bullet?"

"I don't think so. He was shot in the back of the head. I talked to the coroner at church the following Sunday. The doc said the bullet went in here and stayed in his head."

Boyland pointed to the hairline on the back of his neck.

"What did they think happened? Did you talk to the investigators?"

"Sure did. That Thursday afternoon. They didn't think it was a stray bullet. He was so far away from the Lyceum."

"Do they think he was shot on purpose?"

"Yep. We all did. We figured it was the same guy who shot the reporter in the back. That was a close range shot. Powder burns on the reporter's shirt. The Fratelli boy was shot kind of the same way. In the back of the neck."

"Were there powder burns or anything to say how close the shooter was?"

"I don't know about that. Neither the investigators at the scene or the coroner said anything about a close range shot."

"The investigators who worked the Fratelli shooting, do you know if any of them might still be alive?"

"Not around here. None of the locals. The state people, now I don't know about them. The Highway Patrol investigators I saw here, the ones who came to work the Fratelli boy's case, they were all older than me. And I'm eighty-three."

Out of the corner of my eye I saw a mouse run across the passageway in the front room and disappear into the bottom of a newspaper pile. Probably a sign from the heavens I'd been in Boyland Burr's lovely home long enough.

"Can I ask you something, Willie Mitchell?"

"Yes, sir."

"Why are you looking into this now?"

"Russell Fratelli's younger brother Francis is a friend of mine. He's not doing well and his brother's death has been on his mind a lot lately."

"I understand that. You get older, things that happened a long time ago can seem real important if you ain't got much time left."

"Do you know Francis Fratelli?"

"I did a while back. Knew him just to say hello. I know he's got a lot of rent property around town. Haven't seen him in probably ten years, I bet. I don't get out much."

"Thank you, Boyland. Appreciate your seeing me."

"Glad to, Willie Mitchell," he said and reached for the lever on the side of the La-Z-Boy to bring the back up.

"Don't get up. I can see my way out. Thanks again."

He gestured as I passed him on my way to the narrow passageway in the front room. I walked quickly through Mr. and Mrs. Burr's collection of papers, hoping the decaying yellow mounds of newsprint didn't topple over and suffocate me to death. What an ignominious way to go.

CHAPTER TWELVE

When I came to on number eight green, Jimmy Gray's big frame was hovering over me, shielding me from the sun. It took me a few seconds to grasp what had happened. I hadn't had a seizure in over six months.

I mentioned earlier that when I first met him, Boyland Burr had commented on my prosecution of El Moro, whose trial was moved from Sunshine to Jackson for reasons too disturbing to go into here. The second evening of jury selection, while my son Jake and I were jogging, we were struck by a car containing two men who wanted me dead. If it had not been for Jake, they would have succeeded.

It's been five years since the incident. I spent most of the first year enduring multiple surgeries and months of agonizing therapy. I came away with some permanent problems to which I have become accustomed. The vision in my left eye is blurry. A special contact lens clears it somewhat. I have periodic weakness and severe, non-specific aches deep in my left leg. It comes and goes, occasioned at times by a change in the weather. The most serious continuing problem is a type of seizure disorder, *absence* seizures, once labeled *petit mal* seizures. I don't shake uncontrollably. I just blank out for a while, and when it's over I feel completely normal. I can feel them coming on, and when I do, I sit or lie on the ground, or if I'm driving I pull over. At times the seizures have lasted only thirty seconds, but sometimes they can go on as long as six or seven minutes.

This was the first time I had a seizure on a golf course, and it scared the hell out of François and Mr. Potato Head, who with Jimmy Gray made up our foursome that Wednesday afternoon. Jimmy had been with me many times when I zoned out, so when he saw me drop my putter and lie down on the green he knew exactly what was going on.

"He just does it to get attention," Jimmy told François and Potato Head when I came back into the world, "claims he's got some kind of French brain disorder."

I laughed at Jimmy, stood and picked up my putter and knocked in a ten-footer. On the walk to the carts I explained to the men what had happened and gave them a brief history.

"Jesus Christ," François said, "I thought you had a heart attack."

The rest of the round was uneventful, except I won the greenies on nine, eleven, and fifteen, getting the ball closest to the hole on the par threes. Jimmy Gray bought us all a Bud Light "to settle everyone down" when the beer cart girl showed up on number ten. We settled the bets with the other Geezer Group foursomes in the bar, and Jimmy and I got into his gigantic fire-engine red Lincoln Navigator for the drive home.

"Show me where this hoarder Boyland Burr lives," Jimmy said when he entered the Highway 6 bypass heading west.

"Yea, though you walk through the The Valley of the Shadow of Newspapers," I said, "you will fear no evil. I'm going to skip the part about your rod and your staff, if you don't mind."

"I think that's best. I just want to be friends."

"Maybe you ought to go in Boyland's house and check it out. I imagine it was featured in *Southern Living* at some point. Assuming you can get your wide body through the stacks of papers, be sure to get some of those Sugar Wafer cookies he opened this morning. I wouldn't eat the SpaghettiOs, though."

I had described the retired Marshal's living conditions and told Jimmy what Boyland Burr had shared with me earlier in the day. Boyland's most interesting and useful comment was that the Highway Patrol investigators and everyone else at the scene thought it was an intentional shooting, not a stray bullet, probably by the same person who shot the British reporter in the back. Cissy Breedlove and James Butler had described it as a stray bullet. Since no one had solved the mystery of who shot the reporter in the fifty-three years since he died, it didn't bode well for my solving the Fratelli homicide.

Jimmy turned onto South 10th off Old Taylor Road, but before he turned right on Hayes toward Boyland Burr's house, I stopped him.

"What?" he said.

"That black Escalade parked over there near the Marshal's house. That's Buddy Richardson's."

"You sure? Buddy's not the only one drives a black Escalade."

"Drive past it but don't slow down."

Jimmy turned onto Hayes then left onto South 11th. As we passed the Cadillac, I memorized the license number. Its plate said Dundee County. I asked Jimmy to drive north on South 11th for two blocks and pull over. I called Sheriff Lee Jones in Sunshine and asked him to run the license plate. In two minutes he called me back and confirmed the vehicle was registered to Buddy Richardson.

"That's him," I said when I ended the call. "What's he doing at Boyland Burr's house?"

"Maybe he's not. There's lots of houses in walking distance of his car."

I got out of Jimmy's Navigator.

"Where you going?"

"I'm going to walk towards the house and wait a while. You park on South 10th on the other side of Old Taylor and sit tight."

I closed the door and walked toward the black Escalade. Several rolled up editions of *The Oxford Eagle* were in the driveway of the large home across the street and north of the Marshal's house. I figured the family was out of town, so I took up a position in their driveway where I was hidden from view but could see the front of the Burr house and Buddy's vehicle. Within ten minutes, Buddy Richardson emerged onto the porch, shook hands with the retired Marshal and patted him on the back. He laughed and said something to Burr as he walked to his car, but I couldn't make it out.

Five minutes after Buddy drove off, I was sitting in Jimmy Gray's Navigator.

"Why would Buddy Richardson be meeting with Boyland Burr?" I asked, making a note to enter the question on my computer file.

"Who knows? They're about the same age. Maybe they're friends. I've got a better question for you. What's the connection between the dead reporter and Russell Fratelli? Out of all the people in the riot that night, why did the shooter pick out those two guys to sneak up on and shoot in the back, a British citizen working for a French newspaper, and a senior at Ole Miss from Clarksdale?"

"Good question," I said.

CHAPTER THIRTEEN

Late the next morning I got a surprise phone call from Walton and walked to the apartment on the south side of the Square where he said he was staying for the duration of the Buddy Richardson trial. I turned right on Van Buren off South 9th, walked past the Lyric Theater, McEwen's, Old Venice, City Grocery, Square Books, and crossed Lamar. In the next block I opened a door I had never noticed between two high-end clothing stores. I walked up a long flight of stairs through an interior door into a spacious, artfully decorated apartment with a balcony overlooking the Square and the historic Circuit Courthouse in the center of it.

"Man-oh-man," I said, shaking Walton's hand. "Nice place."

"No kidding. Belongs to a friend of mine from law school."

"He must have a pretty good practice."

"He was born with a silver spoon and then married well."

"Two for two."

"I've taken over the dining room table for my work space."

Walton's trial prep covered the table. I recognized his three-ringed file folder with tabs separating his presentation from the defense. He had taken my tutoring to heart, making trial preparation more important than the actual conduct of the trial. I glanced at the small stack of cases he had printed off of LexisNexis under his Response to Pre-Trial Order and Memorandum of Law.

"Looks like you're ready," I said.

"As ready as I'm going to be. I had all this worked up before we started jury selection in Yaloquena ten days ago, so all I've got to do is go over everything again tomorrow and Saturday. I'll get plenty of rest Sunday, then start jury selection Monday."

"Do you have anyone local helping you during *voir dire*?

"The local D.A., Kent Mudson, has loaned me one of his assistant DAs who's from Lafayette County and knows a lot of the venire."

"Good. How are you going to manage your witnesses?"

"Thank God for Lee Jones. He's assigned Sammy Roberts to help me throughout the trial. He's chief deputy now, and will have deputies ferry the witnesses here as needed and take them back to Yaloquena."

"Great. What are y'all doing to protect that low-life Metzger? Without him there's no case."

Lynn Metzger was the hit man hired by Buddy Richardson to kill his granddaughter's husband, the late Carl Sanders, whom Metzger ambushed ten months before on the dirt road to Sanders' residence on his farm in Yaloquena County.

"Sheriff Jones is personally in charge of that. They have him in a safe house somewhere in north Mississippi, a little over an hour from here. That's all I know. Lee says he's got Metzger where no one can get to him."

"I still can't understand why Buddy would hire a Dundee County thug to kill Sanders when he's supposed to have access to all the Dixie Mafia hit men across the South."

"Maybe that organization doesn't exist anymore," Walton said.

"Oh, they're still around in one form or another, even if they're not organized like they were in the old days. They're probably no longer headquartered in Biloxi, but I guarantee you they're out there, stealing heavy equipment, or burning a building for an owner underwater on his mortgage. Glad you have to deal with them now and I don't. Is Gayle coming up for any of the trial or is she too tied up with the twins and Laura?"

"Not exactly," Walton said, averting his eyes.

"What's the deal?"

"She's going to stay with Mrs. Bannerman in West Point until the trial is over. Taking the kids out of school."

"That might be two or three weeks."

"Yeah," Walton said, "thing is, Gayle got a call last Friday before I got home. Caller said if I didn't back off Buddy Richardson she and the kids were going to be as dead as Carl Sanders."

CHAPTER FOURTEEN

At three o'clock in the afternoon that same day, I answered the back door and welcomed Yaloquena Sheriff Lee Jones into the condo. I shook his big hand and thanked him for coming on such short notice. It had been a month since I had seen him last in Sunshine. I noticed for the first time a few gray hairs on the edge of his temples. Hard to believe, but Lee was fifty-two now and in his eleventh year as Sheriff of Yaloquena County. Even so, he was still as fit as he was in his days as a Highway Patrolman, and built like the all-conference college linebacker he was in the Southwest Athletic Conference.

I asked about his wife Yancey and their two daughters, one of whom, Samantha, was a freshman at Ole Miss, a beautiful girl with *café au lait* skin like her mother. Never too big on small talk, Lee said they were all fine, and moved right into the reason I called him.

"I knew about the threat," Lee said. "Walton called me as soon as it happened. We checked into it and found out it was made from a disposable phone whose signal bounced off the tower in the center of town, right by Fite's Bulk Plant. So, that was a dead end."

"I told Walton 99% of calls like that are just empty threats," I said. "I had a few in my day that rattled Susan, but I told her people who wanted to harm me were not going to give me a heads up; they'd just do it."

"Yeah, like the two guys that ran you down on the Reservoir. But this was Gayle's first threat, and we're dealing with Buddy Richardson. I don't put anything past him. Walton told me she was taking the kids to stay with her mother and I said I thought it might be a good idea. I called the Sheriff down there in Clay County and he said they'd do a regular patrol down Mrs. Bannerman's street."

"Good, but I'm more worried about Walton than his family."

"He's prepared the case about as well he could. Talked to all the witnesses. Spent a lot of time with Lynn Metzger. Talk about a lowlife piece of crap. I feel dirty just being around him."

"Walton said you've got him well-secured someplace."

"Yep."

"It's not Walton's trial preparation that worries me," I said. "I spent time with him this morning at the place he's staying on the Square. He's plenty nervous, shook up. That's what I wanted to talk to you about."

"This is his first high-profile case. He'll do fine once trial starts."

"I think so, too. But he's asked me to sit at the table with him."

"In court? During the trial? He didn't say anything to me about that. You're a civilian now."

"Judge Williams wouldn't care. I'm not a D.A. any more, but I'm still licensed to practice."

"Are you going to do it?"

"I told him he didn't need me, that he could convict Buddy without my sitting there, but he kept asking. Ended up I told him I'd sit at the prosecution table with him if he insisted. It settled him down. Come Monday morning I'll revisit the issue with him. His nerves will calm once jury selection starts."

"You said on the phone you wanted to talk to me about Buddy Richardson, too."

"He's been in town since Tuesday. Saw him yesterday on the porch of a retired U.S. Marshall who helped defend the Lyceum in the riot of 1962 on campus. Name is Boyland Burr."

"What was Buddy doing there?"

"I don't know. Jimmy says they might be friends. About the same age."

"I guess it's possible."

"I've got an appointment with the Chief of Police here this afternoon at four to tell him about Buddy's trial starting Monday. Like you to go with me."

"Lafayette Sheriff's office will be in charge of security at the courthouse."

"Walton's already talked to the Sheriff here. The Sheriff has agreed to put more men on the security detail for the jurors and the courthouse in general. But I want to talk to the Chief of Police about keeping an eye on Buddy while he's in town."

"I wish Zelda had never granted him bail."

"Not much she could do about it with J.D. Silver insisting correctly that the law says the only purpose of bail was to guarantee the defendant's appearance. Silver offered to put up a cash bond of a half-million and Zelda agreed. Walton says Buddy's shown up on time for every proceeding they've had so far. He says Buddy acts like he's having a good time in court."

"Maybe all that crystal meth he's been smoking's made him crazy. Let's go meet the Chief."

We rode in Lee's official vehicle, a black Tahoe with the Yaloquena County Sheriff's Office logo on the doors, to the Oxford P.D. on Molly Barr north of Jackson Avenue. We entered the office of Chief Mike Columbus, a fortyish, clean-cut police officer with a military bearing. He had heard about the trial being moved from Yaloquena to the Lafayette County Courthouse, but he knew nothing about Buddy Richardson's background. Lee and I spent fifteen minutes tag-teaming the Chief with stories about Buddy's history. Lee added one at the end of our laundry list that I had not mentioned.

"It was rumored in Yaloquena and Dundee Counties that Buddy had something to do with providing the money for those transvestite prostitutes who claimed to have dated a candidate for governor back in the eighties."

"I forgot about that one," I said. "The politician was from Natchez, and he won the governor's race in spite of the claim. The prostitutes later recanted, admitting they said what they were paid to say."

I didn't mention this to Lee and Chief Columbus because it's such ancient history, but I'll share it with you: the male prostitutes were a political dirty trick allegedly orchestrated by a former employee of the Sovereignty Commission, who was also connected to the Citizens' Councils in the Delta, a.k.a., the White Citizens' Councils.

The Sovereignty Commission was an official agency of the State of Mississippi, established by statute to promote and defend state's rights and fight the federal government's forced integration of public facilities and schools in the state. It was created by the Mississippi Legislature in 1956, which also appointed the Commission members, who were lawmakers and other elected officials, as well as politically-connected private citizens. In carrying out its mission to preserve Jim Crow and segregated schools, the Sovereignty Commission became a statewide intelligence agency, most of its budget spent on gathering information and keeping files on citizens its investigators suspected were communists, fellow-travelers, civil rights leaders, and politically active African-Americans. By the time it was disbanded and de-funded, it had amassed files on over eighty thousand Mississippians. While it existed, it spent much of its annual budget on funding Citizens' Councils' activities in counties all over Mississippi.

The first Citizens' Council was established in the Delta in 1954, two years before the Sovereignty Commission. Its stated purpose was to oppose the civil rights movement in each county, using economic coercion rather than violence to maintain segregation. It held public meetings, professing to be equal in its mission and decorum to local Rotary and Kiwanis Clubs.

Buddy Richardson was young, in his mid-twenties at the time, but was heavily involved in establishing and running the Yaloquena and Dundee Citizens' Councils. He was never an officer, preferring to work behind the scenes, but Buddy controlled the agenda at meetings and orchestrated the groups' activities. The Councils were non-violent on paper, but whenever Buddy thought force or intimidation was necessary to make the Councils' point, he made it happen. No telling what all he did, how many buildings he torched, how many people he maimed or intimidated—or killed. Some of the violence was probably carried out by Buddy's Dixie Mafia buddies.

My father Monroe Banks, banker and model citizen, knew a lot about Buddy Richardson's activities. He shared a good bit of the knowledge with me. I never asked him how he knew so much about Buddy.

I found out six years ago. Monroe Banks was a member in good standing of the Citizens' Council in Sunshine and Yaloquena County.

I learned about his membership the hard way—I read it in the *Clarion-Ledger* the day after the Sovereignty Commission files on Big Al Anderson of Sunshine were released by the FBI. And for those people who did not read in the paper about my father being on the White Citizens' Council in Yaloquena County, *femme fatale* Mary Margaret Anderson screamed it out in the hallway outside the grand jury room in the courthouse. I had just cross-examined her before the Yaloquena Grand Jury in connection with the arson death of her husband, the worthless, wealthy, wheelchair-bound Little Al Anderson.

At that time Susan and I had been separated for three years. While she was away from Sunshine, I got involved with Mary Margaret Anderson. It was the worst personal failing of my entire life. And it's no secret any more. As a result of the death of Little Al and subsequent investigation, the entire town of Sunshine and much of the state learned about my affair with Mary Margaret.

I'm telling you this now because I didn't want you to hear it from someone else.

CHAPTER FIFTEEN

I was on the road at six a.m. the next morning. It was like the good old days. Hard-charging. Up at five-fifteen. Shower, dress, a cup of coffee in the kitchen then one to go in a twenty-ounce Styrofoam cup. It's the best time of the day, my favorite time to drive.

The meeting with Chief Columbus the day before had been pleasant but unproductive. He told us he did not have the manpower to put a tail on Buddy Richardson. Neither was he open to Lee's suggestion that a Yaloquena deputy follow Buddy in a civilian car. It created too many jurisdictional hazards, the Chief said, pointing out that the deputy had no authority to make an arrest in Oxford even if he saw Buddy doing something illegal.

I didn't agree with the Chief on his interpretation of the law, but we were in his town, and his understanding trumped mine. He thanked us for warning him about Richardson, and wished us luck on the trial. He said if the old man committed an offense in Oxford, they'd arrest him for it, but if he didn't, they had no reason to follow him.

I offered the guest room at the condo to Lee, but he said he had to get back to check on the protection detail on Lynn Metzger. He said he'd see me Monday at the courthouse if not before.

Like I knew I would, I had to stop at Batesville to go to the bathroom before I got on I-55 to head to State Police Headquarters in Jackson. A couple of mugs of strong black coffee and a bladder losing its elasticity are not a good mix. Old habits die hard, though, and while at the C-store I poured a little more coffee to warm up what I had left in my Styrofoam cup.

Two hours and one bathroom stop later, I pulled into the parking lot near the Highland exit off I-55, the headquarters of the Mississippi Highway Patrol and its investigative division, now known as the MBI, Mississippi Bureau of Investigation.

I had made a call the day before to Colonel John Austin, with whom I had many cordial dealings in my last two terms as elected District Attorney. He said he would ask his chief administrator to locate the investigative files from the 1962 riot, particularly everything they had on the Fratelli homicide.

I introduced myself to the woman officer at the front desk. She said Colonel Austin had told her to expect me, explaining that he was at the Capitol at a sub-committee hearing on funding, and would be out most of the day. She said the files I had requested were collected in a conference room, and led me down a narrow hallway to it.

She closed the door behind her. On the conference table were three large cardboard boxes of files labeled "University of Mississippi 1962." Set apart from the boxes was a manila folder with a yellow Post-It Note on the front reading "Russell Fratelli Homicide."

The Fratelli file was less than an inch thick.

I leafed through the pages to get an idea of the contents before I began reading. Midway through I found the coroner's report clipped with one photograph of Russell Fratelli dead on an autopsy table. He was lying on his back, covered with a white sheet up to his chest. I studied the photograph and took several pictures of it with my phone camera.

Portions of Russell's face and neck were discolored from the beginning of decomposition, but I could tell he was a handsome, physically fit young man with dark hair. The photo did not show the back of his neck where the bullet entered. And except for decay, no visible signs of injury on the body. I removed the paper clip and set the picture aside. The report consisted of two typewritten, single-spaced pages. The doctor did not provide a sketch of a human body to show the location of the entry wound. Instead, he wrote a detailed description of the bullet hole's location, the upward trajectory, and its terminus inside Russell's brain.

The young coroner described in exact clinical terms his removal of the bullet from Russell's brain during the autopsy. He described it as "flattened, but intact," noting the absence of fragments appearing on the X-ray taken of the victim's head before the physical examination began. The coroner described placing the bullet in a glass vial and giving it to the Highway Patrol investigator present at the procedure. He asked the investigator to deliver it to the State Crime Lab. The coroner did not describe powder burns or stippling near the entry wound. Because of his attention to detail in all other areas of the autopsy, I was confident signs of a "close range" shot did not exist. But I also knew from experience that if the shooter used a handgun, depending on the length of the barrel, caliber, and other conditions, he could have been slightly over twelve inches away and not left any gunpowder burns or stippling.

I put the coroner's report and photograph on the table, where I intended to make a stack of the documents I wanted to photocopy. The next document I read was the report of a Lieutenant Donovan, whom I figured to be the lead investigator for the Highway Patrol because of his rank. Donovan's report was chock full of details as to date, time, location, but very little of substance relating to Russell's murder. Donovan listed the state investigators at the scene, the names of the witnesses questioned, and a summary of what the investigation concluded, which was very little.

I read every report and statement in the file, but added only a few pages to my photocopy stack. The witnesses questioned uniformly added nothing to the case, except for Francis Fratelli, who told the investigators about the phone call that lured Russell away from the apartment. To my surprise, Lieutenant Donovan had obtained the phone company records of the calls to Russell's phone. Only one call was made near the relevant time. Unfortunately, Donovan said in his report the phone records showed the call to Russell was made from a pay phone on the Square that was used over eighty times on the day of the riot and the following three days. Donovan said the investigators checked out the pay phone, but made the decision that it would have been a waste of time to dust for fingerprints. Because of the phone's surface and location, mainly partials would have been available, and any prints lifted would likely be useless. Unless the prints were made by a known suspect or a criminal with his prints in the system, there would be no prints with which to compare.

So, that answered one question. The investigators did consider the call to Russell that Sunday evening to be important, but because it was traced to a well-used public pay phone, the information was of no practical use.

The only other document in the file that shed some light was a copy of the hand-drawn, incredibly detailed sketch by Ole Miss undergraduate Curtis Wilkie the day after the night of violence. He drew the entire scene of the riot around the Grove, from the Lyceum to the Confederate Monument and below. He added handwritten notations, including where the bodies of the French newspaper reporter and the victim from Abbeville were found.

The woman Highway Patrol officer photocopied the reports and statements I wanted, and the Wilkie sketch. I thanked her and asked her to express my appreciation to Colonel Austin. Before I started my truck, I made a call to the Director of the State Crime Lab, Robbie Cedars, with whom I had worked scores of cases as DA. I had called him the day before to ask if he could locate the bullet taken from Russell Fratelli's brain. He told me this morning he hadn't yet, but asked me to stop by the lab anyway to catch up.

Within minutes I was at the Crime Lab. It was good to see Robbie Cedars.

"My favorite D.A.," Robbie said.

"How've you been, Robbie?"

"Good. How's life after politics?"

"I like it. How's it feel to be director after all these years?"

"I keep looking around for someone to tell me what to do, and realize I'm it. It took some getting used to, but things are running smoothly now. Sorry I haven't come up with your bullet yet, but I'm fairly sure I will. When we moved into this building the Ole Miss evidence was something I know was brought over from the old facility, so we'll find it. Just have to go through a bunch of smelly old boxes of evidence."

"I appreciate it. Let me show you something."

I pulled out the coroner's report on Russell Fratelli and pointed to the description of the bullet as "flattened, but intact." Robbie thought a moment.

"That rules out identifying by comparison rifling if the lands and grooves are no longer discernible. You don't have a weapon anyway, so there's nothing to get a comparison shot from."

"Assuming the bullet is too damaged for comparison," I asked, "is there anything you can tell me about it? The size, the weight, anything to narrow down the type of weapon it was shot from?"

"Sure. If I can weigh it and analyze the metal content, I can make an educated guess on the caliber and probably type of weapon. But it's going to be broad generalizations, probably not much help to you."

"Well, just put that big brain of yours to work on it. Anything you can tell me will be more than I have to go on now."

We reminisced for another fifteen minutes about cases we worked on together, the times he testified in my trials. Robbie said he would call me as soon as his people found the bullet and he had a chance to analyze it.

On I-55 heading north to Oxford, I called Cheryl Diamond in Houston. She answered on the third ring.

"I've thought of you several times this past week, Willie Mitchell," she said. "And here you are calling me. It's no coincidence."

"Probably not," I said and laughed. "I need a favor, Cheryl," I said after we had chatted a while.

"Anything for you, Willie Mitchell," she said.

"I'm going to scan a photograph of a murder victim and e-mail it to you, along with a copy of the coroner's report. The young man was twenty-two and was killed in the riots surrounding the admission of James Meredith to the University of Mississippi in 1962. His body wasn't found for several days, and was not included in the official death count the state and feds put out arising out of the trouble. I'm going to send you a couple of links to articles about the riot, too, for background."

"What do you want me to do?"

"Anything you can. I'm looking into this for the young man's brother. Nothing official, just a favor to him. The victim's name is Russell Fratelli."

"You know I can't promise anything. I'll study the photograph of the victim and read the articles, and if anything comes to me I'll let you know."

"I know this is a long shot, Cheryl, but I don't have much to go on in getting to the bottom of this thing. Everything I look at is a dead end."

"And if the spirits are with you, Willie Mitchell, maybe they'll share something with me about his death."

Before you think I'm off my rocker for consulting a sixty-nine-year-old, independently wealthy psychic who lives in Houston and looks a lot like one of the Gabor sisters, let me tell you what Cheryl Diamond did for me. About eighteen months ago, during my final re-election campaign, I prosecuted Ross Bullard in Sunshine for the abduction and murder of seven-year-old Danny Thurman. The boy disappeared at a July 4th political event where my opponent Eleanor Bernstein and I were scheduled to have our first "debate." In spite of a massive manhunt, we could not find little Danny's body.

I won a hard-fought conviction that I worried about holding up on appeal. After the trial, Cheryl Diamond led me to Danny's body in a cave adjacent to an old creek bed in a heavily wooded area many miles south of Sunshine. She had never been to Yaloquena County and knew no one involved in the case.

Cheryl located Danny Thurman's body. No one else could.

CHAPTER SIXTEEN

After I returned from Highway Patrol Headquarters and my visit with Robbie Cedars at the State Crime Lab, Susan and I ate dinner Friday night with Jimmy and Martha Gray at The Snack Bar, in the Mid-Town Shopping Center off North Lamar. The Snack Bar has a lively atmosphere and was Jimmy's favorite because he treated it like a cocktail party, greeting people he knew when they came in, and schmoozing with the patrons at the long, bar-like table that ran the entire length of the upper tier of the split level dining room. We were seated at Jimmy's favorite table in a corner on the lower level. If you were in The Snack Bar that evening, at some point you had to pass our table. If Jimmy knew you, he was going to flag you down for a visit.

Susan looked beautiful as usual—tall, blonde, and elegant—as pretty as she was the day we married. Martha was a quiet, attractive brunette who was devoted to the wild man to whom she was married. We were all about the same age, had been married about the same number of years, and had suffered through good times and bad together. Jimmy and Martha helped hold me together during Susan's three-year sabbatical from our marriage and the Mary Margaret Anderson disaster. Susan and I helped the Grays get through the traumatic loss of their younger son, Beau, who died at nineteen in a hunting accident. His gun accidentally discharged while Beau was climbing over a fence, hunting alone. Beau and our son Scott grew up together in Sunshine and were best friends.

Beau's death was almost the end of Jimmy Gray. His mourning was alcohol-fueled and angry, and I spent as much time with him as it took to keep Jimmy from drinking himself to death. Martha and Jimmy consoled each other through the tragedy and after several years, the pain of Beau's death still lingered, but was not as acute. Their older son, Jimmy Jr., was an internal medicine specialist in

Jackson, and did his best to cajole his father into taking better care of himself, to the extent it was possible for anyone to moderate Jimmy's behavior. He lived life at warp speed.

Jimmy loved people, and had come to know more folks in Oxford than I did, even though Susan and I were living here full-time, while he and Martha were still spending half their time in Sunshine. He was the life of every party, and that Friday night in The Snack Bar was no different.

I spotted James Butler, the retired newspaper man and talented painter I had spoken to at his home the past Monday. He acknowledged me and made his way to our table. I introduced everyone, and after Jimmy Gray quizzed him about his relatives and friends and made several connections, Butler joined me on the curved divan at our corner table.

"Thanks for getting me into the *Eagle* archives," I said. "Lots of interesting articles and pictures. Not much relevant to Russell Fratelli's death."

"I've been thinking since we met earlier, about the troubles in 1962," he said quietly. "This probably won't help you either, but *The Daily Mississippian* also has a room full of old newspapers and black and white photographs organized by each year in their office on campus. I mentioned to you I was a reporter there and covered the riot with some of the other *Mississippian* staff. I could get you in there to have a look-see. I know the young woman who's editor."

"That would be great, James. When could we do it?"

"Best time is on the weekend. It's pretty hectic in there during the week. Sunday morning's the optimum time because these students party pretty hard on Saturday night and they usually don't stir until sometime in the afternoon."

"How about day after tomorrow? This Sunday morning?"

"Fine. I'll get a key from her."

He told me where *The Daily Mississippian* office was on campus, and we agreed to meet there Sunday morning at eight. It's one of the perks of living in a small town I really enjoy. If you need to talk to someone, and if you're out and about, you'll probably run into them sooner rather than later.

After we polished off the second bottle of Louis Jadot Pouilly-Fuisse, Susan and I were ready to leave.

"You're such a short-hitter," Jimmy said.

"My mother always told me to leave when I'm having a good time."

"You two go ahead," he said. "I'll settle up with the bank Mastercard."

"Marketing," I said.

"I'm sacrificing my time for the good of the institution."

Jimmy's "sacrificing" had paid off big for our Oxford branch of Sunshine Bank on Jackson Avenue, just off the Square and west of Bouré. When one of the big regional banks headquartered in Nashville had taken over a north Mississippi competitor of ours two years ago, they consolidated their Oxford operations and the prime location on Jackson came available. Jimmy had become friends with the Chairman of the Board of Directors of the Nashville bank during the big bank's multi-year pursuit of Sunshine Bank and Jimmy Gray. Jimmy had come close to selling out to the Nashville bank at a very favorable multiple of book value when Susan and I made the decision to move to Oxford. It took place after I declined to serve another term as D.A. I told Jimmy the decision was his to make, that I would be satisfied whether he kept the bank or sold it. Neither of us needed the money, and Jimmy finally decided he would miss banking too much if he sold. The Nashville bank wanted a five-year commitment from Jimmy to stay on and continue to run the bank. Jimmy told me he had never worked for anyone, and if he was going to have to run the bank anyway, we might as well continue to own it.

Sunshine Bank acquired the location just off the Square. It required minimal renovation, primarily sprucing up the exterior and interior and changing the signage. Jimmy hit the ground running. Our bank already had customers in Oxford, because many of our patrons in the Delta had moved here. Sunshine Bank had always been a big agricultural lender, financing farmers all over the Delta. The dramatic jump in farmland prices over the past decade had made our agricultural loans super-secured, with the mortgaged collateral exceeding the value of the loan amount dramatically. It's the reason why the Nashville Bank had salivated over acquiring our loan portfolio.

Jimmy's customers were fiercely loyal to him, and were all pleased that he made the decision keep the bank. Since we opened the branch in Oxford, Jimmy had turned over most of the day-to-day operations in Sunshine to the management team he had personally groomed, allowing him to focus on acquiring assets in Oxford and spend more time here. He was having fun growing the branch assets and had become a familiar figure on the Square.

While Susan and I were driving home, I received a text from Eleanor Bernstein, the lawyer who would have been the next District Attorney for Yaloquena County had those salacious photographs not come out. She was now an Assistant U.S. Attorney, recently transferred to the Oxford office.

"Need to C U tomorrow, Willie Mitchell. Important. EB."

CHAPTER SEVENTEEN

I heard a delicate knock on the back door of the condo. Eleanor Bernstein had called me fifteen minutes earlier and said she needed to be discreet. I suggested she park in the back to minimize the possibility of being seen. She had me intrigued with what she wanted to share with me.

"Come in, Eleanor," I said and gave her a hug.

She wore a business suit, a dark gray pinstripe, her blouse buttoned to the top, as usual. Eleanor was always well-dressed and professional in her days as the Public Defender for Yaloquena County. She spoke quietly and carried herself with dignity. She was neatly turned out this Saturday morning, attractive, thin with very dark skin and short hair. She rarely smiled, her demeanor steady and calm. We tried a lot of cases against each other and weathered some highly charged confrontations, but always remained friendly. Her job as indigent defender was much tougher than mine. Her clients were almost always guilty, poorly educated, and consistently ungrateful to her. Eleanor managed to juggle her overwhelming case load while maintaining an even keel. She was now forty-five, still in a long-term relationship with Lynette Nguyen.

"I'm afraid I have some bad news, Willie Mitchell," she said.

"Come have a seat before we get down to business, Eleanor. Tell me how you're settling in up here."

"I'm glad to get out of Jackson," she said. "That office down there is a nightmare. Not very well-managed. The Oxford office is run much better and my case load is lighter. I found a condo over near the cemetery. Three minutes from the office."

"How's Lynette?"

"Fine. Thanks for asking. She's still working as a nurse anesthetist with the group in Jackson. They have a satellite office up here that they're expanding to accommodate the growth they expect when the new Baptist Hospital opens. She comes up most weekends, or I drive down there. We're keeping our fingers crossed about an opening here in Oxford. We think it might be as soon as sometime next month. I can't wait because I'm so tired of driving I-55 with all the construction going on."

"You like some coffee?"

"No, thanks. I can't stay but a minute. There's something coming down that you need to know."

"Let's have it."

"You know I work in the criminal division. There's an ongoing investigation out of Washington into the racial makeup of grand juries throughout the Delta over the past twenty years."

"I know about it. It's been going on a while. Justice began looking into every judicial district in north Mississippi, gathering statistics. We had to send them a lot of information. I say 'we,' but it was mostly Clerk of Court Winston Moore and Walton who put the data together for them."

"There's a line of cases coming out of the Fifth Circuit," she said, "that have overturned convictions going as far back as fifteen years if they can prove a pattern of racial discrimination in grand jury selection in state criminal prosecutions. Most of the cases come through the federal system on a writ of *habeas corpus*."

"Walton seems to think Yaloquena County is all right because in the twenty-four years I was in office there have always been African-Americans on the grand juries. With a county that's seventy-five per cent black, it's not possible to put together a grand jury venire that's not majority black."

"In all my years trying cases in your jurisdiction, I don't think we ever had a jury on which blacks weren't well-represented. Judge Williams was on the bench the entire time, and she impaneled every grand jury. Since she's black and ran the courtroom I can't see how anyone could complain about how you and she handled everything."

"So, has something happened?"

"The Fifth Circuit in New Orleans decided a case out of Natchez last year. The panel extended the reach of the grand jury discrimination cases to include the selection of the foreman."

"Judge Williams always asked me to select the foreman. I would recommend one of the grand jurors and she always went along."

"I know. But the case out of Natchez puts an affirmative duty on the District Attorney in each judicial district to see that racial balance is achieved in the selection of a foreperson."

"Why not the judge?" I asked. "I think that's actually what the law says."

"The Fifth Circuit reasoned that the grand jury is part of the prosecutorial process, and puts the obligation squarely on the D.A.'s shoulders. The case went up to the Supreme Court but *certiorari* was denied."

"So the Fifth Circuit opinion is the law. I swear I cannot believe there can be any legitimate objection to the way we did it in Yaloquena."

"There is, according to the Justice Department. They say the records show Yaloquena had only one black grand jury foreman in the ten years from 2000 to 2010."

"That's going back fifteen years. I know for a fact that I asked a lot of black grand jurors to be foreman and they declined, not wanting the responsibility."

"That's not documented in the records," Eleanor said.

"No. It wouldn't be. It was all informal. Nothing put on the record."

"The head of the criminal division here called me in yesterday to read a memo that had come down from D.C. They've made a decision to target some of your convictions to try to get them overturned."

"What a waste of time and money. You know from your own experience I never sent anyone away unless I was certain they were guilty."

"I know it. That's what I told the chief."

"This is ridiculous. What makes it so bad is Walton's going to have to fight these battles, and his work load is already heavy. It's just plain counter-productive to re-litigate cases from so long ago, especially where there's no doubt the defendant was guilty. Typical Justice Department. They make these policy decisions in their pristine halls in D.C. They say 're-try the case' and have no idea how hard it is on those of us out here in the trenches to convict when the crime happened a dozen years ago. To them it's an academic exercise."

"Overturning the convictions is one thing," Eleanor said. "But the other thing they're considering is even worse. The decision was made yesterday during a conference call between D.C. and the chief of criminal prosecutions here. They're going to open a criminal investigation into your grand jury foreman appointments while you were DA. They're talking about going under Section 1983 to charge a deprivation of civil rights under color of law."

"Criminal investigation? That's insane."

"That's what I told them. You know what the guy in D.C. said?"

"No telling."

"He said they want to make an example out of you."

CHAPTER EIGHTEEN

James Butler arrived at Bishop Hall two minutes after I did. Though he had given me directions during our chance meeting in the Snack Bar, the Pouilly-Fuisse must have flooded my synapses and interfered with my usually unerring cognitive function. I had to consult an online map of Ole Miss to locate the building on the north side of Fraternity Row down the hill from the Paris-Yates Chapel. James and I were the only two humans in sight. If we had encountered students, it would have been more likely they were coming in from a long night rather than getting up to make an early appointment.

He led me inside to the main office of *The Daily Mississippian*, mentioning that the addition of "Daily" to the college newspaper's title was added a few years after the riot. He opened the door with the editor's key and led me back through a hallway to a door with "RECORDS" stenciled on it. We walked inside. The smell reminded me of the day I had recently spent in the *Oxford Eagle* archives—a combination of old newsprint and dust—and the twenty minutes I spent in Boyland Burr's lovely home.

"The editor told me two interns spent all of last semester identifying, organizing, and labeling everything in this room. There's lots of valuable history in these pages, but nobody is interested in going through them. These days, if it's not digital, the students don't fool with it."

"Yep," I said.

Butler studied the shelves a moment and gestured for me to help. We removed four boxes of newspapers and three boxes labeled "PHOTOGRAPHS 1962." He spent ten minutes leafing through the papers and pulled out the editions published in September and October of 1962, placing them on the table in front of me. He spent a moment on the photographs, which were mostly five-by-seven black and white prints.

"The editor said these photographs are supposed to be in chronological order, but I don't think they are. What do you want to do with these?"

"Why don't you just leave all three boxes there on the table and I'll go through them. Do I need to be out of here at any particular time?"

"The editor said she may come in late this afternoon, but I don't think it matters. Spend as much time as you want. The young woman asked me to caution you about removing anything from this room."

"No problem," I said. "I appreciate your doing this, James. No need for you to stick around. I'm going to be here several hours at least. Tell you what, give me your home number and I'll call you when I'm done."

"Naomi and I are leaving after lunch to go see her sister in Mobile. Be gone a few days. Let's do this. Give the key to the editor if she shows up before you leave. If she doesn't, just lock up and keep the key until I get back. I'll pick it up and get it back to her."

"I can bring it here tomorrow."

"No need to do that. The editor has another key. Hell, just about everyone on the staff has a key. We'll talk when I get back."

I shook Butler's hand and thanked him as he closed the records room door. I opened the first paper and sniffed, imagining dust and motes erupting like solar flares from the pages as I turned them. I was certain the little buggers floated menacingly around the room, biding their time before getting sucked in by the powerful gravitational pull of the black holes in the center of my face—my nostrils. Fearless in the face of imminent peril to my sinuses, I bravely forged ahead, comfortable knowing I had confronted much worse.

The Mississippian covered less of the legislative and gubernatorial attitudes about the admission of James Meredith than I had seen in the *Oxford Eagle*. It's what I expected of the student paper. It focused on campus events rather than the saber-rattling in Jackson. The October 1, 1962 edition was devoted entirely to the events of the day before, with plenty of pictures. I read the articles and studied the photographs in the papers, but I saw nothing new, nothing that would help explain the murder of Russell Fratelli. *The Mississippian* put out an issue every day during the week following September 30, with other campus news finally making its way back into the paper in the Friday edition. It contained a cryptically-worded, small article about Russell's body being found off the northeast corner of the Grove in the ravine leading down to the railroad tracks. The paper did not run a photo of Russell. Other than reporting that the investigators suspected "foul play," they did not link his death to the Sunday night riot. In retrospect, it was an odd omission, but was consistent with what I had learned about the effort to tamp down publicity about the incredibly violent riot.

At about eleven o'clock, after almost three hours of going through the newspapers, I turned my attention to the three boxes of photographs, each box approximately the size of a case of copy paper. I lifted a stack of photos from the first box and began going through them, picking up speed as I went. The pictures in the first box were fun to look at but not relevant to Russell Fratelli, so I went through them as quickly as possible. In spite of Butler's observation that they weren't in order, the first photographs appeared to have been taken in winter. The exterior shots showed students bundled up against the cold under denuded deciduous trees. As I neared the end of the first box, photos showed students playing tennis in shorts, and pear trees in bloom.

Encouraged, I moved to the second box, which should have brought me up to early September if the pictures were in chronological order. I skimmed through the first photos, flipping rapidly. I had seen enough shots of students on campus in the summer months. I was anxious to get to box three, which should have contained the riot photos.

The last picture in box two caught my eye. I studied it closely to make sure. After five minutes I was certain I recognized the young man, even though no names were written on the photograph. The handsome young man leaned against a tree in the Grove, his arms around a beautiful brunette held tightly against him. Each gazed into the others' eyes in a pose we've all seen many times—young lovers in a trance, oblivious to everything around them—focused only on each other.

The handsome, dark haired young man was Russell Fratelli. No doubt about it. The girl's uplifted face was in profile. I could not be sure, but I swear she looked like Cissy Summers, the beauty queen, soon to be Miss Mississippi and third runner-up in the Miss America contest.

CHAPTER NINETEEN

When Susan and I moved to Oxford, I was determined to have a go at William Faulkner again. My relationship with him in undergraduate school English courses had been unsatisfying except for *The Reivers* and *The Bear*. In grappling with his major works, even though the writing was powerful and moving, I couldn't understand the narrative. In *The Sound and the Fury,* if it hadn't been for Cliffs Notes, I would have had no idea who the characters were or what was going on.

"Count No-Count" Faulkner remains a hero in Oxford, his personal idiosyncrasies long ago forgiven because of his writing brilliance and widespread fame. His home in the heart of Oxford's oldest residential area, Rowan Oak, is a major tourist attraction. In our first year in Oxford, Susan and I had met some of his relatives, most of whom spelled their family name without the "u" that Faulkner added, so the story goes, when he enlisted in the Canadian R.A.F. after being rejected by the U.S. Army for being too small.

In my first months in Oxford, I read *The Sound and the Fury, As I Lay Dying,* and *Absalom, Absalom!* I did better with *As I Lay Dying* this time, following the story much more closely than I did in college. *Absalom, Absalom!* was still shrouded in mystery, but I managed to follow the story of Thomas Sutpen and his quest to become a celebrated patriarch in the grand manor he constructed on his plantation, Sutpen's Hundred. *The Sound and the Fury,* however, was still impenetrable. Even after I went online to research the story of the Compson family and understood that four different narrators told the story, I still struggled to follow what was going on. Faulkner's description of the constant screaming of the idiot man-child Benji was powerfully written, very disturbing, and extremely confusing.

My grappling with Faulkner came to mind because I was walking the nature trail through Faulkner Woods, the one-hundred-acre undisturbed wilderness adjacent to Rowan Oak now owned by the University. It was late afternoon Sunday after I had spent seven hours in the records room of *The Mississippian*. I accessed the trail off University Avenue behind the University's Mary Buie Museum and followed it through the dense woods and over deep creeks and ravines to exit onto Old Taylor Road next to Rowan Oak.

I took the walk through the woods to clear my head and think. The photograph of Russell Fratelli and the girl who looked like Cissy Summers wrapped up against a tree in the Grove was evidence of a different type of relationship than Cissy had described to me at her townhome. "We dated a few times," is what she said over coffee that morning eight days earlier, which I took to mean they were no more than friends who had a couple of dates and then moved on. No big deal. But the looks in their eyes in the photograph and their body language told me an entirely different story—if the girl were indeed Cissy Summers.

I took a deep breath and reminded myself not to jump to any conclusions. I could easily have been mistaken about the girl's identity. Cissy wasn't the only tall, beautiful brunette on campus that summer. It's also possible that even if the girl were Cissy, maybe the reporter who took the photograph posed them as students in love. Or maybe I was straining at a gnat, reading too much into the picture.

My more pressing concern that Sunday afternoon was what Eleanor Bernstein told me at the condo about the Justice Department's plans for me in connection with the impanelling of grand juries and selecting the grand jury foremen when I was DA. The sad fact was that common sense and practicality were no longer part of the process at the Justice Department. In my lifetime it had become the leading enforcer of political correctness and the tool of whichever party had control of the executive branch. It was now one of the many bloated bureaucracies in Washington D.C. where good ideas and efficiency went to die.

Walking back home I passed Boyland Burr's house on South 11th. I considered knocking on the door to ask about his relationship with Buddy Richardson, but the idea of walking through those newspapers and seeing the dried SpaghettiOs on the dinette table was too offensive for this Sunday night. I turned left on Filmore and right on South 8th to Susan's condo.

CHAPTER TWENTY

I put on a dark suit and tie Monday morning and walked to Walton's combination apartment and war room on the Square, arriving upstairs at 8:30. I knocked and entered at the same time. Walton was busy at the dining room table, going over the jury venire with another young man, whom I assumed to be the Lafayette County Assistant District Attorney loaned to Walton for local knowledge.

"Willie Mitchell Banks, meet Josh Pickett," Walton said.

"Thanks for helping," I said.

"Glad to do it," Josh said. "I've heard a lot about you, Mr. Banks. My boss says you were the best District Attorney in the state for many years."

"Nice of him to say," I said. "How's the panel look?"

"It's fairly typical of our usual venire. There's a handful of people who work at the University and a good number of retired people. Racially it tracks the county fairly well."

"Josh agrees with us on the professors," Walton said. "Avoid them like the plague."

"It's best you don't put them on the jury," Josh said. "They are generally unfavorable to prosecutors, especially the younger ones, and they tend to dominate the other jurors."

"Josh says they're accustomed to lecturing their students, so they go into professor mode when they're picked," Walton said.

"Townspeople and faculty don't always get along," Josh said.

"Just like every university town," I said.

I offered to help carry boxes or exhibits but Walton said he was only bringing what he needed for jury selection, which was his trial notebook and the venire list that he had annotated with information Josh provided. We walked across the street. I glanced up at the south side of the historic courthouse in the center of the Square. Built in

1840 in a combination of Greek Revival and Italianate styles, it was painted white, and seemed to loom over me as we approached. We entered the building under the southern portico. At the risk of sounding like Cheryl Diamond, my psychic buddy from Houston, I felt a distinctly negative vibe—a foreboding.

We walked up the narrow, carpeted wooden steps to the second floor. I admired the masterful woodwork on the bannisters and curved handrail. We entered the Circuit Courtroom on the west side of the building. I paused to take in the majestic beauty of the huge room. The wooden entrance doors were at least twelve feet high, proportional to the height of the wood plank ceiling, which was painted white and soared thirty feet above the floor. Windows stretched fifteen feet on the north and south walls. High overhead I admired the massive, ornate medallions on the ceiling from which ancient chandeliers hung. I made a mental note to ask someone if the chandeliers were originally gasoliers and later electrified.

The courtroom's unique curved wooden benches were two-thirds full with prospective jurors. Walton, Josh, and I pushed through the gate on the rail separating the public from court personnel. We took seats at the prosecution table. The judge's bench was on a riser in front of us, flanked on the left by a door leading to chambers for the trial judge, an elevator, and a holding cell for use in criminal cases where the defendant is in custody. To the right of the judge's bench through the open door I saw the long table and chairs in the empty jury deliberation room. Behind us, people steadily entered the courtroom, eventually filling all the antique, highly-polished benches. Ten minutes later, J.D. Silver and Buddy Richardson walked down the center aisle, trailed by Silver's jury selection expert. I remembered her from the Ross Bullard trial in Sunshine.

The door to the left of the bench opened and into the courtroom walked Winston Moore, Circuit Clerk for Yaloquena County, and Eddie Bordelon, the Chief Deputy Clerk who ran Judge Williams's courtroom. As usual, Winston was resplendent in a navy blue suit with wide, white pinstripes, a cherry red kerchief in the breast pocket matching his tie, and black patent leather loafers. Eddie was a transplanted Cajun from South Louisiana. He was short and wiry, bald and wore rimless glasses. He wore an innocuous gray suit, his typical courtroom attire. Eddie was the most nervous, hyper-organized, and efficient courtroom clerk I had ever encountered. I left the table and walked over to shake hands with Eddie and Winston, greeting them in a hushed tone, almost like we were in church. It was good to see them.

I had not been back in my chair more than a few seconds when Buddy Richardson stood up from the defense table and strode proudly to greet Winston Moore and Eddie like they were the oldest and best of friends. Winston was a politician with a quick smile and welcoming manner by nature, so he stood and chatted cheerfully with Buddy for a moment. Eddie shook hands with downcast eyes, then took his seat began scribbling on a legal pad.

"Asshole Richardson," Walton whispered under his breath.

I didn't blame him. When I tried cases, I stressed to the Clerk of Court and all court personnel they were not to communicate in any way with the defendant in front of the prospective jurors. Sitting there in the courtroom, waiting for their names to be called, each prospect nervously watches every movement in front of the courtroom rail. If potential jurors see Winston Moore chatting and smiling with the defendant, it may cloak the defendant in an aura of decency and legitimacy. Buddy Richardson hired Lynn Metzger to lie in wait, ambush, and murder Carl Sanders, his grandson-in-law. I did not want jurors seeing the Clerk of Court schmoozing with the defendant as if they were old friends. Neither did Walton. But it was too late. The damage, if any, was done.

At 9:05 Judge Williams had not yet taken the bench. I leaned over to Walton and asked him if he had heard anything recently from the Justice Department regarding the inquiries they made while I was still DA about grand jury selection in Yaloquena County.

"No," he said, "not since we sent in all the data. Why?"

"No reason," I said and shrugged.

I glanced over at the defense table. Buddy Richardson was back in his seat after his visit with the Clerk. He and Memphis hot shot criminal lawyer J.D. Silver, a.k.a. Helmet Head, were happily chatting up the woman jury expert, the three of them chuckling at the defense table as if waiting for a Broadway play to begin. It irritated the hell out of me.

Just when I thought it couldn't get worse, Buddy stood up and stretched, then turned and spent several minutes looking over the prospective jurors on the curved benches. He smiled and nodded when any of them made eye contact. Buddy was working the crowd.

"The son-of-a-bitch has a lot of nerve," I muttered to Walton under my breath. "I swear he acts like he's the star of the show on opening night."

The local bailiff entered the courtroom directing everyone to rise. Judge Zelda Williams, my favorite judge of all time, followed him in and took her seat behind the bench. I hadn't seen her in six months. Her hair might have turned a bit more gray, but I wasn't sure. Zelda presided over so many of my trials, seeing her was like reuniting with an old friend. We had a mutual admiration society, but kept our contact professional like we were supposed to.

"Good morning," she said to the packed courtroom. "Mr. Moore, please call the roll."

Zelda made eye contact, acknowledging me with a barely discernible nod. I did the same. Winston Moore took thirty minutes to read each name and account for the no-shows. Walton was busy making notes next to the names on the jury venire list as they were called. Josh periodically leaned over and whispered to Walton. Zelda read the general juror qualifications to the prospects, and asked if anyone had any medical reason they could not serve. Three prospective jurors walked through the rail and lined up in front of the bench. Each whispered, in turn. I couldn't hear what their ailments were, but Judge Williams excused all three.

"Now," she said, "Mr. Moore, please place the remaining names in the box, shake them up, and call the first twelve."

Eddie had been busy separating the perforated strips on the list and placing each prospective juror's name in a metal box. After shaking it vigorously, Eddie held up the box for Winston, who fished out the first twelve strips and read out the names. The prospects followed Zelda's instructions to take their seats in the jury box.

At 10:30, Zelda announced a ten minute break. Everyone stood while she walked to her chambers. As soon as the door closed behind her, the courtroom emptied. I glanced at the defense table. Sonny caught my eyes and winked. I acted as if I hadn't noticed and turned to talk to Walton.

"I'm going to head home for the rest of the morning, Walton, if you don't need me. I've got some calls to make. Be back at one or one-thirty, whenever the Judge reconvenes after lunch."

"Sure, no problem. Would you mind dropping this trial folder off? I don't need it here now. Don't know why I brought it. Here's the key."

I had to wait a bit while the remaining prospective jurors filed out. I walked down the stairs and out the south entrance past the jurors who had gathered to get some fresh air under the towering oaks on the courthouse grounds. It was a pretty day, bright sunshine, a few lonely cumulus clouds drifting high over the Square in a northeasterly direction.

I crossed the busy street and walked up the steps toward the interior door of the apartment. At the top step I noticed the door was slightly open. I had seen Walton lock it earlier when we left. I lightly pushed on the wooden door. As it swung open, I stood on the top step and peered in. It appeared that a tornado had struck inside the apartment.

Walton's neat stack of exhibits had been strewn across the room. His Pre-Trial Memorandum was ripped to shreds on the floor, as were the cases he had printed out from LexisNexis. I didn't go in. Standing on the top step outside the door, I called Mike Columbus, Chief of Police. I walked down the steps and stood on the sidewalk in front of the outside door. Across the street, the last of the prospective jurors were filing back into the courthouse. I didn't have to wait long for OPD to arrive.

Five minutes passed. Two Oxford black-and-whites pulled up at the same time. Chief Columbus hustled out of the passenger side of the first car.

"What's the situation?" he asked.

"I came back here at a break to drop off Walton's trial book. When I got to the top step, the inside door was open slightly. I looked inside and there's stuff thrown everywhere in there. I was with Walton and local Assistant D.A. Josh Pickett when we left here a little after 8:30. I saw Walton lock the door."

"Did you go inside the apartment?"

"No. Stayed on the top step. When I pushed the door open I saw the mess in there and called you."

"Let's have a look."

The Chief walked up the steps ahead of me. One of his officers trailed me, and the two other policemen stayed on the sidewalk. The Chief looked in the apartment for a moment and turned to me.

"How do you want to handle this? It's a crime scene. What kind of crime I don't know exactly."

"Me either," I said. "Even if we went in I wouldn't be able to tell if anything was missing. We need to wait for Walton. They'll break for lunch at noon or 12:30 and we can get him to see what's been taken or destroyed. I don't want to interrupt him during jury selection. You or the Sheriff have any crime scene techs here in town?"

"I've got a couple of guys with some training. They're not crime lab proficient but they're good enough for us to use on property crimes, which is what this looks like."

"This is not random, Chief. This place is owned by a law school buddy of Walton's. He's been sleeping and working here since Thursday. Someone waited for him to leave for court this morning, and did this while he was gone. It had to be someone who knew about the trial and Walton's schedule."

"How about your man Richardson?"

"He's been in the courtroom all morning," I said. "But this has his stench all over it. Buddy had one of his henchmen do it while he had the perfect alibi."

"Why don't you head back to the courtroom and I'll station a couple of men here to watch it. Bring Walton back over at lunch break and I'll have my crime scene men ready to do whatever y'all think needs to be done. We can print the whole apartment, but you know what kind of mess that makes."

"Yeah, and it'd probably be a waste of time. Give me your cell number and I'll send you a text when Judge Williams breaks for lunch."

CHAPTER TWENTY-ONE

I made the decision not to tell Walton about the break-in when I returned to the courtroom. No need to interrupt his concentration on jury selection. I made sure he didn't see me place the trial book on the floor beside the prosecution table where he couldn't see it. I watched the questioning the remainder of the morning, enduring the spirit-deadening, repetitious ordeal of picking a jury in state court. The shame of it is the process is so very important. Picking a jury receptive to your case is just as important as the evidence you present. And I don't care how much investigation you have done into each prospect's background, or how brilliant your jury consultant is, many times the decision to accept or challenge comes down to gut instinct. In every case I tried, I always found out something relevant about a juror during the trial, after he or she was seated and sworn in as a member of the panel. Sometimes it worked to my benefit. Sometimes it didn't.

I made sure my phone was on silent and held it under the table so Judge Williams could not see me texting. I sent a text to Sheriff Lee Jones, telling him what happened and suggesting he put a security team on Walton. I also sent a text to my friend Patrick Dunwoody IV's private cell number. He was the number two man at Justice, his authority exceeded only by the Attorney General of the United States, the political hack Danny Okole. Okole was the first Hawaiian to be named chief law enforcement official for the country, and was so far out of his league it was embarrassing. Dunwoody said Okole had a unique combination of ignorance and arrogance that made him particularly ill-suited for the job. He added that Okole earned his appointment for two reasons: first, he was a very productive fund raiser for the Commander-In-Chief, and second, he could be counted on to do as he was told. In my text to Dunwoody, I was vague, indicating only that I needed to talk. His response was that he was available, and for me to call his cell at my convenience.

Dunwoody was one of the most interesting men in Washington. Almost a dead ringer for British actor Jeremy Irons, he was the last of the Dunwoodys, one of Virginia's first families. His forebears received large land grants from the King of England when they settled in the foothills of the Blue Ridge Mountains outside of Charlottesville, contemporaneous with Thomas Jefferson's ancestors. Patrick lived at Bellingham, an estate of two thousand acres remaining from the original land grants, with his executive assistant at Justice and longtime companion Donald Monroe. Patrick acknowledged he would be the last of the Dunwoodys, adding with a smile "the family line had saved its best for last."

Susan and I met Dunwoody after he intervened to help our son Jake out of an extraordinarily dangerous situation. We became friends and Susan and I had spent several weekends at Bellingham as his guests.

At twelve-fifteen Judge Williams broke for lunch, announcing the Court would reconvene at one-thirty. I waited for the jurors to leave before telling Walton and Josh about the break-in. We met Chief Columbus at the apartment. I suggested that the Chief and Walton go in by themselves. Walton could assess the damage to his work product and evidence, and Chief Columbus would be an independent witness of Walton's conduct in the apartment. After twenty minutes, Walton and the Chief joined the rest of us on the sidewalk.

"Nothing's missing," Walton said.

"You checked the evidence? It's all there?"

"All the evidence is still in the Sheriff's evidence locker in Sunshine. I knew this place couldn't be secure and I would be gone a lot. They destroyed most of my documents, but I've got copies of everything back in my office in Sunshine. The display boards are torn up, but they're easy to reproduce. Everything they damaged I can easily replace."

"You want us to process this place? Check for prints?"

Walton looked at me and shrugged.

"I don't see the need. Do you?"

"Be a waste of time. I sent a text to Lee asking him to assign some security to you."

"I think that would be wise," Chief Columbus said and turned to me. "You knew what you were talking about, didn't you? This guy's a bad ass."

"Yep," I said. "Been bad all his life."

Chapter Twenty-Two

By Tuesday at noon Walton and Helmet Head had seated two jurors. Decent progress considering the defense lawyer's continued abuse of the *voir dire* process. Helmet Head used every question as an opportunity to interject his theory of the case and illustrate the weakness of Walton's. It wasn't Zelda's first rodeo, so after letting him push the envelope all afternoon Monday, she reined him in during a conference before convening Tuesday morning, promising to admonish him in front of the prospective jurors to let them know what he was doing. I didn't participate in the meeting, but Walton told me Judge Williams laid down the law to the big-haired lawyer.

"You don't need to stay, Willie Mitchell," Walton said when he pulled me aside in the most isolated corner of the Lafayette County courtroom. "I appreciate your holding my hand the last couple of days, but my nerves have calmed down. Appreciate your helping me over the hump."

"Just pre-game jitters, partner," I said clapping him on the shoulder. "I'm proud of the way you're handling yourself. It's a big case and like I said, you're up to it."

"I had a good teacher."

"I'll hang around a while this morning, then probably be in and out the rest of the week. But if you need me, I'll never be more than five minutes away. You call or text and I'll be here. And look, stay safe."

Instead of sitting at the prosecution table, I took a seat in the front row behind Walton, but next to the side aisle so I could leave discreetly. I wanted the jurors to see Walton running the show without my sitting at his side. After the jury was selected, Josh Pickett's job would have been completed, and Walton would be sitting there by himself. That's the way I liked to try a case. I didn't want anyone at the table with me. I was certain Walton was the same. I took a deep breath, feeling great pride in Walton

Donaldson, the man and the lawyer he had become while working with me the past eleven years.

Yaloquena Sheriff Lee Jones walked in and waved. He took a seat in the first row on the other end of the curved bench, right behind Walton. Next to him sat Sammy Roberts, a chiseled, flat-bellied thirty-seven-year-old black man in street clothes. Ex-military and former Highway Patrolman, Sammy was now Lee's Chief Deputy, and exactly the man I would have chosen to be Walton's bodyguard. Lee had placed a uniformed deputy, Will Gresham, in Walton's apartment on the Square. Lee told me Sammy would be with Walton for the duration of the trial, and Will would assist, primarily in the apartment. I told the Sheriff I thought it was the right move with the right men.

Helmet Head excused the first prospective juror he questioned after Judge Williams denied his challenge for cause. I walked out of the courtroom as Clerk Winston Moore called the name of the next prospect. On the south side of the courthouse I looked up at the apartment window overlooking the balcony and spied Will Gresham looking down on me. We waved and I walked west on Van Buren and on to the condo.

Susan left me a note saying she was out running errands and would be back about eleven. I listened to a voice message on the land line in my office. I took off my suit jacket and returned Patrick Dunwoody's call, making sure to dial his cell rather than his office number.

"How's the trial proceeding?" he asked.

"Slowly. They'll spend most of this week seating the jury. Have you found out anything since we spoke yesterday afternoon?"

"I'm afraid I have, Willie Mitchell," Dunwoody said in his aristocratic Tidewater accent. "I am sad to report that in these times, this town is as corrupt as the Eighteenth Century monarchies, with all the courtiers and hangers-on living on patronage at the beck and call of His Majesty. My Justice Department, which in the past was a beacon of propriety enforcing federal law in an even-handed manner, has become a political tool. The sycophantic Maori who runs it is as unscrupulous as he is dull-witted."

"I hope you've had your office swept recently."

"Yesterday, in fact, by the tech firm I have on personal retainer. The bad news is this: the Civil Rights section is pursuing a criminal charge against you under Section 1983. The theory is that in your selection of grand jury foremen over your years in office you acted under the color of law to discriminate against African-Americans in your county."

I was glad I was sitting down. The news could not have been worse. I had seen the full force and power of the federal government ruin the lives of good people on a whim. Now I was in the crosshairs. The Justice Department had the deepest of pockets, and when the Leviathan brought its strength to bear against an individual it was formidable. Even without a conviction, the result of the investigation and charge was often financial ruin and loss of good name.

I had a good friend, a prosecutor in rural North Louisiana, who was killed by the Justice Department. I know that's a strong statement, but it's true. He had been in office over twenty years and ran a very tight ship. We met at a regional meeting of the NDAA in Dallas. Neither of us was active in the National District Attorneys Association, but the meetings included valuable updates on recent trends in criminal law. We sat next to each other, struck up a conversation, had lunch, and spent the rest of the conference talking about our offices, which were similar in many respects. I could tell immediately he was an honest man, a man of integrity. He was not a bulldog prosecutor, wanting to win at all costs. It sounds trite, but my friend was interested in dispensing justice, not just for victims, but for defendants, too.

He invested with a Shreveport developer in a real estate venture. The developer had been extremely successful in the past. My friend did not know, however, that the developer was using money to fund this particular project that he had withdrawn from other LLCs and partnerships, which he had set up to launder profits from other ventures and evade taxes. The development my friend invested in was clean. It was not connected to the money laundering schemes of the other entities controlled by the developer.

My friend had been talked into investing by a respected Shreveport banker whom he trusted.

Without any warning, an indictment came down from a Federal grand jury. All of the investors were charged as conspirators under the RICO statute, and a separate count of the indictment was added to accuse my friend of violating his duty to provide "honest services" as a public official.

The Shreveport, Monroe, and Alexandria papers blasted the news of the indictment, complete with photographs of my friend selected intentionally to make him appear to be a shady character, which was the opposite of the truth. As soon as I heard the news I called him. He said he was confident he would be vindicated, that he had no knowledge of the developer's LLCs and partnerships used to hide profits from other ventures. He had retained a Shreveport lawyer who specialized in white collar criminal law. I recognized the name and asked him how much the retainer was.

"One hundred thousand," he said.

I offered to help any way I could. He said he would keep me posted. When I hung up I had a bad feeling. I could feel the despair in my friend's voice. I didn't know he had a family history of depression.

Stories continued to fill the North Louisiana newspapers, mentioning my friend in connection with allegations about the developer's past projects, even though the DA had not even known the developer at the time. I drove to Shreveport to be there at my friend's arraignment, spend some time with him and make sure he knew he had my support. Waiting in the U.S. District Courtroom that morning, I read in the Shreveport paper that a well-known lawyer in my friend's jurisdiction had announced his candidacy for DA, pledging to rid the office of corruption.

My friend did not show up for his arraignment that morning in Shreveport. He had hanged himself at his camp on a scenic North Louisiana river. After the funeral I continued to follow the case. At a hearing three months after the indictment, the cases against all of the indicted co-conspirators were dismissed. A plea arrangement with the developer had been agreed upon whereby he paid back taxes, penalties, and interest on the profits he laundered and was sentenced to three years of supervised probation. The District Judge said in his sentencing statement that probation was appropriate because the developer had made full restitution to the government and taken full responsibility for the laundering scheme, exonerating his partners and investors from any involvement. In his allocution, the developer admitted that none of the alleged co-conspirators in the indictment had any knowledge of the legal taint on the funds the developer was using for the current project.

All charges against my friend, including the "honest services" count in the indictment were dismissed by the Justice Department. But no apology to my friend's widow and children was forthcoming from anyone in the government. This all happened before I became friends with Patrick Dunwoody IV. While Susan and I enjoyed his hospitality at Bellingham one weekend, I related the story and its deadly consequences to him. I asked how it could have happened.

"Many of these decisions are made by children, three or four years out of law school, anxious to make a name for themselves in the Department. They particularly like to go after public officials. The U.S. Attorneys are political appointees, sometimes highly unqualified. They rubber stamp decisions like this made by their staffs. If you asked one of them, he or she would tell you it was nothing personal."

On the phone in my office that Tuesday morning in Oxford, I asked Dunwoody if he had any idea who was pushing the allegations against me.

"I'm sure you remember Leopold Whitman."

I certainly did. Leopold Whitman used to be the U.S. Attorney for the Southern District of Mississippi headquartered in Jackson. He and I had butted heads fighting over drug runner and budding Islamic terrorist El Moro, who murdered a deputy sheriff in Yaloquena County while on the run. Whitman wanted me to deliver El Moro to him so he could go after the drug cartel financing El Moro's operations. I said no, that I was prosecuting him for murder. We went round-and-round in the coterminous state and federal legal system. I came out on top, but only momentarily, because two of El Moro's confederates ran over me in an old Chevrolet, taking me out of action for a year. Whitman got the jurisdictional ruling he wanted while I was in the hospital, but his prosecution of El Moro did not turn out well, resulting in his "promotion" to a desk job at Justice in D.C. where he eventually led the Office of Inspector General. Dunwoody referred to OIG as "the rat squad."

"Well," Dunwoody continued, "Leopold Whitman has taken a particular interest in the grand jury process in Yaloquena County during your tenure. My sources tell me he was summoned to a meeting in a certain senator's office, a senator from your state, for well over an hour last week. I am told that the renewed interest of the Department in the once dormant investigation of you has been revitalized since the meeting."

"Which senator did Whitman meet with?"

"Senator Chad Breedlove. Do you know him?"

"Not personally. But I've met his mother."

Chapter Twenty-Three

I woke up Wednesday morning because I felt a seizure coming on. I opened my eyes long enough to see the clock radio read 6:00 in big, red numerals on my night stand. I closed my eyes quickly because I knew from experience the longer my eyes stayed open the dizzier I became. I was experiencing the aura that preceded all my seizures. I treasured it, because my aura had kept me from injuring myself many times. When I had the seizure on number eight green the week before, the one I mentioned it to you, I felt it coming on. So, I dropped my putter and lay down on the green.

I did some research on my own when I first began having the seizures during my recovery from being struck by the Chevrolet driven by El Moro's men. I did an online search for "pre-seizure symptoms" and found a description of the "aura" reported by many seizure patients. Some of them experience bright light flashes, or odd smells; some feel light-headed and strange. Put me in the latter category. What I feel is hard to describe. At the onset of my aura, my perception of the world around me changes. I seem to be floating in place as my brain slowly shuts down. Movement becomes increasingly difficult. I know this will sound strange to you, but inside my head, it's as if I'm experiencing a painful, loud noise. But there's no noise and no pain.

Since I was already in bed that Wednesday morning, I was in no danger of falling and hurting myself. I remained on my back as the aura washed over and through me. Then I was out. Gone elsewhere, into some vast nothingness. When I regained consciousness and felt up to it, I rolled on my side and looked at the red numbers: 6:07. Seven minutes. It felt much longer. I remembered sensing the aura, the clock reading 6:00, then nothing. No lights, sound, movement, or thoughts. It was as if I didn't exist.

I glanced over. Susan had slept through it. She worried about my seizures more than anything. We had both grown accustomed to the pain in my leg and the blurred vision in my left eye, but not the seizures. The one on the eighth green was the first I had experienced in quite a while. I didn't tell Susan about that one, and I didn't mention this one either. But I knew if the seizures continued, I would have to tell her.

I rested on the side of the bed for a moment, then rose slowly to avoid the light-headedness that sometimes followed the seizure. When I was certain I was in control, I walked into the bathroom to start my day. James Butler was supposed to have returned from Mobile the night before, and I wanted to show him the copy of the photograph I made on the Xerox machine in *The Daily Mississippian* on Sunday. I was tempted to remove the original, but I didn't have permission and did not want to give the editor a reason to deny me further access to the photographs. I planned on going through them again, just to make sure I hadn't missed anything.

I wanted to visit with Walton at his apartment before Court convened, so if I were going to exercise, I needed to start right away. Ten minutes later, I was jogging westward on University Avenue toward the Ole Miss campus. I made a mental note when I passed the Confederate Monument to call my son Scott.

I arrived at Walton's apartment at 8:45 and took the stairs two at a time. Deputy Will Gresham answered my knock, and let me inside where I greeted Chief Deputy Sammy Roberts and Walton, whose head was buried in his trial notebook.

"Still at two?" I asked.

"We seated one more in the afternoon," Walton said looking up. "It's like pulling teeth to get Helmet Head to move along."

"How is he on peremptory challenges?"

"He's got plenty left. I've only used one."

"You'll get the jury seated and two alternates by Friday afternoon," I said. "It's funny how it works out like that. Everyone gets a little tired by the end of the week, even J.D. Silver."

"The man's got some serious hair," Sammy Roberts said. "Looks too much like a television preacher for me. I wouldn't trust him as far as I could throw him."

"I don't trust him one bit," Walton said. "We get along, but I learned my lesson in the Ross Bullard trial. If a lie will help the cause of his client, Helmet Head will use it. Doesn't bother him a bit."

"That's the job of a good defense lawyer," I said. "He's paid to mislead and obfuscate, to trot out to the jury alternate theories he knows are not true."

"I couldn't do that," Walton said.

"Me either," I said.

There it was. The real reason I had no interest in becoming a criminal defense attorney, white collar or no collar. I had never articulated it before. The reluctance to join the other side, no matter how lucrative the offers, was rooted in my character. I could not argue to a jury something I knew to be false. Period. I could not, and I would not. And don't accuse me of being sanctimonious. It's just the way I am.

I walked across the street to the courthouse with Walton and Sammy and entered through the crowd of prospective jurors gathered outside in the pleasant morning sun. Inside the courtroom, I stayed outside the rail, sitting on the first row next to the side aisle to facilitate my inconspicuous exit sometime during the first hour. Helmet Head left the defense table and walked toward me. I stood and shook his hand over the rail. I was cordial, but unsmiling, minding my own rule to avoid displaying camaraderie with the defense attorney or defendant in front of jurors.

"My client asked me to give you this," Helmet Head said, holding up a small, sealed envelope. "It's against my better judgment, but he's the boss."

"What is it?"

"Not a clue. I asked him and he said it was a note for you. Before you look at it, I need a commitment from you that if it's anything inculpatory, you'll give it back to me and not use it in the case. Deal?"

"All right," I said, knowing Buddy's ways well enough to know he would do nothing to incriminate himself.

I opened the envelope and read it while Helmet Head stood there. It was only one sentence, printed in a clear hand.

"I would like to buy you a cup of coffee this weekend. Buddy Richardson."

I showed the note to Helmet Head. He read it and shrugged.

"Why?" I asked.

"My client doesn't explain much to me. He doesn't do what I ask most of the time. He says he's paying me to do what he tells me. Having a cup of coffee with you is about the last thing I would want him to do, but if he's dead set, I can't keep him from doing it. Got a head like a rock."

"Tell him I'll think about it," I said. "I'll let him know Friday."

Helmet Head walked back to the defense table. He whispered to his client, who listened while looking at me over his lawyer's shoulder. I stuck the note in my pocket and listened to Walton question the first prospect. He was an older man, a farmer from around Water Valley. Walton accepted him, but Helmet Head began a challenge for cause I knew was going to take a while. I left my seat as quietly as possible and walked out.

Fifteen minutes later, I parked in James Butler's driveway and knocked on his carport door. He let me in and offered me a seat at the kitchen table. I gave him the key to *The Daily Mississippian* offices and placed the Xerox copy of the black and white photo of the young lovers in the Grove on the table.

"That's Fratelli for sure," he said. "But the girl, I don't think that's Cissy. Cissy's taller. This girl is looking up at Fratelli, and my recollection is Cissy was about as tall as the Fratelli boy." He picked up the photocopy and studied the girl in Russell's arms. "This copy is not as clear as the picture, I'm sure, but I'm fairly certain looking at her from the side that's not Cissy."

"Do you know who it might be?"

"No. The campus was full of pretty brunettes that summer. It's hard to say. I don't recognize her. Maybe if I saw the original."

I thanked Butler again for his help with getting me into the archives of both the *Oxford Eagle* and *The Daily Mississippian*.

"Sorry I couldn't be more help," he said.

I called my son Scott's cell as I drove back to the condo. It went to voice mail, so I asked him to call me back. When I walked into the condo my cell dinged and I answered.

"What's up, Daddy?" he asked.

"I need your help, and Skeeter's. You remember Leopold Whitman?"

"I see that little weasel on occasion on the Hill. I have to fight the urge to run up to him and punch him out."

"He's involved in dredging up something that's been dormant for over a year, the process of grand jury selection in Delta counties from 1995 to 2010. I've gotten the word that they've drawn a big target on my back."

"Why you? This is such crap. I remember when it first came up."

"My information is Whitman is behind it somehow. He met with Senator Breedlove last week or so. I'm thinking Whitman was giving him a heads up of what was coming down."

"Or worse," Scott said. "I'll talk to Senator Sumrall this afternoon. See what we can find out."

"Set up a call or a meeting between Skeeter and Patrick Dunwoody if you can. Dunwoody knows about Whitman's meeting with Senator Breedlove, and knows the charges they're considering filing against me."

"I'll call you back," Scott said.

"Hold on, Scott. You and Skeeter need to tread lightly. They'd be quick to claim obstruction of justice or interference with an investigation if they find out you're nosing around where you're not supposed to."

"I got this, Daddy. We won't leave any footprints. But we need to head this off if we can. That s.o.b. Whitman hates you."

"I know. But we have to do this legally."

"Right. Just like always. We play by the rules everyone else ignores."

"That's the way I want it. You talked to Jake?"

"Not in a month. He's on some kind of mission. I have no idea where."

"Okay. Call me back."

I hung up and took a deep breath.

"Why would Buddy Richardson want to talk to me?" I asked myself.

CHAPTER TWENTY-FOUR

I took the Xerox copy of the photograph to the golf course with me to show to François. He was strapping his clubs to the golf cart when I pulled up and parked. I walked over and showed him the copy.

"I don't know if that's Cissy or not, Willie Mitchell. I'm sure that's my brother. But I can't tell about the girl. I never met her until the funeral."

"She was there? In Clarksdale?"

"Yeah, I'm pretty sure she was. It's been a long time, but...."

His voice trailed off as if he were thinking about something from his past.

"Do you have any photographs taken at the funeral?"

"I don't think so. People didn't take pictures like they do now, with their phones and all." He paused. "Have you found out anything?"

"Not really. Been running down pig trails that turn into dead ends."

"I'm sorry. If it's too much trouble...."

"It's got me hooked now, François. I've still got plenty of things to check out. I got a call driving out here from my pal at the State Crime Lab. They've located the bullet that was removed from Russell's head. He's going to take a look at it this afternoon and call me."

"I'll be damned. They still have it after all this time?"

"They do. Took a while to find it. It's flattened out, all misshapen, but it's intact."

Thirteen of us comprised the Geezer Group that afternoon. My foursome included "Carlos," a retired restauranteur from Greenville who loved Ole Miss sports with an unbridled passion, and two other refugees from the Delta, Edgar "Nicene" Creed, and Bubba "Rabbit Ears" Todd. I called Creed "Nicene" for obvious reasons, though he never went to church. "Rabbit Ears" had acute hearing, especially over a putt. He would back off at the slightest hint of a sound. Jimmy Gray said "Rabbit Ears" could hear a rat wee-weeing on cotton a hundred feet away. Nicene and Rabbit Ears had played in my group at Sunshine Country Club for years, and both had moved to Oxford a few years ago. They weren't regulars in the Geezer Group because both still worked, Nicene selling farm chemicals all over the Delta and Rabbit Ears running cement plants in Yaloquena and Dundee counties.

A few of the Geezer Group regulars, including Duck, Brainer, Tiger Woody, Victim, and Otis populated the other groups. Ole Miss and New Orleans Saints legend Archie Manning, the greatest gentleman athlete the NCAA ever produced, joined our group for the back side, having given a speech at the Inn at Ole Miss for the Second Chance Mississippi group, a foundation put together by Dickie Scruggs to raise money to fund GED applicants and trade school students all over Mississippi.

I didn't play well. Lost eleven dollars. My mind was not on my swing. The Justice Department threat was eating at me. I knew I had done nothing wrong in the grand jury foreman selection process, but Justice had a way with statistics and data that could make something innocuous look malignant. Like their theory of "disparate impact" in housing and employment, where they did not have to offer an iota of evidence of actual discrimination. All they had to show was that the policies of an employer or housing authority resulted in jobs or housing disproportionally low for a protected class of people. If applied to grand jury selection in Yaloquena, since the county is 75% black, the "disparate impact" theory demanded that 75% of the grand jury foremen had to be black, or discrimination is presumed.

My gloom and doom imagination was working overtime. Thank God that on the drive home, Robbie Cedars called with the results of his analysis.

"It's so smashed and flattened, no way we can do a comparison, Willie Mitchell, even if you had the gun. But I can tell you this about the bullet. It's not a .38 caliber, and it wasn't manufactured in the United States."

their wars up to and including their disastrous adventure in Afghanistan from 1979 to 1989. It was the Russian infantry's pistol in World War II, and was widely distributed to armies throughout Asia and used in the Korean War, the Laotian Civil War, Vietnam, and just about every conflict on the Asian Continent in the Twentieth Century.

The identification of the bullet and murder weapon was the first original piece of circumstantial evidence I had uncovered in the two weeks since I began looking into Russell's murder. It also confirmed what a shoddy investigation had been done in 1962. The same type of analysis of the bullet could have been done back then. The pressure from the feds and the state to separate Russell's death from the riots must have had the side effect of minimizing the need for a thorough investigation.

I went to bed that night encouraged by the new evidence. It led me to believe that with enough effort, I might be able to discover other facts leading to the identity of the shooter.

The next morning I walked into the courtroom at ten-fifteen, anticipating Judge Williams would break at about ten-thirty. I took my seat next to the side aisle in the first row and was pleased to see seven jurors in the jury box. Zelda recessed at ten-forty-five, and I walked through the rail gate to join Walton and Josh Pickett at the prosecution table.

"You've made good progress," I said, taking a seat next to Walton.

"Thank God Helmet Head's out of peremptory challenges. You were right. We're going to finish this selection process tomorrow and start the trial Monday morning. I know Josh will be glad to get back to his own work."

"It's been educational for me," Assistant D.A. Pickett said. "We've never tried a murder-for-hire in this Circuit Court, at least while I've worked here. Walton's taught me a few things about picking a jury."

"Good," I said. "Josh, will you excuse Walton and me a second?"

"Sure. I've got to make a call," he said and walked out of the courtroom.

"I wanted to let you know the Justice Department is renewing its investigation into grand jury selection in Delta counties."

"I thought they dropped that after we sent in all the information."

"It's now on the front burner again."

"How do you know? I haven't gotten anything on it at the office."

"I found out last Saturday. Doesn't matter how, but it seems they're targeting me for discriminating in the selection of grand jury foreman going back as far as 1995."

"You should have told me."

"You've had your hands full here. And I don't want you to think about it while you're trying this case. The only reason I brought it up the other day was to find out from you if you had heard anything."

"Not a word. Like I said, I thought it was over."

"Leopold Whitman is involved somehow in pushing it."

"That little creep? What a prick."

"I've talked to Scott and he's going to do some looking into it. He'll get Senator Sumrall working on our side up there."

"Soon as this case is over I'll do anything you need."

"One more thing," I said. "Helmet Head gave me a note from Buddy Richardson yesterday."

"I saw y'all talking. What did it say?"

"Buddy wants to buy me a cup of coffee this weekend."

"Why?"

"I have no idea. I wanted to run it by you."

"What are you thinking?"

"Helmet Head is trying to keep Buddy in line, but he says Buddy's going to do whatever he wants regardless of his high-priced advice. I know it's weird, but I think I'd like to sit down with him."

"I think you should, too," Walton said after thinking a minute. "He's the one making the overture, so he can't complain about it later. He's too shrewd to say anything that I can use against him, but I'd like to get your take on his demeanor, his mental attitude in case he gets on the witness stand."

"Which he probably won't," I said, "considering Helmet Head's spent so much time explaining to the jurors that Buddy has the constitutional right not to testify. Yesterday, I heard him call it 'a sacred right'."

"I don't think he will, either. You have to promise me you'll call me as soon as your meeting with Buddy is over and fill me in."

"You bet," I said.

I watched J.D. Silver say something to Buddy and walk out of the side door of the courtroom. Probably going for a bathroom break. I followed and caught up to him before he reached the men's room.

"J.D.," I said, "would you pass along to your client that I'll meet him at nine a.m. at the Starbucks on West Jackson Avenue. It's likely that neither of us will be recognized there. I'm sure I won't know anyone in the place."

"Yeah," he said. "Hope you have better luck communicating with him than I do. Remember, our deal is whatever he says, Walton can't use it."

"That's right," I said. "Looks like you'll start testimony Monday."

"We'll finish next week," he said. "Between you and me, I can't wait to get away from him. I deal with a lot of low-lifes, but this guy takes the cake."

"What do you mean?"

"I'll only say this. If he's got a conscience, I haven't seen any sign of it."

CHAPTER TWENTY-SIX

Walton and Helmet Head finished picking the jury Friday, seating the second alternate at five-thirty. Walton took off to see his wife and family at her mother's home in West Point, about two hours away. He called me on his way out of town and said he'd be back early Sunday a.m. to spend the day getting ready for opening arguments Monday morning. He asked me if I had a chance to look over the report and exhibits he had submitted to the Justice Department over a year ago relating to the grand jury inquiry. I told him I had looked at everything once, and was about to go through it again.

"Thanks for having Louise get it to me," I said. "We only had one black foreman over the period in question," I said. "That doesn't look good."

"But I went back over each venire, and pointed out the times that you had recommended a black grand juror who declined to serve as foreman. That happened five times in that fifteen year period."

"I was real happy to read that part of the report. Nothing was in writing at the time of selection. It was all done informally with Zelda. But when I read the names of the men and women who declined to serve as foreman, it jogged my memory. How in the world did you reconstruct that?"

"Judge Williams," he said. "I saw her in the Circuit Clerk's office when I was meeting with Winston Moore to piece together as much information as I could going back to 1995. She asked us what we were doing. I told her about the Justice Department's investigation."

"What did she say?"

"She didn't use the word 'bullshit,' but it's a good summary of what she thought about Justice's inquiry. Judge Williams asked me to meet with her when I had the grand jury venires collected. I did, and she went through each one, read the names of the grand jurors, and pointed out a total of five black jurors who turned down your request that he or she serve as foreman. Zelda knew them all. She has a good memory."

"I'll have to give her a hug next time I see her outside a courthouse. That information makes me feel much better, but Justice is going to emphasize the stark statistic that we only had one in fifteen years. Disparate impact kind of argument, you know. *Res ipsa loquitur.* The thing speaks for itself."

"You've got to be wrong about that, Willie Mitchell. No way."

"I know from experience when the Justice Department wants to come after you, they do it regardless of whether there might be evidence to exonerate you. They can get anyone indicted, and when they indict a public official, it makes a big splash on television and in the papers."

"Then they dismiss it a year later and the media barely mentions it."

"You got it. Give my regards to Gayle and the kids. I'll check in on you Monday at the apartment."

By the time Walton and I ended our call, it had begun to rain. Susan and I spent a quiet Friday night at home, dining on a smorgasbord of leftovers. I drifted off to sleep about nine-thirty and woke up at six Saturday morning to go over Walton's report and exhibits again to see if I missed anything. At eight-forty-five I left the condo for my meeting with Buddy Richardson at Starbuck's.

He was already seated at a small table in the corner when I arrived. I bought a small cup of dark roast coffee and joined Buddy at his table. I didn't extend my hand. Neither did he.

"I wanted to let you know my wife Susan is doing fine, Buddy. You asked about her the other day. You mind if I call you Buddy?"

"That's my name. Just like I imagine you don't mind me calling you Willie Mitchell. Dale Carnegie said the prettiest sound a person can hear is his own name. I read that in his book."

Buddy made a point of looking me straight in the eye.

"I guess you and Susan worked out the problems you went through a few years back. Really glad to hear it," he said with a crooked smile.

I studied him a moment. His white hair was long, well over his ears, and his full beard was solid white. Above his beard were rosy red cheeks and dark, intense eyes resting on puffy, heavy bags. He seemed on edge sitting there, all wound up. I wondered if he had smoked a little crystal methamphetamine to jump start his brain before the meeting.

"You know, Buddy, I was thinking. I've seen you around Sunshine, known who you were for most of my life, but I don't think we've ever had a conversation. I'm wondering how you would know something personal like that about Susan and me."

"Aw, Willie Mitchell, you know how news travels in the Delta. Information has always been important to me. I've made good money many times because I acted on some information that came my way."

"Like the head start you got on your video poker truck stop in Louisiana."

"Absolutely. But you have to be willing to act decisively once you find out something like that. I know other truck stop owners who found out what was going on when I did but waited to see if the legislation really would pass. Then they waited some more because they weren't sure the governor would sign it. I jumped out there early before they even took up the bill, and beat them all to the punch. Sure it was risky, but taking a chance is the only way you can hit a big lick in this world."

"Why did you want to have coffee with me?" I asked.

"Lighten up there, Willie Mitchell. Let's have a civilized conversation before we get down to business. A little foreplay never hurt nobody. You know, your old man was on the Yaloquena Citizens' Council same time as me. I always liked him. He was a man of his word. Smart, too."

"I wish he hadn't been on the Citizens' Council, but I guess things were different then. I didn't know until a few years ago."

"You cain't judge what we did by today's standards. The federal government back then was a fraction the size it is now. Regardless of how anybody felt about integration, it wasn't right for the feds to push the states around like they did over all that civil rights bullshit."

"You're not including yourself in the moderate category, are you Buddy? They say you fought for Jim Crow and segregation harder than anybody."

"Sure did. And I'm proud of it. Look at what their culture has done to this country. The black bastards ruined the education system, bringing the white kids down to the niggers' level. Now they're all stupid, blacks and whites, not learning anything in school because the goddamned unionized teachers don't do anything but preach political correctness and civil rights crap. Look at the trash we got on television and in the movies now. And the universities are just as bad with the Goddamned liberal professors and all."

I sat there, wondering how long he would rant and how much redder his face would turn. It was ironic to hear a man responsible for so many murders and immoral acts, most recently the killing of his own granddaughter's husband, expound on moral and racial issues. I thought of his drug-fueled night of violence and passion described by the young Dundee mother in my office in Sunshine when I was District Attorney. Buddy still hadn't told me why he wanted to meet with me, but if he wanted conversation, I was game.

"I've been reading a good bit on the integration of Ole Miss, the admission of James Meredith in 1962 and the riot it caused."

He leaned back and stared, waiting before he commented. I sensed a mood swing. He was getting himself under control.

"Yeah," he said, much calmer than just moments before. "More federal interference."

I sipped my coffee in silence for a minute. Buddy stared at me with his dark eyes, then flashed what Jimmy Gray would call a shit-eating grin.

"What was it you wanted to discuss, Buddy?" I asked.

"Aw, nothing really," Buddy said. "I just wanted to meet you and chew the fat, that's all. I guess I wanted to tell you what a fine man your father was. Nothing else in particular.

I'm just an old man, trying to get through this rough patch you and your boy Walton are putting me through. Just an eighty-five-year-old has-been, trying to make it through my golden years in peace."

"Right," I said rising from my chair. "I'll be seeing you."

On the drive back to the condo, I replayed parts of Buddy's conversation in my head. There was nothing he wanted to talk to me about. He was sizing up the opposition, a thrust and parry to test my mettle.

I wondered how I performed.

CHAPTER TWENTY-SEVEN

I had a lot on my mind, but played golf anyway that Saturday afternoon. Jimmy Gray was my cart partner, and he liked to drive. Riding in the passenger seat, I kept a tight grip on the roof because the cart listed left under the weight of the big banker.

"Next time we might want to get them to put some more air in the tires on your side so I don't keep leaning on you."

"Aw," Jimmy said, "I thought it was because you liked me so much."

"How many times do I have to tell you? I just want to be friends."

I had dropped by Jimmy's house after leaving Starbuck's to fill him in on the meeting with Buddy and get his take on it. Jimmy Gray was a clown, but he was highly intelligent and insightful, especially in dealing with people. It was part of the reason he was such a successful banker.

"I wish you had talked to me before you had the meeting," he said. "I don't think it was such a good idea."

"We were in a high-traffic, high-visibility location. To tell you the truth, it was curiosity more than anything. Walton was all right with it."

"He's just a boy and has no idea how sinister Buddy Richardson is. You ought to know better. And what did you get out of it—nothing."

"No, that's not true. I did get a glimpse into the man."

"Like Bush forty-three looking into Vladimir Putin's eyes."

"Not exactly. I've been thinking how to describe what I sensed in him." I paused a moment. "I guess the overriding impression I got was volatility—a volcano about to erupt. I expected him to raise his voice or pound his fist on the table, but he forced himself to stay cool. I'll tell you one thing. He doesn't act like an eighty-five-year-old. I had the feeling he was as physically capable as you and me."

"Probably the dope."

"Maybe that's part of it, but I left Starbucks with the feeling that Buddy's an angry, malicious old gangster with plenty of fight left in him. And he had that meeting for a reason. I thought at first he really was going to tell me something. But sitting across from him, I could feel what he was doing. He was sizing me up as if I were his adversary, not Walton."

"He's right. You still the big dog, Boudreaux. You ought to start carrying your pistol at all times," Jimmy said. "I put Big D back in the Escalade."

"Big D" was Jimmy's nickname for his custom-made .50 caliber titanium gold Desert Eagle semi-automatic pistol, one of the most powerful handguns in the world. When I tested it with Jimmy at the shooting range out in Yaloquena County, it took both hands for me to fire it because Big D weighed almost five pounds and kicked like a mule. Jimmy was strong enough to fire it with decent accuracy using only one hand. He kept Big D resting in a foam cutout in an expensive aluminum case. The .50 caliber bullets were as thick as my finger and weighed a remarkable 300 grains, almost four times heavier than the bullet that killed Russell Fratelli. Jimmy pays over forty dollars for a box of twenty of these massive bullets. I know because I've been shopping with him at the gun store.

I hadn't carried in a long time. When I was District Attorney I kept a loaded 1911 Springfield semi-automatic in my desk in the right hand top drawer, laid in there in the most efficient position for quick removal. The one time I thought I might need a pistol for self-defense in my office, when Little Al Anderson showed up in his wheelchair to confront me with a pistol grip protruding above his belt, my pistol wasn't in the drawer. I had removed it thinking it was no longer necessary to have it handy. In spite of many heated discussions and confrontations with constituents who were angry with me about how I handled a case in my first twenty years as DA, I had never had occasion to pull the pistol in self-defense. The day after the Little Al episode, I put the Springfield back in the drawer.

Riding on the cart path looking out at the lush, green golf course, I was grateful I no longer had to endure heartrending, tearful meetings with relatives of victims who wanted retribution that I could not deliver. Many times the events leading to the death of their loved one did not constitute a crime defined by law. Some DA friends of mine who were better politicians used delay to make delivery of the bad news more palatable. But I could not bring myself to mislead grieving relatives into believing that as soon as the investigation was complete I would bring charges if I knew it wasn't true. In almost all cases, it's obvious from the outset whether criminal conduct caused the death of the victim. When it was clear there was no evidence of a crime as defined by state law, I felt an obligation to tell the family as soon as I was sure. I think it accelerates the grieving process, helps them achieve finality. Other DAs disagree. They string the family along, postponing the inevitable.

This early notice process I followed is no doubt another reason I was on everyone's top ten list of the world's worst politicians.

"Your phone's buzzing," Jimmy Gray said and stopped the cart.

I jumped out, unzipped the pocket in my golf bag, and removed my phone. I didn't recognize the incoming number, and neither did my phone.

"Hello," I said.

"Is this Mr. Banks?" the woman asked.

"Yes. Who's calling?"

"This is Naomi Butler," she said, her voice shaking. "I got your number from the pad my husband keeps by the phone on the kitchen counter. He had your name written out and your number next to it."

"Oh, hello, Mrs. Butler. That's fine. What can I do for you?"

"I'm sorry to bother you, but I've been calling everyone I know who's talked to my husband recently."

"Has something happened?"

"I'm not sure," she said, her voice cracking. "He didn't come home last night and didn't call. I'm afraid he's gotten sick or something, and maybe is some place in need of help and I don't know where."

"Have you called the police?"

"I called Chief Columbus first thing this morning. He and a young detective came over and interviewed me. I gave them all the information I had. They asked me to call anyone he spent time with in the last week or two."

"Well, I was with him at *The Daily Mississippian* on Sunday morning, the day y'all left for Mobile. He seemed fine. Then I saw him on Wednesday before noon at your house."

"I know he showed you the room where they keep the old newspapers and photographs at the University."

"That's right. He was nice enough to get the key from the editor. I brought the office key to him Wednesday."

"He went back to *The Daily Mississippian* yesterday afternoon to return the key, and we ate an early supper. He received a call on his cell phone and said he had to go out for a minute and would be right back." She started crying. "I haven't heard from him since."

"I'm sure he'll turn up, Mrs. Butler," I said. "Is there anything I can do to help?"

"I don't guess," she said after a moment. "If he calls, could you let him know I'm worried sick about him?"

I assured her I would and returned the phone to my golf bag. I told Jimmy what Naomi Butler said about her husband.

"That doesn't sound good," Jimmy said.

"No. It doesn't."

I pulled my seven-iron out and took a couple of practice swings. I hooked my Titleist ProV1 into the trap. The bad shot didn't surprise me, because my mind was far removed from my game. I was thinking about the retired newspaperman and talented artist, James Butler. I had a very, very bad feeling in the pit of my stomach.

CHAPTER TWENTY-EIGHT

We finished the round about four-thirty. I asked Jimmy Gray to settle my bets for me. I drove straight to the Oxford Police Department on Molly Barr. I had a feeling the Chief would be in because of James Butler's disappearance. The policewoman at the desk said Chief Columbus was in the office and asked me to have a seat. I wasn't in the chair a minute before the Chief appeared in a doorway and motioned me into his private office.

"Naomi Butler called me, Chief. She told me she talked to you this morning about her husband."

"That's right," he said, his demeanor serious, troubled.

"What have you found out?"

"Nothing," he said.

I was relieved to hear courtesy in his voice. I'm a civilian now, so he would have been within his rights to grill me about my interest and protect what information he had on the status of the investigation.

"Mrs. Butler called me because I was with him last Sunday at the college newspaper office and again at his house on Wednesday."

"Are you two friends?"

"No. I just met him. I've been looking into the riot at Ole Miss in 1962 and someone gave me his name as a person who would know a good bit about it. I had a visit with him at his house Monday before last and he suggested I go through the archives at *The Oxford Eagle* and *The Daily Mississippian* to look at the articles that were written contemporaneously with the riot. He made some calls and got access to both places for me. I read some of the articles and went through all the old photographs."

"What is it about the riot that interests you? You writing a book?"

"No. A friend of mine asked me to look into the death of his brother. He was found in a ravine off the Grove the Thursday following the riot."

"Russell Fratelli," the Chief said. "Mr. Francis's brother."

"That's right. How did you know?"

"Mr. Francis rents to a lot students and we deal with him from time to time on routine landlord things—locating a tenant, checking out vandalism, bad checks, the kind of things you get in a college town. And my father was one of the Highway Patrol investigators who helped carry his brother's body out of the ravine."

"Small world."

"I was born thirteen years after the riot and as soon as I was old enough my old man started telling me war stories about the good old days."

"What did he tell you about Fratelli?"

"He said they all figured a real bad actor from out of state skulked around the Grove that night figuring he could kill that reporter and the Fratelli boy and he'd never be caught. Use the riot as cover. The investigators thought the mysterious back-shooting redneck was good for both murders."

"That's what I've been told," I said. "But they were wrong."

"How do you know?"

"I had the bullet analyzed by a friend of mine at Crime Lab, best ballistics expert in this state. He said Russell Fratelli was killed by a Russian manufactured bullet from a pistol the Soviets used for most of the twentieth century."

"Your friend is Robbie Cedars, the Director?"

"That's right.

"If Mr. Cedars said the bullet was Russian-made the gun must have been a TT-30 or 33. Those were real reliable pistols. You didn't have to keep them all that clean, like a Glock. Low maintenance and plenty deadly enough."

"You know your weapons. That's what he said, a TT-30."

"Always been kind of a hobby with me," the Chief said. "You made any other headway?"

"No. Bunch of dead ends."

"If I can help you any way on that let me know. Mr. Francis is a nice man and I'd like to help him. I know he's sick."

"Thanks," I said. "James Butler doesn't strike me as the kind of man who would run off and leave his wife. And I know from talking to him he doesn't have any dementia or Alzheimer's. He didn't drive off and get lost."

"No. You're right. I got to know him when I was a young cop working around here and he was still at *The Eagle*. He's sharp; a man who keeps his t's crossed and his i's dotted."

"Have you seen his paintings? Unbelievably talented."

"No, but it doesn't surprise me."

"What have you been able to do so far?"

"All my men on regular patrol duty are on the lookout. I brought in two of my investigators to call on every person who had contact with him in the last week or so. You're probably on the list. Mrs. Butler made it up for us. I've notified law enforcement in the area through this alert system we've developed. Notified the Highway Patrol."

"Sounds like you've touched all the bases. Did he have money?"

"Mrs. Butler says they live on his pension and Social Security and what little savings they have in the local banks."

"He's got all his faculties so he didn't wander off," I said. "He doesn't have the kind of money that would make him a kidnap or extortion target. That leaves a personal grudge or vendetta...."

"Mrs. Butler says he doesn't have an enemy in the world. Says he stays home and paints most every day."

"What about another woman?" I asked. "Could he have run off with somebody?"

"You've talked to him. Does he seem like that kind of guy?"

"No. Comes across as a faithful husband and happy retiree if you ask me. But my mother used to say all the time, "You don't know what's cooking in somebody else's pot.""

"You got that right."

"Would you mind if I check in with you from time to time to see if you've come up with anything?"

"Text me," the Chief said and gave me his cell number. "I hear that testimony in the Buddy Richardson trial starts Monday."

"Nine a.m. They finished picking the jury Friday afternoon. You ought to stick your head in the courtroom if you're downtown any next week. Probably the first time in the history of Lafayette County Courthouse there's been an eighty-five-year-old gangster on trial for murder."

I drove home, happy to have a chance to get to know the local Chief of Police. You never know when it might come in handy. I cleaned up and Susan and I walked three blocks to McEwen's on the Square for an early dinner. We had a table by ourselves in the back of the restaurant. The beautiful young woman *maître d'* said they were fully booked beginning at seven.

We ordered vodka tonics with lime. Susan asked me to bring her up to speed on the Buddy Richardson trial, the Russell Fratelli investigation, and the Justice Department witch hunt. By the time I finished we had drained our second VT and ordered dinner and a bottle of E. Guigal Cotes du Rhone, my favorite of the restaurant's reasonably priced reds, a wine recommended by my Oxford oenophile pal, Lowry Lomax. I began to tell Susan about the disappearance of James Butler and my meeting with Chief Mike Columbus, finishing the details as the waiter poured Susan her first glass of Cotes du Rhone.

I raised my glass and toasted Susan, describing her, and I think this is a direct quote, as "the most beautiful woman I have ever known," and thanking her for putting up with me all these years. She toasted me as "the most handsome, intelligent, and sexy man she had ever met," and thanked me for waiting for her to come home from her self-imposed three-year "sabbatical" from our marriage a few years back.

Obviously, the VTs had kicked in.

"You know," she said sipping her wine, "I thought you were through with all that law and order stuff once we moved up here and you were no longer District Attorney."

"I was," I said, "but apparently it's not through with me."

CHAPTER TWENTY-NINE

Sunday morning I woke up with a mild headache and discomfort. Not really a hangover, just not operating at one hundred per cent.

Okay. Okay. It was a hangover. But not a bad one.

I walked outside to get the Jackson paper and looked up at the overcast sky. I wouldn't have minded a little rain to keep me indoors. I usually feel guilty if I stay inside on a pretty day. I made a beeline for the Keurig and popped in a K-Cup, the strongest I could find in the McCarty's bowl on the counter.

"Caffé Verona," I muttered with pleasure after my first sip, the coffee addict that I am.

I turned on the lamp next to my easy chair. After I removed the ad inserts from the swollen Sunday *Clarion-Ledger*, the paper was two-thirds smaller, consisting only of six slender sections and the comics. I turned on a Memphis station for local weather and immediately muted it to avoid waking Susan. I sipped my coffee and waited. While looking over the rim of my mug I saw a banner scroll across the bottom of the screen. OXFORD MAN DISAPPEARS—LOCAL POLICE FEAR JAMES BUTLER, 74, ABDUCTED. Butler's picture appeared at the end of the scroll.

I heard movement in the kitchen and turned to see Susan groping for her mug and a K-Cup. In couple of minutes she joined me.

"I guess we had a really good time last night," she said.

"You told me it was the best time you ever had," I said smiling, a reference to a local lawyer friend of ours who insists on describing each function he attends as "the best time I ever had," to the delight of every host.

The land line rang. In accordance with our negotiated, time-honored early morning protocols, since I had drunk the most coffee, I had to answer. I listened, cupped my hand over the phone and whispered to Susan "It's Skeeter

Sumrall," and walked into my office in my pj's, shut the door and pulled out a legal pad and a Bic pen.

"How are you, Senator?"

"Fair to middlin', Willie Mitchell. How about you?"

"I've been better."

"I bet. Retirement suiting you?"

"It was, but I've been busy lately. I take it you've done some sniffing around this thing at the Justice Department staring me in the face."

"Yeah. I've been dancing the light fantastic up here, trying not to add to the crap that's already out there. You sure have a vindictive enemy in that little sawed-off bastard Leopold Whitman."

"I know. It goes way back."

"Scott reminded me. Well, he sure enough did call on the Junior Senator at his office in the Russell Building. Spent an hour or better with him."

"Talking about me?"

"So I'm told."

"Who asked for the meeting?"

"According to Chad's people it was Whitman."

"And the ostensible reason?"

"To gauge the public reaction to the possible prosecution of my favorite retired District Attorney for a Section 1983 civil rights offense."

"Why would Whitman care what the public thinks?"

"Good question. Why indeed? To tell you the truth, I don't trust the information we've gotten on this point. Justice Department people don't give a rat's ass about what the public thinks. And Whitman's not a political appointment. He's civil service and can't be fired even if they catch him with an underage goat in a compromising position."

"It must be Whitman," I said. "Senator Breedlove would have no reason to call the meeting."

"I agree, but none of this makes any sense. Have you ever gone against Breedlove in any way?"

"No. I've only met him once and that was when he came through the Sunshine Courthouse in a whirlwind Delta tour that was mostly about photo ops in front of dilapidated shanties. I shook his hand and wished him luck. I didn't get involved in his election. I have one good friend in the U.S. Senate. I don't need another."

"Now, this is just between us boys, Willie Mitchell. I don't trust young Chad. He's a Harvard man with a lovely mother and a scoundrel for a father. He's a distant sort, hard to get to know. Kind of standoffish, cold. The apple doesn't fall far from the tree."

"Which tree you talking about? Cissy or her husband?"

"The husband. I've talked to him at official and social functions in Jackson, and I swear the man seems pissed off all the time."

"I can't say. I've never met him."

"The grapevine's not yielding much on this thing, so I'm going to take the direct approach. I'm going to see him."

"Who?"

"Why, Chad Breedlove, of course. This one time I'm going to violate my policy of staying out of the Justice Department building. Those people give me the creeps over there. If you ever hear this fat boy's in their building it's because I've been subpoenaed for something."

I laughed, because Skeeter wasn't fat. He was short and stocky, with a Fred Flintstone kind of build. Not much neck. And he wasn't crooked. He was a good politician, and politics is a transactional game. You do something for me. I do something for you. But my son Scott verified what I already knew: Skeeter kept his horse-trading legal and ethical.

"Have you talked to Dunwoody?"

"Scott did. Drove over to Bellingham with that beautiful young lady he's married to. Over brunch Dunwoody told Scott that Whitman's keeping the number of lawyers involved really small, and spreading out assignments and information on a need-to-know basis inside the group. Bad news is Dunwoody doesn't have anyone inside that loop."

"Yet."

"We hope."

"Any idea of the time frame?"

"Dunwoody told Scott they're trying to expedite it up the chain of command to get permission to present the case to a federal grand jury."

"Weeks? Months?"

"I don't know."

"What should I do, Skeeter?"

"Go on about your business. Whitman's little gambit ain't out in the public yet, not even being whispered by Mississippi people in the know up here. I'm going to do everything I can to put a stop to this absurd prosecution before it goes too far."

"Don't get yourself in trouble on my behalf."

"Don't you worry, Sonny boy. I know a little bit about maneuvering up here in Gomorrah on the Potomac. A lot more than the Junior Senator or Leopold Whitman."

"All right, Skeeter, thanks."

"I'll be in touch."

I walked out the office and made another cup of coffee. Susan was moving around upstairs in our bedroom. I turned off the television and tried to read the sports section.

My eyes moved over the pictures on the first page, then a couple of paragraphs of a story about the New York Yankees' pitching woes, but the words did not register. My mind was focused on the Justice Department investigation. Nothing else.

CHAPTER THIRTY

After the call from Skeeter I went upstairs. In her thick, pink terry cloth robe, Susan was making the bed. When she leaned over to stretch the sheet, the robe gapped open. I couldn't help but notice she wore nothing underneath.

"Are you trying to seduce me, Mrs. Robinson?" I said. "Aren't you?"

She straightened up and with a hand on one hip winked at me.

"What took you so long to notice, Mister?"

I walked around the bed and took her in my arms. She pulled on the fuzzy pink belt around her waist and the robe opened. I stepped back and admired her for a moment, then put my arm around her waist. We danced slowly. I leaned back and looked into her eyes.

"You are so beautiful," I said.

"Even with my hair in a mess and no makeup?"

My eyes moved down her naked body.

"I hadn't noticed."

She slipped out of her robe. While I took off my shirt over my head she pulled down my pajama bottoms around my ankles. We kissed—a long, deep kiss, then moved onto the bed, and....

Well, I think that's enough. You can imagine the rest. We've been together a long time, but making love to Susan is still a wonderful, passionate thing. She was the perfect partner that Sunday morning, giving in and pushing back as needed; submissive, aggressive, quick with a suggestive word or two to heighten my arousal.

I'm not sure what heaven is like, but I think I have a clue. We ended together in what I can only describe as a quasi-religious experience involving our mutual invocation of the Supreme Being.

We don't smoke, so we lay naked and motionless, nothing on the bed but the fitted bottom sheet.

"Well," she said in a low voice, "how do they say it in sports? You left it all on the field." She rolled against me and lay her head on my chest, her hand patting my stomach, which is not as flat as it used to be.

"I love you," I said. "I always have."

We fell asleep together. I was at peace, satisfied and grateful, until ten minutes later when the image of Leopold Whitman intruded and ruined the moment. He was a small man with round glasses, balding with a reddish-brown beard he kept closely trimmed. He was an arrogant and pushy know-it-all, attributes that kept him in good stead in D.C., especially in the Justice Department.

I rolled out of bed and pulled the sheet over Susan. I slipped on a tee shirt and sweatpants and quietly walked downstairs. I made another cup of coffee and walked into my office. Susan would sleep another twenty minutes before she showered and dressed to start the day. I noticed I had a missed call on my cell, which I had muted and left on the top of my desk.

Cheryl Diamond had called.

"Good morning," Cheryl said when I called her back. "I hope I'm not calling too early."

"Not at all. I've been up for a while. My phone was in my office on silent."

"I've read several of the articles you sent about the unrest in 1962 on your campus there. I really had no idea that went on."

"Most people don't. It was a long time ago."

"I was sixteen years old," Cheryl said in her child-like voice.

"It's a miracle more people weren't killed."

"I've studied the photograph of the young man, Russell Fratelli," she said, "for hours. I've seen him in my dreams, standing among those trees."

"In the Grove?"

"Yes. But he's alone. He wasn't part of the crowd that Sunday night. I mean he was there, but not for the demonstration. He had no malice in his heart. That's what I sense."

"That's right, Cheryl. He was in favor of letting Meredith in school."

"But I wouldn't have called just to tell you that. You already knew he wasn't there to protest. I saw him again last night."

"Did you dream about him?"

"It wasn't exactly a dream. I may have been asleep, but this was more like the visions I receive in my waking hours. To tell you the truth, I'm not sure what it is or how it happens."

"All right."

"I saw a dark figure walking toward the young man, coming up from behind. The darkness was coming only for Russell."

"So he wasn't picked out of the crowd at random as an easy target?"

"I think that's what I saw. This dark force wanted Russell Fratelli, and no one else. It was something personal, Willie Mitchell."

CHAPTER THIRTY-ONE

I sat on the first curved bench on the prosecution side. I was next to the side aisle again in anticipation of a quiet exit from the Circuit Courtroom. I wore a coat and tie, not sure why. Maybe out of habit. Walton was seated alone at the prosecution table. Josh Pickett's jury selection work was done, but I saw him sitting in the back row when I walked in. I was sure he was there to watch the opening arguments.

I sat alone, thinking about what Cheryl Diamond told me the day before. She gleaned from her "vision" what I already suspected. Unlike the murderer who targeted the British reporter for the French wire service, Russell's shooter came to the Grove that night with the specific intent to kill Russell Fratelli. The Brit was murdered probably because he was a foreign reporter with a camera, but his assailant did not know anything about him personally. Russell's shooter had a grudge against him—a very personal, deadly grudge.

Police Chief Mike Columbus sat next to me. I shook his hand.

"That's your former assistant?" he said, pointing to Walton.

"He's the Yaloquena District Attorney now. Very good trial lawyer." I said and paused a moment. "Any news on Mr. Butler?"

"No. It's very frustrating. It's like he just dropped off the face of the earth. I passed along to my investigators your suggestion of the possibility of a girlfriend. They went back to see Butler's friends they felt they could talk to about it, and everyone said no way. Said he's just what he appears to be, a happily married retiree who loves to paint."

"He didn't run away," I said. "I know he didn't."

"I agree with you. We'll keep looking."

The Chief and I stood when the bailiff walked through the door calling the courtroom to order. Head down and eyes on the carpet before him, Deputy Clerk Eddie Bordelon walked in behind the bailiff, followed by Judge Zelda Williams. Winston Moore's duties in jury selection had ended, and he was back in his office in Sunshine. Judge Williams nodded to the bailiff, who entered the jury room on the right side of the bench and reappeared a minute later leading twelve jurors into the jury box. He seated the two alternates in chairs next to the box. The bailiff gestured to Judge Williams when they were all seated.

"Good morning, ladies and gentlemen of the jury," she said. "The first stage of the trial is opening arguments, first by Mr. Donaldson representing the State of Mississippi, and then by Mr. Silver, representing the defendant Buddy Richardson."

"May we approach, Your Honor?" Helmet Head said.

"Certainly," Zelda said as J.D. Silver and Walton stepped up on the riser and stood before the Judge.

"So, that's the badass Buddy Richardson," Chief Columbus whispered to me, gesturing to the defense table. "He doesn't look like much to me."

"Looks can be deceiving," I said.

"Ready to proceed, Mr. Donaldson?" Judge Williams asked when the lawyers returned to their tables.

"Ready, Your Honor," Walton said and walked to the temporary podium in front of the jury box.

"I would like to thank each of you for your patience last week during the jury selection process," Walton said, and praised them for "their willing participation in one of their most important civic duties."

Like most things said by lawyers to ingratiate themselves with jurors, it could have come across as patronizing if not done right. Walton exuded integrity and sincerity when he said it, so I was confident it had its desired effect. The truth is, after spending a week in the courtroom with Walton and Helmet Head, each juror already had a distinct impression of each lawyer. And make no mistake, J.D. Silver did not get the big bucks because of his hair. He was a first-rate lawyer, up on the relevant statutes and current case law. Moreover, he was an entertainer with a relaxed, folksy demeanor that was genuine and connected with many jurors. I went up against him in the Ross Bullard prosecution for the abduction and murder of seven-year-old Danny Thurman, and believe me, he was a formidable opponent in court. It's a given that the District Attorney has the law and the evidence on his side. Moreover, the defendant is usually not an upstanding sort. The good defense lawyers know all this going in. They depend on their ability, strategy, and personality to squeeze out the tiniest reasonable doubt from a juror or two. Moreover, they know their client will be a disaster on the witness stand, and do whatever it takes to keep him or her from testifying.

In all my years of trying cases before juries, I never saw a single defendant help himself by taking the witness stand. Not once.

"Eight months ago," Walton began, "on a lonely farm driveway in Yaloquena County, about eight miles from Sunshine city limits, a young farmer, Carl Sanders, age thirty-five, was ambushed in the early evening darkness less than a hundred yards from his own house after putting in a hard day's work on his place, getting his crops ready for the harvest season."

Walton named the law enforcement witnesses he intended to call to describe the investigation that took place at the Sanders's home that night, including the names of the team members from the State Crime Lab who arrived at one a.m. to work the crime scene and gather evidence under the blinding glare of the portable light towers Sheriff Lee Jones and his men set up.

Walton said the Yaloquena County Coroner would testify about the autopsy of the body of Carl Sanders and would identify the two bullets taken from the deceased, one that entered through the victim's left arm, pierced his heart, and lodged in his right lung; and a second bullet that entered Sanders' left temple and came to rest in his right frontal lobe.

"No witnesses saw the shooting death of Carl Sanders, except for the man who shot him. You might think it would be very hard for investigators to find the man who killed

Carl Sanders, given these circumstances. Well, ladies and gentlemen of the jury, you would be right, except for an incredibly lucky break.

"I will call to the witness stand a man from Dundee County, an insurance salesman who happened to be driving by the Sanders place while it was still daylight. This witness saw another man from Dundee County with whom he was well-acquainted, a man he knew to be Lynn Metzger. The witness will testify that Lynn Metzger was driving slowly on the county road that ran past the Sanders place about an hour before dark, and appeared to be studying the Sanders gravel driveway. In fact, Metzger was so busy casing the driveway he didn't notice the other Dundee County resident when he passed.

"The witness from Dundee County who recognized Lynn Metzger will testify that when he saw the news about the Carl Sanders murder the next day, and the video of the scene taken from the news helicopter, he realized he had driven past the Sanders farm. He put two and two together, and figured out why Lynn Metzger was at the scene. The witness called Yaloquena County Sheriff Lee Jones and at the Sheriff's request, drove to Sunshine and gave a complete statement of what he saw the previous day.

"The witness will testify that he recognized Lynn Metzger that day around Carl Sanders' farm, because he had been in a boundary line dispute with Lynn Metzger. It involved a forty-acre tract in the hills the witness owned that adjoined Metzger's property. He will further say that less than one month before Carl Sanders' death, Lynn Metzger drove to the witness's house and threatened him, face to face, arriving in his truck. He will testify that he saw Lynn Metzger drive past the Sanders place in that same truck just hours before the murder, and he has no doubt it was Metzger. You will hear the Dundee County witness relate all of this, ladies and gentlemen, and you will be convinced that the witness is telling the truth.

"You will hear from Sheriff Jones that his men confronted Lynn Metzger with this information, and that a subsequent search of Metzger's home in Dundee County pursuant to a search warrant issued by a Dundee County Judge, turned up a semi-automatic .22 caliber Baretta pistol, which weapon was identified by the ballistics analyst at the State Crime Lab as the gun that fired both .22 caliber bullets taken from the brain and lung of Carl Sanders in the autopsy.

"Ladies and gentlemen of the jury, I will establish through testimony that Lynn Metzger had no prior relationship with Carl Sanders, and in fact, did not know the victim. So the question arises: why would Metzger do such a despicable thing to a man he did not know?"

Walton paused a moment to let the question simmer.

"Lynn Metzger is going to take the witness stand, ladies and gentlemen, and from that chair," Walton said, pointing to the witness stand, "he will tell you why." He paused then spoke much louder. "HE WAS PAID TO KILL CARL SANDERS, Ladies and gentlemen. HE DID IT FOR MONEY. MONEY PAID TO HIM BY THE DEFENDANT BUDDY RICHARDSON."

The courtroom was silent as Walton pointed at the defendant. Helmet Head had no reaction. He continued to take notes on his legal pad as if he were trying a contract dispute, not a heinous murder. Buddy stared straight ahead at the wall next to Judge Williams' bench, at times closing his eyes and bowing his head.

"I want you to know that Lynn Metzger is testifying under a plea agreement with my office. He will tell you from the witness stand that if he testifies truthfully about his role in the death of Carl Sanders, he will be allowed to plead guilty to second degree murder, and receive a sentence of forty years imprisonment in the State Department of Corrections.

"You may ask why I would make such an agreement with the cold-blooded killer Lynn Metzger. And you are entitled to know. It is the only way, ladies and gentlemen, to get to the person that set all of this in motion, to get to the person who paid Lynn Metzger $50,000 in cash to kill Carl Sanders, and that person is the defendant Buddy Richardson."

I don't know if he did it on purpose, but Buddy Richardson was yawning at exactly the same time Walton said his name.

"Judge Williams will instruct you at the end of the trial that the State does not have to prove motive. In other words, I do not have to prove WHY Buddy Richardson paid Lynn Metzger to kill Carl Sanders. But ladies and gentlemen of the jury, I am going to. I will put on evidence, testimony from the defendant's own granddaughter Lisa, that Buddy Richardson detested her second husband, Carl Sanders, accusing Sanders of interfering with his relationship with Buddy Richardson's great-grandson. She will testify that Buddy Richardson threatened to kill Carl Sanders twice in her presence, if Mr. Sanders did not agree to let the defendant take the six-year-old boy to his plantation home High Hope in Dundee County to spend a week, free from the alleged interference of the boy's step-father, Carl Sanders."

It was a powerful opening statement, one that kept the jurors on the edge of their seats. I made a point of observing them so I could report what I saw to Walton. So far, so good. Unless Helmet Head pulled a rabbit out of his hat, I saw no way Buddy Richardson could win over this jury.

Walton wrapped up quickly and sat down. J.D. Silver took his time gathering his things and walking to the podium. On his way, Buddy Richardson stood up at the defense table. I thought it was odd, to say the least, because the Judge had not declared a recess.

I watched Buddy raise his hand to Judge Williams as if he had something to say. He opened his mouth, then closed it.

He teetered a moment, then fell backwards, striking the floor hard, first with his head, then his back. He must have been unconscious, because he made no attempt to break his fall.

Everyone in the courtroom seemed to gasp at the same time. Silver rushed back to Buddy's side when he realized what happened. He knelt on one knee, tapped Buddy lightly on the cheek, then turned to the bailiff standing over him.

"Call 9-1-1," Helmet Head said. "Tell them to hurry."

CHAPTER THIRTY-TWO

As soon as it became obvious Buddy Richardson would not be getting back on his feet, Judge Williams asked the bailiff to remove the jurors to their deliberation room. She remained on the bench and Eddie Bordelon sat at the minute clerk's desk—their eyes glued to the defendant.

When Buddy hit the floor, Chief Mike Columbus immediately rushed through the rail and knelt beside Helmet Head. I watched him adjust Buddy's head and neck to make sure his breathing passage was unobstructed. He listened to his heart, took his pulse, and whispered to J.D. Silver kneeling next to him. Silver stood up, looking relieved to turn Buddy over to someone who appeared to know what he was doing.

EMTs burst through the back door of the courtroom. No more than fifteen minutes had elapsed since the bailiff made his 9-1-1 call. Chief Columbus spoke quietly with them a moment, then backed away and watched them work.

Silver walked over to me.

"It looks serious," he whispered.

"Has he been sick?" I asked.

"Not that I know of. You saw him Saturday morning. How did he seem?"

"On edge. Jumpy."

"He's been like that every time I've been with him. Nervous as a cat in a room full of rocking chairs. I bet you he's had a stroke."

"How's his blood pressure?"

"I have no idea. We never discussed his health."

I looked past Helmet Head at the pretty, thirty-something blonde woman standing outside the rail, looking down at the old man. I had never met her, but I knew from Walton she was Lisa Richardson Bailey Sanders, whose six-year-old son, Robert Edward Lee Bailey, was the apple of

Buddy's eye. Buddy's belief that Carl Sanders, Lisa's husband, was keeping the old man from spending time with the boy was the proximate cause of the murder. She remained behind the rail and looked down on her grandfather with detachment, as if looking at a stranger.

Lisa Sanders turned toward me. We made eye contact. She shook her head slightly and pursed her lips. She no longer appeared aloof. She was disgusted. Lisa's eyes were as dark and piercing as Buddy's—raptor's eyes. She turned away from me, glanced down at Buddy, and sat down in the front row. She went through her purse dispassionately, pulled out her phone, and began sending a text.

"I don't think Mrs. Sanders is very upset," I said.

"No kidding," Silver said. "She wouldn't talk to my investigator, other than to tell him she hoped her grandfather burned in hell for what he did to her husband. Between us, my investigator said from the people he interviewed it seemed Carl Sanders was a decent sort of fellow."

"Can't say the same about your client. I can see why Lisa and Carl would want to keep the boy away from Buddy."

"You know, in my business, I don't get to represent many nice people. At least Buddy pays promptly and up front." Silver looked down at his client. "In light of the circumstances, I think my policy in that regard is very wise."

"You know," I said, "I've been watching Buddy since he hit the floor. He has not moved, or even blinked an eyelid."

"I believe he's had a massive stroke."

"Or too much crystal meth," I said.

Helmet Head ignored my comment. We watched the EMTs count to three and lift Buddy onto the collapsible gurney. They strapped him in and wheeled him through the rail gate and out of the courtroom. I looked down on him as he passed. Between the oxygen mask and his beard, most of his face was covered. His eyes remained closed.

Silver walked back to his table and began to gather his files and documents. Walton left the prosecution table and joined me at the rail.

"Anything like this ever happen to you?"

"Never," I said. "He hit that floor hard."

"I was watching Silver put his tablet on the podium when I heard the *whump* behind me. I turned and he was already down."

"Mr. Donaldson, Mr. Silver," Judge Williams said. "Please approach the bench and let me enter something into the record."

They walked up on the riser and stood in front of her.

"At approximately 9:40 a.m., this Monday, April 26, after District Attorney Walton Donaldson had completed his opening statement, Mr. Silver arrived at the podium to address the jury. Before he uttered the first word, his client, Mr. Buddy Richardson, the defendant, stood at the defense table, then fell backwards onto the floor, where he has remained unconscious and unmoving from the time he fell until the EMTs removed him on a gurney from the courtroom at approximately 10:05.

"After Mr. Richardson did not get up from the floor, I instructed the bailiff to remove the jury. The twelve jurors and two alternates have been in the jury waiting room under the supervision of the bailiff."

Zelda looked over her reading glasses at the two lawyers.

"Would either of you like to add anything to the record?"

Walton and Silver said no.

"Mr. Bordelon," Judge Williams said, "please go to the jury room and instruct the bailiff to bring the jury back in."

Eddie jumped up and hustled past the Judge's bench.

"I'm going to instruct them that they are still under oath as jurors, that they are temporarily excused to go about their business, and to call the automated number in the Circuit Clerk's office at 3:00 p.m. today for further instructions. I will instruct them that they are not to discuss the case with each other or anyone else, and they are not to watch any television news reports or read any newspapers or websites that might have information about this case. Anything else, gentlemen?"

Walton and Silver shook their heads as the bailiff re-seated the jury. Judge Williams gave the instructions and released the jurors. She waited until the jurors were gone and said "Court is adjourned" before walking off the bench.

On her way out, she stopped at the rail and extended her hand to me.

"How are you, Willie Mitchell?"

"Good, Zelda. You?"

"The same. This was certainly unforeseen." She paused. "We miss you in the Sunshine Courthouse."

"I miss you, Zelda, and everyone else. But I have to tell you, Oxford is a really cool place to live."

"It is," she said, looking over her shoulder to see if anyone else was in earshot. "I've never seen so many good restaurants in such a small town. Philip and I had planned on eventually eating at every one of them during the trial. We ate at quite a few last week during jury selection. With this unfortunate development today, I'm not sure we'll be able to reach our goal."

"Tell Philip hello for me," I said.

"I will," she said, then looked over at Silver at the defense table. "Mr. Silver, I assume you're going to the hospital to be with your client?"

"Headed there right now, Your Honor."

"Please call me at noon, then on the hour after that, and let me know his condition. I'll notify the clerk and we'll put instructions on the machine accordingly. I hope this is not as serious as it appears and we are able to reconvene in the morning."

"Will do, Your Honor."

Zelda walked out. Eddie Bordelon walked over to Silver and scribbled the Judge's cell number on a light green Post-It Note pad he kept with him at all times. He shook hands with me on his way out of the side door. Silver walked out, leaving Walton and me alone in the empty courtroom, which now seemed cavernous.

"What did Zelda say?" he asked.

"Nothing. Small talk about local restaurants."

"She seems pretty calm about all this," Walton said.

"Zelda's seen it all in her days on the bench. Besides, she knows what kind of man Buddy Richardson is. A fatal stroke would be a nice coda to all of this. Justice would be served for a change."

"Yeah," Walton said, "but I can't imagine we'll be that lucky."

CHAPTER THIRTY-THREE

Walton and his security crew, Deputies Sammy Roberts and Will Gresham, were sitting at the dining room table in the apartment when Sheriff Lee Jones and I walked in. Walton was in his shirtsleeves, his tie loosened.

"You heard anything?" the Sheriff asked.

"Not a word," Walton said. "We were talking about lunch."

"Actually it was Will talking about lunch," Sammy Roberts said, lightly jabbing the stomach of the pudgy white deputy seated next to him.

"How's our star witness?" Walton asked the Sheriff.

"Metzger's entertaining the odd couple with Dixie Mafia stories," Lee said, "most of them made up, I'm sure."

I smiled at Lee's reference to the odd couple. Robert "Smitty" Smith, was a fifty-five-year-old white Deputy Sheriff who acted and sounded like a cast member of *Hee Haw*. Delroy Robinson, a thirty-year-old black Deputy, was an accomplished local deejay and rapper wannabe in his spare time in Sunshine joints. They were partners, taking their comedy routines in their patrol car on the Yaloquena County roads, entertaining each other and the citizens they encountered while enforcing the law, more or less.

"I wish we had them on tape," I said, "the hit man and the odd couple, holed up and swapping tales. We could make some money."

"Be a hit reality show," Walton said.

"Smitty and Delroy are funny," Sheriff Jones said, "but that Lynn Metzger is one cold-hearted son of a bitch. Last time I was there he was telling us about how Buddy and he came to terms on the contract on Carl Sanders. Said he had done jobs for Buddy before, but nothing this big. Metzger said he told Buddy he'd do it for a hundred thousand, and Buddy offered him twenty-five. He said they negotiated for a couple of days, going back and forth, until they came to terms at fifty. Metzger said, and I'm quoting here, 'The old man wore me out, finally jewed me down to fifty thousand, and I said okay, partly because I was fed up with the old bastard'."

"Metzger's a peach, isn't he?" I said. "An equal opportunity hater."

"I didn't want to make the deal with Metzger," Walton said.

"You had no choice," I said. "It was the only way you could get to Buddy. And it was also smart for you to take the death penalty off the table. You might get a jury to impose it, but with all the appeals, Buddy wouldn't live long enough for it to be carried out."

"From the looks of him when they rolled him out of the courtroom," Walton said, "maybe the Man Upstairs has done our work for us."

"Wouldn't that be justice?" Sammy said. "The Lord sending the old Klukker to hell to burn with his friends in white sheets."

"Don't count him out," I said. "He's a tough old bird."

I heard somebody clomping up the wooden stairs to the apartment. So did everyone else. Sammy Roberts tapped Will Gresham on the arm. The two of them jumped up from the table and took positions next to the interior door at the top of the stairs.

"Don't shoot," hollered the visitor through the closed door.

"Aw, hell," I said. "It's Jimmy Gray."

Sammy opened the door and Jimmy Gray trundled his big frame into the apartment grinning from ear to ear.

"This a private conference? Seems to me y'all are violating the Open Meetings statute. Y'all on the public teat getting paid with my tax dollars, so I have the right to attend."

"We're not paid enough to do our job *and* have to put up with the likes of you," Lee Jones said, grabbing Jimmy by his big bicep and shaking him.

"I'm not on the dole anymore," I said. "What have you heard?"

"Delbert, my junior loan officer, his sister works at Baptist. She told him Buddy was in I.C.U. and they were stabilizing him. Said they'll probably run some tests on him this afternoon when his family doctor gets here."

"Family doctor?" Walton asked.

"It's old Doc Finstermayer from Kilbride," Jimmy said. "He's almost the same age as Buddy. Older than dirt. He's been taking care of Buddy for years."

"You know him?"

"Just a little. Seen him once or twice at the bank in Kilbride."

"This isn't good," I said. "If he's been his doctor for that long he knows Buddy's a dangerous man, probably knows some of the things Buddy's done."

"You think the doctor will protect him?" Walton asked.

"I figure Doc Finstermayer will do whatever Buddy tells him to do," Jimmy said. "Probably keep him in that hospital long as he can."

"I'm going to ask Judge Williams for a conference about this," Walton said. "I'm sure Helmet Head will go ballistic."

"Telling Zelda about your concerns in a conference with Helmet Head is a good idea," I said, "but I'd wait until tomorrow to ask. Maybe Buddy's situation looks more serious than it is—maybe it's just dehydration or something—and he can be discharged in time for trial tomorrow."

"I wouldn't count on it," Lee said.

"Who's hungry?" Jimmy said. "I took the liberty of ordering sandwiches and sides for everybody from The Blind Pig. Ought to be here any minute."

"Sounds good to me," Sheriff Jones said. "Nice of you to do that."

"Courtesy of Sunshine Bank," Jimmy said.

The sandwiches hit the spot. So did the gallows humor around the dining room table. No one felt guilty about wishing Buddy the worst. He had dealt so much misery to so many people in his lifetime, it would be rough justice for a stroke or heart attack to take him out just as he's about to go to trial for the murder of Carl Sanders. Making Buddy pay for his crimes was long overdue.

Jimmy and I left together. I didn't have my truck, so I asked Jimmy to run me by to check on Mrs. Naomi Butler before dropping me off at the condo. We were at the Butler house in five minutes. Jimmy asked if I wanted him to stay in his Navigator and wait. I told him to come in with me, that Mrs. Butler probably needed the comic relief.

"We won't stay but a second, Naomi," I said standing in her kitchen. "This is Jimmy Gray. He runs the Sunshine Bank on Jackson close to the Square. We just wanted to see if how you're doing. I spoke to Chief Columbus earlier this morning."

"Not good," she said in a shaky voice. "I have the feeling that something bad has happened to James. Something really bad."

CHAPTER THIRTY-FOUR

I got a call from Chief Columbus at four o'clock that same afternoon. As soon as he identified himself, my stomach knotted. I didn't know the exact details, but I sensed he was going to tell me James Butler was dead.

"We found him," the Chief said, "or I should say a farmer over in the Delta found him and called Sheriff Jones's office. The dispatcher called me. I've sent my crime scene people over. Appears to be a suicide."

"Damn," I said. "I just find that hard to believe."

"We're going to check everything closely. I told my men it might have been staged and to proceed accordingly."

"They should bag his hands as soon as they get there. That's important."

"They know. There's one more thing."

"Have you told Mrs. Butler? I stopped by at noon. She's fragile."

"I'm going over there now. But I thought you'd want to know where they found him. It's on a dirt road west of Highway 49 north of Sunshine. The dispatcher said it's the road to your duck camp."

I thanked the Chief and called Jimmy Gray. He was at the condo to pick me up in less than ten minutes. I had never been in an automobile moving as fast as Jimmy drove that Monday afternoon. On straight stretches with no traffic he kept it between ninety and a hundred. The Navigator was heavy and held the road well at that speed, but I wouldn't want to do it again. Ninety minutes after leaving the condo, we turned west on the farm road and drove about a mile before we saw the law enforcement vehicles bunched up in the last curve before my camp. Jimmy parked behind a black Oxford Police Department SUV and we walked the rest of the way. I briefly said hello to the four Yaloquena deputies at the scene. They had turned Mr. Butler's Buick Lacrosse sedan over to the two

OPD investigators for what processing could be done on the dirt road.

James Butler was slumped in the driver's seat, his body against the door, his head leaning on the door post. The driver's window was open. Jimmy and I walked around the Buick in a wide arc and stopped on the driver's side. An exit wound gaped at James's left forehead and temple. We watched the OPD technicians, one in the back seat and the other standing next to the open passenger door.

After a while the officer backed away from the passenger door. I waved to him and walked over to speak.

"I'm Willie Mitchell Banks and this is Jimmy Gray. Chief Columbus called me to let me know about this. I knew Mr. Butler and I've spoken with Mrs. Butler several times since he disappeared."

"Yes, sir," he said, removing his latex gloves and pointing in the direction of my duck camp. "I've seen you at the station talking to the Chief. You were the DA over here. The deputies tell me that's your camp house."

"It is. I've owned the place about thirty years. Built the camp in the nineties. Used to be a pretty good duck hole, the black water lake on the back with all the cypress trees, but I haven't hunted it in a long time." I paused. "What's this look like to you?"

He motioned for me to follow him to the Buick. Jimmy hung back and watched as the technician led me to the open passenger door. I was pleased to see plastic bags over each of Mr. Butler's hands. The officer pointed to the passenger seat.

"Someone was sitting in the passenger seat when the bullet went into Mr. Butler's head."

"How can you tell?"

"You see this back spatter?" he said, pointing to drops and specks of blood on the inside of the passenger door and the passenger floor mat. "Now, look at this passenger seat. Not a drop on the seat or the back of the seat. The void is created because somebody was sitting there and got the spatter on them. Took it with them on their clothes when they left. It's the first thing I noticed when I opened this door. Back spatter everywhere but on the seat."

"You've got plenty of pictures?"

"First thing we did. Took photographs for the first twenty minutes. I didn't bag his hands until I got plenty of shots of him just as he was when we got here. Then took a couple more with his hands bagged. We'll tow the car to Oxford, take fingerprints inside and out, do some other things we can't out here. By the way, these deputies did exactly what they were supposed to do. They didn't go into the car, just secured the scene. Someone taught them well."

"Sheriff Lee Jones," I said. "Anything else?"

"Did you see the gun?" he asked. "It's on the driver's side floor. Revolver. Looks like a Chief's Special, .38 caliber, but I haven't examined it yet."

"Is it unusual for the gun to be on the floor?"

"No. You never know where the gun is going to land. Doesn't mean anything. People think it ought to be right by the victim's hand, but with the recoil and the body's reaction to the shot, you just can't predict."

I heard vehicles approaching us on the dirt road and turned to see the Yaloquena County Coroner's wagon and a tow truck from Sunshine.

"Here comes Quincy, Medical Examiner," Jimmy Gray said as Al Revels, Yaloquena's non-physician elected Coroner walked toward us on the dirt road.

I spoke to Al and introduced him to the OPD investigators. They conferred a few minutes and Al walked over to the Lacrosse's driver's window and studied the exit wound.

"I pronounce this man officially dead," Al said. "When did he go missing?"

"Friday evening. He lives in Oxford."

"Why'd he drive all the way over here to do this? They got back roads in Lafayette County."

Returning to Oxford at a more reasonable pace, Jimmy and I were quiet at the outset. No matter how many times I've seen murder victims, I can't get used to it. I can bring up a detailed mental picture of the deceased at the scene of every homicide I was called out to.

"You know," I said, "Al raised a very good question."

"That might be a first."

"Assuming the OPD tech is right, and someone in the passenger seat shot Butler and tried to make it look like a suicide, why would they drive all the way over here to stage it?"

"The better question," Jimmy said, "is why they staged it on the dirt road right in front of your duck camp?"

CHAPTER THIRTY-FIVE

Jimmy and I stopped by Mrs. Butler's home when we returned to Oxford. I was relieved to see so many cars parked in her driveway and on the street. When I knocked on the door, a woman Naomi's age answered. Over her shoulder, I saw several other older women working in her kitchen and a few solemn husbands gathered at the table drinking coffee. I explained to the woman who I was and that Jimmy and I had stopped by to make sure Naomi was all right. The woman said she and other friends of the Butlers from church came to support her and help out as soon as they heard. She said Naomi's doctor had come by to check on her and given her something to help her sleep, and Naomi was resting quietly in her bedroom. The woman asked my name again, thanked me, and said she would make sure Naomi knew I came by.

Back in the Navigator, I was grateful Naomi was with friends. She was going to need them, especially when she learned it wasn't a suicide. I wondered what would be worse for the frail, shaky widow who had just lost her companion of probably fifty years, being told her husband killed himself or that someone murdered him? I asked Jimmy what he thought.

"She'd have more guilt if it had been suicide," he said. "She would wonder what she did to let him down, how she could have missed the miserable state of mind he was in. If someone kills him, it lets her off the hook, guilt-wise. Nothing she could have done to prevent it."

"Maybe so. But whoever murdered him had a reason, and when she finds out the motive, I guarantee you it's going to be because Butler was involved in something she knew nothing about. I think it's a more serious betrayal than suicide. Mental illness is not something a person is responsible for." I paused a moment. "Let's go by the hospital."

On the drive back to Oxford I had called Walton and told him he had another homicide in his jurisdiction. I described what we had seen in and around Butler's Buick on the road to my duck camp. Like Jimmy, he thought it more than coincidental that the murder was staged on the road to my duck camp. I agreed, but suggested we not jump to any conclusions.

I asked the status of Buddy Richardson. He said Buddy was still in intensive care and Judge Williams had the local Circuit Clerk change the voice message to the jurors to advise them to call again at noon the next day for further instructions. Walton said Zelda and her husband Philip had driven back to Sunshine. She planned to coordinate updated instructions to the jury with the Lafayette County Clerk of Court. I asked Walton how he was getting medical updates.

"Only through J.D. Silver," he said. "And that's starting to bother me. Silver says I'm not to contact the physicians directly, going on about privacy bullshit. I'm not comfortable with Helmet Head being the gatekeeper for finding out Richardson's medical status."

"You're right," I said. "I would make sure you let Zelda know your concerns in a conference call with Silver first thing in the morning, but be sure you couch it...."

"I'll be diplomatic. If the man is truly ill with a life-threatening condition, there's no way we can proceed. But if he's faking this to buy some time, I've got to do something about it."

"Zelda should speak directly with the physician. Is it Doc Finstermayer?"

"There's a young internal medicine guy, Dr. Grillette, who's on staff taking care of him. Finstermayer doesn't have privileges at Baptist so all the orders he suggests have to go through Dr. Grillette."

"Jimmy and I are going to stop by the hospital to snoop around."

"Good. Let me know what you find out."

"Where's Lee?"

"Gone to check on Metzger then back to Sunshine. He'll call me first thing in the morning. No need for him to come back up here unless we know something about how we're going to proceed."

"You talk to Gayle?"

"Probably five or six times. She wanted me to drive to her mother's to spend the night with her and the kids. I told her I had to stay here until I knew what we were going to do with this jury."

"Jury's been sworn in so double jeopardy attaches. Zelda will have to declare a mistrial if the trial can't go forward."

"Silver's already talked to the Judge and me about it. He's priming the pump. This medical event is convenient timing for Richardson."

"Makes you wonder, doesn't it," I said. "I'll call you after the hospital."

"I'll be here at the apartment with my new best friends Sammy and Will. Will's gone right now to pick up pizza and a Red Box movie."

"Don't let your guard down. Whoever trashed the apartment knows you're staying there. They don't wish you the best. Call you later."

Jimmy parked the massive fire engine red Navigator in the Baptist parking lot. Construction was underway on a new $350 million Baptist Hospital on the recently opened throughway connecting Taylor Road and South Lamar, but it would be a couple of years before the existing hospital was converted to another use. I had only been here a couple of times for brief visits to members of the Geezer Group having knees replaced or shoulders rebuilt, and did not know the layout or the location of the ICU.

"I heard they're going to convert this place to some kind of facility for old folks," Jimmy said, "nursing home, assisted living, and Elderhostel type thing. Ought to be perfect for the Geezer Group—they're all elderly and hostile."

"Different spelling," I said as we arrived at the information desk.

We exited the elevator. I spotted Helmet Head at the ICU nurses station, leaning over the counter, flirting with the nurse. We shook hands and Silver led us to the ICU waiting room.

"What's his status?" I asked.

"The young doctor, Grillette, says he's stable. I can't get much out of Doc Finstermayer. He looks at me when I speak to him, but he gives me no indication my questions register with him."

"How did he know to come up here from Kilbride?"

"Beats me. I didn't call him. He said he's been taking care of Buddy the last forty years. I've been talking to Grillette to get information."

"Did he have a stroke?"

"He's not sure. Buddy's blood pressure was sky high according to the information the EMTs passed along to the hospital."

"They do a CT scan or MRI?"

"Grillette said they did both. Said they were inconclusive. He did an echocardiogram and some blood tests, too. Nothing definitive. He said Buddy might have had a TIA that's hard to diagnose with the tests."

"Sounds like old Buddy might have just fainted," Jimmy said.

"That's possible. Grillette wouldn't rule it out. But he was unconscious for quite a while. Old Doc Finstermayer said, 'Buddy ain't never fainted once in all my years tendin' to him,' and that's a quote."

"When did he come to?" I asked.

"Maybe thirty minutes after he got here."

"You talked to him?"

"Sure did."

"Did he seem back to normal?"

"You know, I don't know. He was more or less responsive to my questions. Whether he's back to normal or not, I don't know. Dr. Grillette has him hooked up to two or three monitors in there in his room."

"You realize what kind of position this puts us in."

"What do you mean 'us'," Silver said with attitude. "Are you some kind of co-counsel? You don't have any legal status in this case. I don't even know why I'm talking to you."

I felt my face flush. I locked eyes with the high-priced prick and invaded his space. It was all I could do to keep from clocking him. I felt Jimmy grab my right arm and pull me back.

"You're the kind of pimp that makes me hate lawyers," Jimmy Gray said to J.D. Silver.

I turned my back to Helmet Head to cool down. I didn't need to get into it with him and create a scene that would work to his advantage. After all, he was right. I had no official capacity, no right to demand anything. I had become the person I used to avoid: A CONCERNED CITIZEN.

"You're right," I said to Helmet Head, being submissive for the good of the team. "I'm just trying to help Walton. He's young, and never gone up against a lawyer of your stature and ability."

Helmet Head pretended to soften and turned on his "we are all in this together"*shtick* I recognized from going against him in the Ross Bullard case. Like all successful defense lawyers, he was a good actor, taking on whichever demeanor suited his needs at the time. This one could be particularly effective, encouraging a false camaraderie that he would use to win a concession or fool a prosecutor into revealing something damaging to the State's case. I guess it was no different than what I did from time to time in pursuit of a conviction.

"Look," Silver said, "we're all on edge here. I don't want to be in this hospital playing nursemaid to the old racist. I've got a pile of work and I'm up against deadlines on briefs and motions in a half-dozen cases. If you can get Grillette to talk to you, be my guest. He's hard to catch and doesn't like talking to me. Maybe you'll have better luck. I'm going to make some calls."

Helmet Head headed to the elevators. Jimmy and I turned to the young lady at the nurse's station whose eyes remained wide from the exchange she witnessed between Silver and me. I introduced us and asked if we could see Dr. Grillette for a minute.

"He'll be here sometime tonight to make his rounds, but I can't tell you when. You're welcome to wait for him."

"What about Doctor Finstermayer?" I asked.

"I don't know," she said. "He left an hour ago. He mumbled something to me as he walked by the station but I couldn't understand what he said."

"He's been around a long time," Jimmy said.

"He looks as old as Mr. Richardson," she said. "Seventy, maybe even eighty. It's hard to tell. His big shock of white hair could use some combing."

Jimmy and I rode the elevator down to the ground floor and stepped out of the automatic doors to stand on the sidewalk under the *porte-cochere*. The spring air was fresh and mild, welcome after the harsh Oxford winter we had just endured.

"What now?" Jimmy said.

"I'm going to stick around upstairs and wait for Dr. Grillette," I said, "to see if I can get him to talk to me. No need for you to be here."

"If you're staying I'm staying."

A white Lexus crossover entered the circular drive and slowed as if to drop someone off, then sped up without leaving the passenger, an old man in his late seventies or early eighties with a bushy mound of unruly white hair. On the bumper of the Lexus, a partially torn Ole Miss sticker flapped.

I got only a glimpse of the driver, a slightly built older man with a hooked nose. I couldn't be sure, but I thought it was Cissy Breedlove's husband.

Chapter Thirty-Six

"So what is Cissy Breedlove's worthless drunk of a husband doing driving around old Doc Finstermayer?" Jimmy Gray said as we rode up the elevator to return to the ICU.

"I'm not sure that was Gavin Breedlove," I said, "I've only seen him that one time in their little courtyard, and I was looking through the window."

"Well, I'm sure that was Finstermayer in the passenger seat. Kind of odd for Breedlove to drive around the circle and not drop off the old Doc."

Jimmy articulated what I had been wondering since the Lexus made the drive through.

"Maybe Doc Finstermayer recognized you," I said, "and didn't want to talk to you for some reason."

"*Moi* ? I can't imagine that being the case. Everyone wants to talk to me. It's probably you he was avoiding."

"I've never met him."

"Yeah, but your face has been on the nightly news in the Delta at least two hundred times over the past two decades, and in the paper, too. Everyone who owns a television in north Mississippi recognizes you."

"Never met Gavin Breedlove, either," I said.

"Maybe there's just something about you that pisses everyone off."

I laughed as we exited the elevator. No one in the nurses' station. I gestured for Jimmy to follow me. We stopped outside Buddy Richardson's room. I listened a moment, then pushed the door slightly. I couldn't see Buddy through the crack in the door because a wall blocked me. I pushed it further open and stuck my head in. Buddy spotted me.

"Well, come right in, Willie Mitchell. I'd welcome the company."

I walked inside with Jimmy trailing me.

"And your banker friend is welcome, too."

I felt awkward because I knew I had no business being in Buddy's room.

"How are you feeling?" I asked.

"Strange," he said. "They say I might have had a stroke, a little one. All I know is my mind's not feeling right. I kind of come and go, all kind of unusual thoughts in my brain. Sometimes it's like I'm not me but someone else lying in this hospital bed. I think my memory's been affected, too. Maybe it'll come back after a while."

"Here we go," I thought.

Buddy was setting up a new defense—the inability to understand the nature of the proceedings against him, one of the two basic inquiries in an insanity defense. The second is the inability to know the difference between right and wrong at the time of the commission of the offense. If the defense can establish through medical testimony, usually psychiatric, that the defendant lacks the capacity to understand the proceedings being conducted against him, he cannot be tried for the offense. I was certain Buddy's claim that his brain wasn't working had been thought out in advance. But I wasn't sure that Helmet Head was complicit. He might have explained the two prongs of the insanity defense to Buddy, but Buddy was shrewd enough to come up with this ploy on his own. Based on what I knew about Buddy's past, I was convinced he would do anything he thought he could get away with.

"I feel like that sometimes," Jimmy Gray said with a big grin, "but it's usually related to being overserved with alcohol."

"You young folks can still party," Buddy said, "but I'm too old for that now. Just biding my time until the Lord calls me home. Lying here almost helpless, sometimes my mind goes blank, just like I guess yours does when you have one of your seizures, Willie Mitchell."

Buddy was smug, almost cocky in letting me know he knew all about me. I wanted to throttle the old murderer, but the door behind us flew open.

"What are you doing in here?" the young physician demanded. "Get out right now."

Jimmy and I skulked out past the sign on Buddy's door that said NO VISITORS. We stopped at the nurses' station, which was still unattended.

"That old bastard's faking," Jimmy said. "No doubt in my mind. He hasn't had any stroke."

"I wasn't sure when I saw him on the floor in the courtroom, but I am now. He's playing possum."

"And he's good at it. We leaving?"

"I want to wait until the doctor comes out."

Ten minutes later, Dr. Grillette walked out of Buddy's room.

"You're not allowed in there," he said.

"We spoke to Mr. Silver earlier," I said after I introduced myself and Jimmy. "He said he had no problem with my talking to you about Mr. Richardson's situation."

"Mr. Silver doesn't have that authority," he said.

"Do you understand the situation we're in?" I said. "The jury had been sworn and seated and the trial begun when he..., was brought here."

"Mr. Silver explained it. Wish I could help you but I cannot discuss my patient's medical situation with you."

"I understand that, and I know you're awfully busy, Dr. Grillette, but take a moment to consider that your patient is accused of the very cold-blooded killing of his grandson-in-law. The man he hired to do it was about to testify against him as early as tomorrow, if it hadn't been for this delay."

He looked down a moment. He finally seemed more sympathetic.

"I'm not going to share any details about this particular patient unless a judge somewhere makes me. What I'm about to say holds true in a lot of cases where a stroke or TIA is suspected. Sometimes the CT scan or MRI is definitive and clearly shows the site of the damage, bleeding, or other evidence that is quantifiable. But not always. Sometimes there are cerebral events that actually occur but cannot be verified by scans or any tests. Those are generally diagnosed based on observation of the patient or what he reports he felt at the time of the incident or continues to feel. You understand what I'm saying?"

The gestures he used to punctuate his explanation was clear. Buddy's "cerebral event" fell in the latter category. Dr. Grillette was treating him based on what occurred in the courtroom and how Buddy said he was feeling lying in the hospital bed. Left unsaid was Dr. Grillette had the professional obligation to take at face value what Buddy was relating to him. He had no other choice.

"When I am presented with a patient who may have had a stroke, but there are no test findings to corroborate, the standard of care is to assume an ischemic event and immediately introduce tPA intravenously. Again, I am only saying what the standard of care is in these *types* of events. I will share with you that I've asked for a neurological consult," he said. "The physician I've talked to is the best neurologist in Oxford, in my opinion. But I have to warn you, his opinion is probably going to be the same as mine."

"But it's possible he didn't have a stroke," I said.

Dr. Grillette shrugged.

"Don't go back in there," he said and walked off down the hall.

His message was clear. Absent a court order, he had said all he was going to say about the medical condition of the murderer Buddy Richardson.

CHAPTER THIRTY-SEVEN

I walked my usual route Tuesday morning beginning at eight. I had a lot on my mind, which resulted in a quick pace and the rapid passage of time. I planned on calling Patrick Dunwoody IV at Justice after I showered to see if he had learned anything else about Leopold Whitman's vendetta. Sunday morning's phone conference with Senator Skeeter Sumrall describing the meeting of Leopold Whitman and Senator Chad Breedlove irritated me each time I pictured the two of them in the Senator's office, talking about *me*. The last thing I needed was the grand jury witch hunt exploding into a full-blown criminal civil rights indictment. As absurd as the claim of discrimination was, I had seen many federal prosecutions where the truth mattered little.

The image of the exit wound on the left side of James Butler's forehead was indelibly imprinted in my mental hard drive, filed alongside other murder victims I had seen *in situ*. I had gotten enough of a look at the .38 revolver on the floor mat at Butler's feet to know it was an old gun. Chief's Specials had been around a long time, introduced in the early fifties and still being produced. Many times I carried my own .38 caliber Chief's Special in a leather holster in the small of my back as a primary or a backup to my Springfield 1911 .45 caliber I wore in a shoulder holster under my arm. In my twenty-four years as District Attorney, I felt the need to be armed many times. I did not want to be outgunned.

I felt sorry for Walton. I knew how it felt to get all geared up for trial, coordinating the evidence and witnesses, then at the last minute having the case continued. It was such a waste of time to have to start the process all over again a few months down the road. And after talking to Dr. Grillette, it was clear that Buddy Richardson was in control of the timing of his trial. As long as he stayed in the hospital in the care of the physicians, he was calling the shots. When I passed through the Square on the final leg of my walk, I looked in on Walton. I had called him the night before when I left the hospital with Jimmy, and described the room visit with Buddy and the unofficial, hypothetical comments of Dr. Grillette.

"How'd we sleep?" I asked when Deputy Gresham unlocked the door to the apartment. "Pleasant dreams?"

"Not hardly," Walton said, sitting at the dining room table in jeans and a tee shirt and pushing aside the two empty boxes from Square Pizza on the table.

Walton and Deputy Sammy Roberts held mugs of coffee. Will Gresham took a sip of Mountain Dew.

"We're not going to be trying this case," Walton said.

"Have you talked to Zelda?"

"Spoke to her a few minutes ago. She had already talked to Dr. Grillette. He told her about the same thing he told you. She said if Buddy is not released from the hospital today, she's going to consider Helmet Head's request for a mistrial based on medical necessity. We'll have to do this all over again."

"Has she set a hearing?"

"If there's no change by noon today, she's asking the local Circuit Clerk to put a message on the machine instructing the jurors and alternates to be in the courtroom at ten o'clock Wednesday morning. She scheduled a hearing an hour earlier to take medical testimony and had the clerk issue a subpoena today for Dr. Grillette to appear."

"He's not going to like that."

"Yeah, well, too bad for the busy doctor. They think they're above all the crap we deal with."

"I can't blame him," I said. "Is Zelda going to re-set the trial for Oxford?"

"She didn't know. She's going to talk to the Clerk about their summer trial schedule."

"Sorry about this, partner," I said. "I'm going to the condo to clean up. I'll be around all day if you need me. Otherwise I'll see you at nine in the morning."

"Before you go, are the OPD crime scene guys positive it wasn't a suicide? I mean, those guys aren't trained like State Crime Lab techs."

"I watched them work. They seemed to know what they were doing. And I could see what he called 'the void' of back spatter on the passenger seat when he pointed it out to me. And what little I knew of James Butler, he sure didn't seem depressed. He seemed upbeat, in fact."

"Lee's got a couple of his detectives coming up here today to go over everything with the OPD techs. We'll probably have to tow the Buick back to Yaloquena if OPD won't keep it stored for us."

"Talk to Chief Columbus. He'll probably accommodate you. They don't have many murders up here, and he knew Butler."

I walked down the wooden steps and got back on my route, which took me down South Lamar then right on Buchanan, and left on South 11th to Hayes. As I neared Hayes, I noticed a man carrying newspapers out of Boyland Burr's house and dumping them in the back of a pickup truck parked in his driveway. I waved at the man, who appeared to be Mexican or Central American, and looked in the truck bed as I passed. It was full of yellowed newspapers. I glanced at the house and saw Boyland Burr on the porch. He waved and I veered off the sidewalk and met him on his porch.

"Looks like a serious housecleaning, Boyland," I said.

"Better late than never, don't you think? I been putting this off for years."

I glanced in the door. The Valley of the Shadow of Newspapers had disappeared, revealing a well-protected hardwood floor in the front room. A Hispanic woman was cleaning the next room, probably having to chisel the hardened SpaghettiOs off the dinette table. The man passed us on the porch headed for the truck, his arms stacked high with newspapers.

"Hey," I said to Boyland, "I thought you might want to know. Mr. Buddy Richardson fell out in court yesterday. Might have had a stroke."

He looked at me as if I were talking about a stranger.

"You know," I said, "Buddy Richardson from Dundee County."

"Don't know him," he said.

"Hmm," I said and almost scratched my chin, but decided it would be overacting. "I could have sworn I saw him on this very porch talking and laughing with you almost a couple of weeks ago. It was a Wednesday."

For a moment I saw the real Boyland Burr. It wasn't the jovial, slovenly ex-U.S. Marshall who looked and talked like Andy Devine. This Boyland Burr was a big, sinister man with a threatening demeanor, not a person you'd want to cross. His dark visage dissolved as quickly as it appeared, and Andy Devine was back.

"The fellow on the porch you saw, my brother sold some cattle to him maybe ten years ago. We delivered them to this big plantation over in Dundee County. My brother called him 'Mr. Buddy.' I didn't know the man's last name and, tell you the truth, that day he came up on my porch I didn't know who he was at first. But he said he remembered me and my brother and was riding by and just stopped to speak a minute. Nice old fellow, seemed to me. Must be pretty well off."

"I think he is. Well, let me get on with my walk. Good seeing you again."

I walked down the steps and back into the street. Half a block from the house, I turned and saw his eyes still on me. I waved and grinned. He raised his hand half-heartedly. Even from a hundred feet, I could tell Andy Devine had disappeared again, leaving the real Boyland Burr staring at me.

Chapter Thirty-Eight

Patrick Dunwoody IV had no update for me on the Justice Department investigation. I told him what Skeeter Sumrall had shared with me Sunday morning. Patrick promised to dig a little deeper, lean on his sources harder. There was little I could do in Oxford to fight the Justice Department.

I called François but couldn't get him. I hadn't talked to him since the previous Friday, when I called to tell him about Russell being killed with a bullet from a TT-30 manufactured in Asia. He asked me the significance, and I told him the only thing it proved was that Russell was killed with a different weapon than the reporter for the French paper and the young man from Abbeville, who were both killed by .38 caliber bullets.

I spent Tuesday afternoon re-reading parts of the Doyle and Eagle books, focusing on the chapters dealing with the riot. I thought there might have been helpful information in there that I had skipped over. Susan and I had an early dinner. I had asked her to make one of my summer favorites, the vermicelli salad that I loved. She did, and I ate too much. I went to bed with Cormac McCarthy's *Blood Meridian,* though I had read it twice before. Now that I had slogged through Faulkner again, I thought I might have a better appreciation of McCarthy's stream of consciousness descriptions. *Blood Meridian* was the most violent narrative I'd ever read. The story followed bloody encounters in the mid-nineteenth century on the border and inside Mexico, by the scalp-taking gang led by The Judge, a balding giant of a man, an enigmatic warrior genius.

The next morning I woke at five-thirty and hit the pavement an hour later after two cups of Caffé Verona. The morning paper said the service for James Butler would be on Wednesday morning at eleven at the Methodist Church downtown. I planned on attending.

Walton had called me at five o'clock the previous afternoon. He said Dr. Nathan Clement of Sunshine had associated a forensic pathologist from Jackson to conduct the autopsy with him at noon Tuesday, all under the watchful eye of ace Coroner Al Revels. Nathan had not produced a written report, but he told Walton that the pattern of gunpowder residue and back spatter on Butler's wrist was consistent with someone else holding the gun in Butler's hand and pulling the trigger to make it look like a suicide.

I commented to Walton that Butler must have been unconscious at the time he was shot. Walton said he asked Dr. Clement if Mr. Butler suffered head injuries that might have caused him to be knocked out at the time of his death. Dr. Clement said the victim might have been, but he didn't find any evidence of a serious head injury. He added that he had sent off blood, vitreous, and urine to the State Crime Lab for a series of tests and would include all those results in the written report. Nathan Clement was one of my best friends in Sunshine, a brilliant physician the town was fortunate to have. Coroner Al always associated Nathan to autopsy routine gunshot or stabbing deaths. In a complex case where Nathan knew there would be significant public interest, he insisted on associating a board certified forensic pathologist, and Al had the good sense to go along with Nathan's request.

I walked into the courtroom at eight-forty-five Wednesday morning and took my seat in the front row next to the side aisle. Walton was working at the prosecution table and I didn't want to interrupt him. Helmet Head sat by himself at the defense table, texting or e-mailing. Knowing him as I did, I figured he was already working on his next case.

Judge Williams entered the courtroom behind the local bailiff and Eddie Bordelon right at nine o'clock. She said for the record she had convened the hearing on her own motion to determine the medical status of the defendant to decide if the trial could go forward with the jury that had already been selected and sworn. I heard the back door open and watched Dr. Grillette walk impatiently down the center aisle. Judge Williams gestured for him to take the witness stand.

"Gentlemen," she said, "I assured Dr. Grillette that we would take his testimony immediately if he were here promptly at nine a.m., and I intend to keep that promise. Since the Court issued the subpoena to the doctor, I will question him first, then each of you may ask additional questions as you deem necessary, but this Court will not permit undue repetition."

Helmet Head and Walton nodded, and Zelda had Eddie swear in Dr. Grillette. She asked him how he came to treat the defendant Buddy Richardson. Grillette didn't need questions. He glanced at his copy of the hospital records on occasion, but testified primarily from memory about seeing Buddy in the emergency room and admitting him to ICU immediately. He gave a concise description of the examination he conducted, the patient's condition, and the diagnostic tests he ordered or administered.

"Is it your medical opinion, Dr. Grillette, that the defendant suffered a stroke?" she asked him.

"The CT scan, MRI, and other tests I conducted revealed no bleeding or damage in the brain, but that is not unusual in ischemic strokes or TIAs. Based on the description of what occurred in the courtroom, the comments of the EMTs, particularly with respect to the patient's blood pressure, and my physical examination on admission, I treated Mr. Richardson immediately with tPA intravenously, the standard of care for stroke patients."

"Is the defendant able to talk to you?" she asked.

"Yes, Your Honor. He regained consciousness in ICU approximately an hour after his admission. I asked him what he remembered had occurred in the courtroom. He said he had no recollection. I then asked him questions about his physical condition."

"Again, Dr. Grillette, is it your opinion that he had a stroke or TIA?"

He paused and looked at his notes in the medical record.

"Although there is no objective evidence resulting from the scans and tests, the patient presented as a patient who had suffered a mild stroke or TIA, and his responses to my questions were consistent with that, so I would say in my professional opinion, yes, Mr. Richardson probably suffered a small stroke."

"Does his medical condition affect his memory?"

"He says he has no memory of falling in court, and has had periods in the hospital in the last day and a half where he cannot remember what just occurred. For example, he said he could not follow the plot of a television show he watched yesterday morning, a re-run of *Criminal Minds*, I believe he said. You must understand, Your Honor, that the effect on his memory of which he complains is entirely subjective. There's no test I can administer to verify that."

"I understand, Dr. Grillette," she said. "One final question. As his treating physician for this event, do you have an opinion about whether it would be harmful to the defendant's current medical condition to return to the courtroom and sit through his trial at this time?"

"Out of an abundance of caution, I feel the defendant's returning to the trial at this time would place him in jeopardy medically and perhaps induce another cerebral event of some kind."

Zelda looked at Walton.

"Any questions for Dr. Grillette, Mr. Donaldson?"

"Just one, Your Honor. Dr. Grillette, do you have any idea how long it will be before Mr. Richardson will be able to return to stand trial without it being a threat to his health?"

I could tell in Walton's voice he had thrown in the towel. I didn't blame him. He and I tried so many cases in front of Zelda, we both recognized when she had her mind already made up about something.

"It's impossible to tell. Assuming good aftercare, I would guess a few months perhaps."

Walton thanked him.

"Mr. Silver?" she said.

"Nothing, Your Honor."

"How much longer will he be in the hospital?" she asked the doctor.

"If he continues to progress, I expect to move him from ICU to a regular room no later than Friday. The length of his stay there will depend on his progress."

I heard the back door close and watched old Doc Finstermayer walk slowly down the center aisle and sit on the front row behind Helmet Head.

"Is there anything you'd like to add, Dr. Grillette?"

"No, Your Honor, except that Dr. Finstermayer, who just entered the courtroom, has assisted in the care of the patient in the hospital, and I would hope after Mr. Richardson leaves the hospital that he will remain under close supervision by his long-time physician."

Judge Williams acknowledged Doc Finstermayer, who nodded agreement.

"Considering this testimony, the Court will entertain a motion."

"Move for mistrial," Helmet Head said without looking up.

"Granted," Zelda said and turned to the doctor. "You may go, Dr. Grillette. Thank you for your testimony."

As he walked out, Judge Williams turned to Eddie Bordelon.

"Direct the bailiff to notify the Court as soon as all twelve jurors and the two alternates have arrived in the jury room. The Court will convene, advise them of these proceedings, and dismiss them from further duty."

CHAPTER THIRTY-NINE

James Butler's funeral began at eleven at the United Methodist Church on University Avenue a block from our condo. Judge Williams had dismissed the jury an hour earlier. Before I left the courtroom, I spoke to Walton briefly. He planned on leaving for Sunshine within the hour to meet his wife and children at home. I felt for him. An unwanted continuance in a major case was always a disappointment. Once I had prepared, I was ready for battle.

Sheriff Lee Jones dropped me off at the condo. He was irritated at a system that allowed a defendant like Buddy Richardson to call the shots.

"The old s.o.b. is faking it," Lee said. "Zelda probably knows it, too."

"She has to play the hand she's dealt," I said. "The law says she has to decide based on the testimony and evidence before her, not her feelings."

"I know," he said. "It's just a damned shame."

"What are you going to do with Lynn Metzger?"

"Good question. I can't tie up two men or more on his security detail for an indefinite time. Don't have the manpower or money in the budget for that. He's going back upstairs in the jail as soon as I have a one-man cell available, which the jailer tells me should be the end of this week."

"May not be pleasant for Metzger, but it'll keep him alive."

"I've been thinking. If the old man had actually died from a stroke, would Walton have to stand by the deal he made with Metzger for his testimony?"

"Since Metzger's already pleaded guilty and his lawyer and Walton entered the terms of the plea agreement into the record in Zelda's court in Sunshine, I'd say yes. As insurance Walton required that sentencing be delayed until after Buddy's trial so everything would be negated if Metzger didn't testify truthfully against Richardson. But if Richardson had died, Metzger's deal would remain intact, in my opinion."

"Stay in touch," I said to Lee as he pulled away from the condo.

Susan was dressed and ready for the funeral. I took a moment to change into a dark suit and muted tie. We walked the block to the church, which was packed. The usher led us to seats in front, right behind the pallbearers' pew.

The service was mercifully brief and the eulogy general, apparently in light of the perception that James Butler took his own life. The preacher praised the good works the journalist did in his career, and mentioned the joy James took in his painting. He said we would never know what was going through James's mind in his final days, and we should remember James as we knew him in life, vibrant and enthusiastic.

The silence after the preacher said "Amen" was broken by the sounds of throat-clearing and barely discernible sniffles and whimpers. As the pallbearers led the way out of the church with the casket, I turned to see Naomi Butler leaving her pew with the help of a man who resembled a younger version of her dead husband. She was crying, dabbing her eyes with a crumpled Kleenex, and leaning hard against her son for support.

Three rows behind the family section, I saw Cissy Breedlove stand to leave, her hook-nosed husband Gavin by her side. She was well-turned out and pretty. Gavin's hair needed combing and his slight stoop made his suit appear too big for his wiry frame. Though he was fifty feet away, seeing him again made me certain he was the driver of the white Lexus who motored through the circular drive at the hospital Monday night without dropping off his passenger, old Doc Finstermayer.

We shuffled slowly out of church. I whispered to Susan that I wanted to hang back from the departing crowd to watch the Breedloves. We lingered in front and spoke to a few people we knew, then walked casually toward the parking lot. In the line of cars waiting to pull out onto

South 9th Street, I spied a white Lexus crossover driven by Gavin, Cissy in the passenger seat. When the Lexus pulled into the street, I recognized the partially torn Ole Miss bumper sticker on the back, the same one I saw under the hospital *porte-cochere* two days earlier.

We walked to the condo. I changed into jeans and a knit shirt and called Francis Fratelli. He answered in a weak voice on the fourth ring. I told him I had called the other day but couldn't get him.

"I've been feeling pretty low," he said. "Didn't feel like getting out of bed to answer it. Did you need something?"

"I've been thinking about the Xerox of the photograph I showed you of the young couple in the Grove, how grainy it was. You feel well enough to go with me to the college newspaper office and look at the actual photo?"

"When?"

"Today," I said and waited for his response, which took a moment.

"Maybe after lunch," he said.

"Can you meet me there at one o'clock? You know where it is?"

"I do. I'll see you there."

I arrived at *The Daily Mississippian* fifteen minutes before one to introduce myself to the editor who had loaned the office key to James Butler. She was all business, hustling to make a deadline. She wore jeans and an overlarge tee shirt, short, spiky hair and no makeup.

"I was wondering if I could access the archives again?" I asked.

"Sure," she said as she handed a sheet of paper to a staffer walking by. "Help yourself."

"I just came from James Butler's funeral."

"Oh," she said. "That's so sad. He was just in here last Friday."

"Was he returning the key he used to let me in the Sunday before?"

"That's right. And he spent a couple of hours in the archive room, too. He seemed in a good mood, like always. He was a wonderful man. Whenever I needed to know something that happened around here years ago, I called him."

"You sure that was last Friday?"

"Positive," she said. "He was in there at least two hours."

"I'm meeting a friend here, an older fellow. I'm going to show him something in the archives. Would you send him back?"

She said she would. I walked to the records room and removed the three boxes of photographs from the shelf and placed them on the table in chronological order. I opened the second box and removed a stack of photos to get to the one on the bottom I was looking for, Russell and the brunette against the tree with love in their eyes.

I rifled through the photos at the bottom and didn't see it. Assuming I just overlooked it, I went through them again, this time more slowly. It wasn't there. I removed all the photographs from the box and placed them on the table in front of me. One by one, I looked at each photograph then turned it face down on the table. I made sure none of the pictures were stuck together.

The photograph of Russell Fratelli and the brunette was gone.

Chapter Forty

It was a little after three o'clock when I finished going through the three boxes of photographs. I had called François when I discovered that the picture of his brother was gone. He was still at home, and thanked me for calling to cancel. He said he was feeling so badly he had fallen back into bed after my earlier call and didn't think he had the strength to keep our appointment.

I asked the editor if anyone had spent time in the archives recently besides James Butler and me. She thought a minute and said not while she had been there, and she had been in the office every weekday in the past two weeks. I thanked her and left.

I concluded that James Butler removed the photograph the previous Friday afternoon. He was murdered the following Monday.

I knew what I needed to do next, but wondered if I had the *chutzpah* to do it. No doubt James Butler's house was full of friends and relatives consoling Naomi and eating the food delivered there in the last two days. I decided to conduct a reconnaissance visit to pay my respects to the widow, and determine whether I could find out what I needed without seeming like a totally insensitive jerk.

I parked at the Butler's home at about three-thirty. A dozen cars lined the driveway and the street in front of the house. I walked inside through the carport and introduced myself to the woman who appeared to be the gatekeeper in the kitchen. She told me it was nice of me to drop by, and said Naomi was holding up as well as could be expected, that I would find her in the dining room. I entered the room and swiped a Frito through what was left of the seven-layer dip on the table, biding my time while Naomi spoke to an older couple.

"I'm very sorry for your loss," I said to Naomi when the coupled drifted away. "I only knew James a short time but he was a fine man."

"Thank you for stopping in," she said in a shaky voice, her eyes and nose red from crying and sniffling.

"I enjoyed going through the old *Mississippian* photographs with James last week," I said, throwing propriety to the wind. "Did y'all ever look at old newspaper photos here in the house to reminisce about old times?"

"Oh, no," she said. "He never brought his work home."

A woman stopped and hugged Naomi, who smiled at her friend. I patted Naomi on the shoulder and excused myself, easing out of the carport door. I drove slowly away in my truck, trying to figure out why Butler would have removed the photograph from the archives. I called François and asked him if I could drop by. Ten minutes later I was seated in his den, asking him whether Russell had any connection with James Butler.

"They were in school about the same time," he said, "but they weren't friends as far as I know. Probably were acquainted with each other. It was a small university back then."

"What about Cissy? Butler told me he knew Cissy went out a few times with Russell that summer."

"You showed him the copy of the picture, didn't you? The same Xerox you showed me. You told me Butler said it wasn't Cissy."

"That's what he said. I remember his saying he was 'fairly certain,' in fact. Went on about the girl in the photo not being as tall as Cissy."

"I wonder who she was," François said. "Russell must have really liked her, the way he was looking at her."

"You playing tomorrow?" I asked.

"Not unless I'm feeling better. Maybe Saturday."

"See you then," I said and left.

I phoned Jimmy Gray and asked him if he could get his loan officer with the sister working at Baptist Hospital to find out what was going on with Buddy. I drove home and spent time in my office catching up on e-mails and returning phone calls to the few people who called me on our land line. A little before six, I heard a knock on the back door. Susan let Jimmy inside.

"Delbert talked to his sister," he said, sitting in my office. "She said nothing's changed. Same orders in place since Tuesday. She said Dr. Grillette only looked in on him once today, in the afternoon."

"How'd she know that?"

"She looked at his chart."

"So much for HIPPA," I said. "Grillette said he'd probably move Buddy from ICU to a regular room on Friday."

"I never realized what poor manners you have."

"What are you talking about?"

"I've been here all of five minutes and you ain't had the common damn courtesy to offer me a cocktail."

"My apologies, Thibodaux. I can fix that."

I fixed Jimmy a Maker's Mark over ice with a small splash of water and made Susan and me a VT. I invited Susan to join us on the front porch to watch the students drive by in their Beemers and Mercedes, but she declined. It was a wonderful late April afternoon. Light green leaves on crepe myrtles and water oaks shimmied in the breeze, a welcome sight after Oxford's winter.

"Our business sure is good," Jimmy said. "This town is growing fast."

"I see construction everywhere. It's outpacing the infrastructure."

"It's a good problem to have. We've been making some good commercial loans. You heard any more on Leopold Whitman's bullshit?"

"Nothing new since I talked to Skeeter Sunday morning."

"I just refuse to believe Skeeter can't get it shut down."

"He said he's doing all he can."

"You ought to see if Eleanor Bernstein knows anything else."

"I will."

"I'll come see you in the joint," Jimmy said after a moment, "if they don't send you too far. Martha don't like me staying away from her very long."

"I can certainly understand why."

"Yep." He scratched his big stomach. "The woman is wild about me."

CHAPTER FORTY-ONE

I don't know why I hadn't followed up on it before. I guess it was because I had been busy, and perhaps because Cissy was an ex-state senator, possible candidate for governor, and Miss America third runner-up. She said she had not gone to Russell's funeral in Clarksdale fifty-three years ago. François said she had. Maybe it was an innocent discrepancy. The passage of time has a way of molding memories to suit our own perception—we remember things not as they happened, but as they should have happened. I'm not talking about the big hands that life deals us, but the little details insignificant to everyone else.

I considered her personality. She was very proper and lady-like, but a real Steel Magnolia, having prospered in the legislature in Jackson, which I considered a Keystone Kops environment where fools are not only suffered gladly, they're exalted. So are liars. I wanted to ask Cissy about the funeral in Clarksdale, and one other thing François mentioned.

I decided to cold call Cissy.

That Thursday morning at eleven I knocked on her townhouse door, surprising her. I stood on her small porch, Cissy in the open door. Standing there in a short, form-fitting navy blue skirt and a diaphanous silk blouse, I was once again taken aback. She looked much younger than her age.

"Good morning, Mr. Banks," she said. "This is a surprise."

"I apologize for just showing up without calling, but I was at the Square and you were only a couple of blocks away."

"Well, come in please. I just washed out the coffee carafe but I can certainly put on a fresh pot."

"No, thank you. I've had enough coffee, Mrs. Breedlove."

"Please call me Cissy," she said, leading me to the back room in the town house, the combination office and den where we sat for the last visit.

"If you'll call me Willie Mitchell."

"All right, Willie Mitchell. Have a seat."

She sat and crossed her shapely legs. I could not help admiring the well-toned flesh at the bottom of her thigh. Cissy smiled and leaned forward.

"What can I do for you this morning, Willie Mitchell?"

"I saw you and your husband at Mr. Butler's funeral yesterday."

"What a tragedy," she said. "I would have never expected him to take his own life. He seemed so happy in his retirement, especially with his painting."

"One thing I wanted to see you about was to say thanks for your suggesting I contact him. He was a wealth of information on the riot, and he helped me access the old articles and photographs at *The Oxford Eagle* and *The Daily Mississippian*."

"I hope you've been able to learn something."

"Not much," I said. "I don't know how much further I can look into this. There just doesn't seem to be anything to help me clear up what happened to Russell Fratelli."

"Another tragedy. How is Francis doing?"

"I saw him yesterday. He's not doing well."

"I'm sorry to hear that."

"And that's another reason I'm here. Francis told me you were at the funeral in Clarksdale, Russell's funeral."

"Did he? When you asked me I felt sure I wasn't. I had never met his parents and can't imagine why I would have gone. But it's been a long time ago, and I find my memory's not what it used to be. If Francis says I was there, perhaps I was. It was such a loss to the University family, maybe I went with some friends. I'm sorry to be so vague. I just don't recall."

It was the perfect answer to keep a trial witness out of trouble. Preparing witnesses for trial, I always emphasized that if the other attorney asked a question he or she could not answer, I said: "DO NOT SPECULATE. If you don't know the answer, just say I DON'T KNOW or I DON'T RECALL." I had suffered through many damaging lines of questions kick-started by my witnesses speculating, opening areas that I had hoped would remain off-limits.

"I'd like to show you something," I said.

I stood up and removed from the inside pocket of my sport coat the Xerox copy of the photograph of Russell and the brunette against the tree in The Grove. I unfolded it as I walked the few steps to her chair. She remained in her seat and studied the copy. Looking down, I noticed for the first time the top two buttons of her blouse were not fastened, and much of her youthful-looking breasts were fully exposed to me. I could not help staring while she examined the picture.

I don't know how it happened, but the next thing I knew, she was looking up at me staring at her breasts. She was not disapproving. She smiled and looked into my eyes, not adjusting her blouse. In fact, I'm pretty sure she moved slightly and exposed even more of her lovely chest for me to admire.

I don't mind telling you I was rattled. I didn't intend to stare, but I couldn't help it. I cleared my throat and sat down. With the Xerox in her hand, she uncrossed her legs and left them slightly open, wide enough for me to admire more of her upper thighs if I chose to. I fought off the animal instincts passed down to me from thousands of previous generations of male *Homo sapiens*.

This was serious business I was about, the unsolved murder of Russell Fratelli, and here I was, checking Cissy out. I was upset with myself at the ease with which she disarmed me, using her very attractive breasts to put me on the defensive. Sitting there, I had a new appreciation of this woman. Cissy Summers Breedlove was still a formidable player when she wanted to be.

"Where on earth did you get this?" she asked.

The change back to her proper, lady-like mode was remarkable. She was no longer sending the "come hither" vibe. If pressed, it would be difficult for me to explain to someone else exactly what just happened. Moreover, the pheremonal exchange between us was so subtle, occurring at the subliminal level, that even a videotape of the entire event would not be conclusive.

"It's a copy of a photograph in *The Mississippian* archives. It was taken in the summer session before the riot in 1962. The paper has its editions and the photographs taken in any particular year organized chronologically. James Butler took me in there Sunday before last."

"This wasn't in the newspaper. I'm sure of that."

"No, it wasn't. I looked through all the 1962 editions. Many of the photographs I saw in the archives never made the paper—just like you would expect. But apparently they kept the pictures anyway."

She gave the Xerox copy back to me.

"Are you the girl in the photo?"

"Yes," she said wistfully. "*The Mississippian* photographer saw Russell and me walking through the Grove one afternoon that summer and asked us to pose as if we were young lovers, hopelessly enthralled with each other."

"You two were awfully good actors."

"If you're not a good actor, you'll never be successful in a beauty contest. Believe me, Willie Mitchell, it takes a supreme effort to be gracious during some of the paces they put you through."

"I don't think Russell was acting."

"Russell liked me very much. I liked him, but more as a friend."

"Did James Butler take the picture?"

"No. But he told me he was involved in making the decision to keep it out of the paper. He thought it was too risqué. James was like that. Almost prudish I would say."

"You know," I said, "the funny thing is, I went back to the newspaper office on campus yesterday and the original photo is gone. This copy is all I have now."

"Maybe it's just misplaced."

"No. The editor told me James and I were the only two people in the archives in the last ten days. I know I didn't remove the photo. I should have, but I didn't think I had the authority to take the paper's property."

"I'm sorry. Well, at least now you know who is in the photo. I shouldn't think the original is important to anyone else. James, rest his soul, is deceased. And I haven't given this a thought in many years. A lifetime, really."

She glanced at the slender gold watch on her wrist.

"I am afraid I have to start my husband's lunch," she said. "You're welcome to join us."

"No, thank you. I've got to be going."

Cissy walked me to the door and opened it. She took my hand in both of hers, rubbing the back of mine. The gentle aroma of the light cologne she was wearing drifted to me, along with the pheromones she exuded. She held my eyes for the longest time, then kissed me lightly on the cheek.

"I am glad you've moved to Oxford," she said. "I enjoy our visits. Gavin is gone a good bit, busy with his projects. Please stop by anytime."

CHAPTER FORTY-TWO

I drove home and had a light lunch with Susan, then led her into the bedroom for a little afternoon delight. Don't wag your finger at me. I couldn't help myself. She didn't need to know right then that an older ex-beauty queen had revved me up. Susan would not have appreciated learning that she was the beneficiary, or victim, of Cissy's antics. I'm not proud of myself, but there it is. I'm reporting it just the way it happened. And if you don't mind, I would prefer that Susan do any finger-wagging I deserve. For the record, I did eventually get around to telling her about Cissy's behavior.

At around three that afternoon I phoned Jimmy Gray to get his loan officer Delbert to call his sister again. Jimmy called me back in twenty minutes. The nurse told her brother nothing had changed, except that Dr. Grillette had entered an order in the chart that Buddy was to be moved out of ICU and onto a regular ward Friday, the following day.

I went online and did a search for "Buddy Richardson." I was surprised at how little I found. I did learn that there are a lot of "Buddy Richardsons" in the world. Mississippi Farm Bureau ran an article in its magazine mentioning Buddy and High Hope Plantation in connection with a mind-numbing story about the jurisdictional problems of managing farms or ranches spread across two or more counties. I did a search for Citizens' Councils in Mississippi and found Buddy's name mentioned several times in scholarly works about the origin of the Citizens' Councils, but Buddy was named only in connection with other members. He did not figure prominently in any of the articles and books. My online search did reveal a reference to a brochure put out by the Citizens' Councils with the title *Operation Ole Miss,* which reported the riot in a light most favorable to Governor Barnett and the Mississippi

Legislature. By any editorial measure, the brochure was a stretch.

Dundee County had no local paper, so I called Jack Ray Weldon, the longtime owner, publisher, and editor of the *Sunshine Courier*. Jack Ray was irascible; we did not always see eye to eye. It was natural that conflicts arose in his coverage of my trials in Yaloquena County and in his accurate, but vicious coverage of our hapless Board of Supervisors. The Yaloquena County Attorney was the Board's statutory counsel of record, but the supervisors had little confidence in his legal ability or intellect. I shared their lack of enthusiasm for his opinion, so when any supervisor met with me privately for unofficial, off-the-record legal advice, I offered it. Their chronic lack of funding and intelligence invariably led them to ignore my unofficial advice from time to time, getting them into hot water with the Mississippi Legislative Auditor and various federal agencies over the use of grants.

"Don't you talk to Walton anymore?" he asked, chuckling. "He imposed on me to do this a month ago. By the way, I spoke to him yesterday morning when he got back here from Oxford. He sure was disappointed the trial was short-circuited, but it made a good story for *The Courier*. I wish old man Richardson lived in Yaloquena County so I could do a better job covering his shenanigans."

"I still get *The Courier* here but it's a day late, sometimes two."

"That's the post office for you."

"So what does your clippings file on Buddy Richardson look like?"

"That's just it," Jack Ray said. "Not much. There are a few articles from the sixties about Citizens' Councils meetings he attended, but there ain't much to them. And get this. There's only one picture of Buddy Richardson in the *Sunshine Courier* going back over fifty years. You remember the man I bought the paper from, Mr. Bill Malone? Before he died I talked to him about it, and he said Buddy Richardson had a thing about getting his picture taken. Almost a phobia. I'm not saying he merely didn't like his picture in the newspaper. I'm talking about anyone taking his photograph for any reason. He would not permit it. Period."

"The one picture you have, is it in an article?"

"Yeah. 1960. Something about a Citizens' Council meeting. You know the paper back then covered them like the Board of Supervisors or School Board. It was just another local meeting, routinely reported as a matter of course. Buddy was pictured speaking to the group. I don't have the original photograph or negative, just the edition of the paper that has his picture."

"Could you scan that and e-mail it to me?"

"No," Jack Ray said and paused. "But Mary could. You still have the same e-mail address?"

"Right," I said and thanked him. "By the way," I said, "do you know anyone at the *Clarion Ledger* I could talk to about their files on Buddy?"

"I do," he said, "but it won't do you any good. I made a call down there for Walton last month. Their clippings file on Buddy is about like ours. The man has stayed under the radar."

"Okay. Thanks, Jack Ray. Ask Mary if she can e-mail it today."

I picked up a Cobb salad and a grilled chicken sandwich from Newk's for Susan and me to split for supper. And when I say "split," I mean she ate a third of the salad and a third of the sandwich; I ate the rest. I put the Netflix disk of *L.A. Confidential* in the Blu-Ray. Susan read a book on the couch while I watched Russell Crowe as Bud White intimidate every other character in the movie and make love to Kim Basinger. It's on my top ten favorite movies of all time.

We went to bed early. I fell asleep reading *Blood Meridian*, unaware that I would be visiting a crime scene the next morning every bit as savage and bloody as anything Cormac McCarthy ever wrote, or Bud White ever wrought.

CHAPTER FORTY-THREE

I ran Friday morning. It was warm for the first day of May, so I worked up a good sweat, eliminating some poisons from my systems. I cooled down on the front porch before I went inside. Susan had recently replaced the wrought iron furniture. She bought a round table and the bouncy kind of chairs, which were much more comfortable than the old ones. I spoke to an older couple, the Kowalskis, walking their Chinese Pug on the sidewalk in front of the condo. The first day we met on the street we exchanged introductions, and I said their Pug reminded me of J. Edgar Hoover. Since then, I've been unable to remember the Pug's name, so I continue to call him J. Edgar, much to the Kowalski's delight and J. Edgar's indifference.

The Kowalskis and J. Edgar headed east. I heard a tapping on the front window and turned to see Susan, wide-eyed on the phone. I motioned for her to come out, gesturing that I was too sweaty to come in. She walked out the front door and gave me the phone, saying only, "It's Walton." I gestured for her to sit and bounce in the new wrought iron chair next to me.

"Have you recovered from the continuance?" I said, smiling until the enormity of what he was saying sunk in.

There had been an attack on the safe house. Lynn Metzger, Walton's star witness, was dead. So were the odd couple deputies, Smitty and Delroy. It happened sometime early that morning. Someone driving by on the highway a mile away heard the explosion and gunshots and called 9-1-1. A deputy patrolling the area drove to the camp and called it in. Lee's men taped off a couple of acres around the murder scene. They were keeping everyone out until the crime scene techs from the State Crime Lab arrived, along with the MBI. Walton added that the crime lab techs were bringing some National Guardsmen who had bomb squad experience from Iraq in case more explosives were hidden around the camp.

"Explosives?"

"It was an IED or land mine of some kind, maybe several. They don't know yet. I'm on my way out there now. Lee called me fifteen minutes ago and gave me the bare bones, asked me to let you know.

"Where did it happen?"

"Out at old man Fite's fishing camp on the Tallahatchie, just inside Yaloquena County. You've been there. I took you to the fish fry some of us put together as a fundraiser for Lee the last time he ran. There's only one road in."

"Very remote," I said. "Remind me how to get there."

Because the park had no address for me to type into my SYNC map system in my truck, Walton gave me precise directions. He added that the drive leading to the camp was private and didn't appear on any navigation program, including his. I concentrated on Walton's instructions and told him I would be on my way as soon as I got dressed.

I gave my phone to Susan and asked her to call Jimmy Gray to tell him what had happened, and that I'd call him when I got on the road.

I ran inside to shower and dress. Ten minutes later, I was cranking my truck. Susan brought me a fresh coffee in a Styrofoam cup and asked me to keep her posted.

Racing toward Batesville on Highway 6, I slowed to seventy as my adrenaline level subsided. No reason to kill myself on the road getting there. No one was going to be let into the scene until the crime lab techs arrived and established a perimeter.

I called Lee. His phone was busy. I knew he would call me back when he got off his other call. I called Jimmy. He had spoken to Susan. I answered his questions, filling the gaps in information as best I could. He was in Sunshine, and offered to meet me, help me in any way. I asked him to sit tight, that I would call him later. Lee's incoming call beeped. I told Jimmy I had to go.

"Walton told me what happened," I said.

"It's rough, Willie Mitchell. I can't believe it."

"You're out there now?"

"Waiting on the private road to the camp. We've got everything blocked so no one can get in there. MBI and crime lab people should be here an an hour."

"They're all dead?"

"It's a massacre. The bodies are torn up from the blast. Just to make sure, I checked the three bodies for a pulse. Smitty and Delroy's bodies are outside the car lying on the road, all mangled. Metzger's inside the vehicle. There's a lot of blood." He paused a moment. "I think the explosion would have killed them instantly. It tore off one of Metzger's legs. Bomb must have gone off right under him. Smitty's missing part of his torso. And just for good measure, the sons-of-a-bitches put a bullet in each one's brain. Contact shot to the temple, looks like."

"My God, Lee."

"Never seen anything like this except in war."

"I'm on my way. Be there probably in an hour."

"Take your time. We'll be out here all day, probably tonight and tomorrow too. There's a lot of ground to cover."

"All right."

I thought he was going to hang up, but after a moment, he spoke quietly, his voice cracking with guilt.

"I was careful driving in and out of this place, Willie Mitchell. I kept my lights off until I got to the main road, even drove by the entrance twice each time to make sure no one was tailing me."

"It's not your fault, Lee. If these guys are good enough to plant an IED or a mine, and blow it at just the right time to take out all three men, they have the expertise to operate a drone or plant a tracking device on your Tahoe. You can buy the things online now. If they had enough money, they could contract with a private satellite surveillance company in Europe and follow you anywhere."

"I didn't think an eighty-five-year-old Dixie Mafia segregationist would be that sophisticated."

"We've all underestimated Buddy Richardson, Lee. All of us."

CHAPTER FORTY-FOUR

When I described Mr. Fite's fishing camp as remote, I didn't do it justice. Jurassic is more like it. Near the eastern edge of Yaloquena County, the Tallahatchie River meanders through brakes and swamps like a drunken water moccasin, creating bogs and u-shaped oxbows along its erratic trail. The river changed directions more often than the Mississippi, leaving behind small bodies of water that rose and fell with the water level in the Tallahatchie.

Following Walton's directions, I left the state highway while still in Dundee County, and drove through milo and soybean fields on a poorly maintained county road with no shoulders. Unlike the sandy loam that supported a cotton crop, the soil here was a gumbo of clay and sand that drained poorly and cracked in summer droughts. It was land that was never cultivated until the federal government price support programs made it profitable to plant soybeans.

I slowed when I saw a Yaloquena deputy's patrol unit stopped on the county road to restrict access to Fite's camp. The solemn deputy recognized me and said yes when I asked him if this was the place where it happened. I turned on the rutted dirt and gravel road, glad I was driving my F-150. After a mile, turn rows on either side turned into a primeval forest of trees with no commercial value to anyone—willows, hornbeams, locusts, and an occasional hackberry growing on higher ground—a worthless no man's land.

I moved slowly through a curve. Bald cypress, some standing in casual water, began to crowd out the other trees. Another hundred yards through the cypress trees and knees, I came to the opening in the swampy landscape I recognized from the one time I had been there before. When Walton drove me to the small gathering for Lee's re-election, there had been pickup trucks scattered around, having ferried locals there for fried catfish, beer, and a bit of light politicking. This time, at least two dozen law enforcement vehicles were parked in each spot dry enough to support their weight.

I pulled off the gravel and saw Walton walking toward me. I stepped out of my truck a hundred yards from the fishing camp. The building was constructed of rough-hewn cypress harvested on the place, with a screened-in porch wrapping around all four sides to keep the mosquitos at bay.

"This is really bad," Walton said, shaking his head. "The National Guardsmen are almost finished checking the area for any other explosive devices. The State Crime Lab people are ready to move in as soon as it's clear."

"Let's take a look," I said.

I nodded at the Mississippi Bureau of Investigation men leaning on their vehicles, spoke to Yaloquena Coroner Al Revels waiting next to his coroner wagon, and waved at the crime lab techs waiting around their step van. Walton and I joined Lee at the bright yellow crime scene tape marking off the area to be searched and processed. I patted Lee on the shoulder and surveyed the scene.

The camp building was built on a spit of land between the Tallahatchie and the narrow oxbow. Its back porch overlooked the river. The front porch faced the inlet, which was the shape of a flattened U, a thick crescent moon. A forty-foot cypress beam and plank bridge provided access the house. It was wide enough only for pedestrians. Visitors parked near where we stood and walked across the bridge over the oxbow to the camp. Because of the control structures that Mr. Fite had built where the oxbow met the Tallahatchie, water surrounded the camp like a moat. Unless you arrived by boat on the Tallahatchie, the cypress bridge provided the only ingress to the camp building. In retrospect, what seemed like a perfect place for a safe house turned out to be a death trap. There was only one way in or out, across the bridge and onto the narrow gravel and dirt road. Smitty's and Delroy's vehicle was isolated on the land side of the bridge, easily available to the killers without their being detected by the deputies or Metzger inside the camp house.

"The guardsmen say it wasn't an IED or a mine," Lee said. "It was a car bomb with a remote electronic detonator. A really powerful bomb. 'Overkill' the bomb experts said. Whoever did it could have been hiding anywhere in the trees you drove through and pushed the button when the three of them got in."

"A car bomb makes more sense," I said. "A lot easier to control."

What remained of Smitty and Delroy lay in the dirt on either side of the vehicle, which was upside down, torn almost in two by the blast. Through the wreckage I could see a charred depression in the ground. To protect whatever physical evidence might be on the deputies' bodies, they had not been covered. Smitty was lying on his back in a pool of blood that had darkened until it was almost black. He was missing a large portion of his side between his pelvis and rib cage, as if ripped away by a shark. Delroy lay on his stomach. His back, buttocks, and legs were shredded, bones exposed. A severed leg lay next to him, but it wasn't his or Smitty's.

"It's Metzger's leg," Lee said.

Standing there, I wished I smoked. Lighting a cigarette, thumping ashes, and blowing smoke would have given me something to do. I glanced behind me at the deputies standing in clumps, speaking only in reverential tones. Some of them were smoking, some chewing tobacco and spitting into Styrofoam cups or empty plastic Coke bottles.

When I turned back to face the camp, the guardsmen were walking across the cypress bridge. They gave the demolished car and the bodies a wide berth, then huddled with Walton and Lee outside the crime scene tape. They were joined by the leaders of the MBI and crime lab teams. I hung back. I was an unofficial observer without status in the investigation. My presence was tolerated because of my relationship with all the players, but I was technically a civilian so I didn't want to press my luck. Walton and Lee stepped away as the crime lab technicians lifted the tape and began to photograph and measure the area around the upside down car.

"This is going to take a while," Lee said.

"Probably into mid-afternoon," I said.

"I'm going to have my men spread out and walk through all the wooded area this side of the oxbow. If they find something, they'll tape it off and preserve it for the crime scene techs when they get finished inside the tape."

I heard another vehicle drive up. My friend Robbie Cedars, director of the State Crime Lab, exited his state car. I walked over and told him what I knew, which is what Lee and Walton had shared with me. He said he didn't visit crime scenes any more, but this case was exceptional. Robbie said he was going to join his team inside the tape, but as he walked toward the camp, he stopped to ask me about the Fratelli investigation.

"Anything new on your riot shooting?" he asked.

"Not really. Thanks for your report on the bullet."

"Any time, Willie Mitchell. Let me know if I can do anything else."

I milled around with Walton for another hour while Lee and his deputies combed the swampy woodlands between the camp and the county road. Walton stepped away briefly to take a call. I was surprised to have cell service.

"I'm going to drive on to Sunshine," I said.

"I'll stay through lunch but then head back to the courthouse. Nothing for me to do out here but get in the way. Check in with me this afternoon and I'll update you on what Lee or the MBI people tell me."

"All right," I said and began to walk to my truck.

"Willie Mitchell," Walton said. "That phone call just now. It was Leopold Whitman. Son-of-a-bitch will be in Sunshine on Monday. He's going to take a formal statement from me about the grand jury thing—under oath with a court reporter."

"Just tell him the truth," I said and walked to my truck.

CHAPTER FORTY-FIVE

I spent the afternoon in Sunshine, where I had lived most of my life. Even if I had not already been feeling low, spending time in Sunshine would have depressed me. The town was on a steady decline. The big employers were gone. The primary source of income was now the federal government, its checks and benefits arriving the first of every month. It was a damned shame.

In contrast, the agriculture industry out in Yaloquena County was thriving. The price of farmland had plateaued recently, but overall it had more than doubled in the previous ten years. Ownership was continuing to consolidate, with corporate farmers and real estate investment trusts gobbling up acreage throughout the Delta. Jimmy Gray had told me some of the best cotton land, the "ice cream" loam that was the most coveted soil, had sold for $5,000 an acre.

I spent ninety minutes riding my family farm with the Hudson brothers. They rent my nine-hundred-ninety acre place for one-fourth of the gross value of the harvested crops. It's cotton land quality, but they said they were planting corn, beans, and milo this year, because the pathetic price of cotton no longer brought enough to cover the cost of production. They had picked well over two bales an acre several years in a row, but the worldwide price let them down year after year. The Hudsons took good care of my farm, requiring no supervision.

The rest of the afternoon I was at my house in the oldest residential part of Sunshine. It was a wooden structure built in 1910 in the Neoclassical Revival style, with large, circular wooden columns topped by Ionic capitals. The columns rose two stories from the concrete floor of the raised front porch. Gigantic red oak and water oaks covered much of the yard. Like my farm, I inherited the house from my parents, together with my mother's extensive collection of English antiques. The house remained as Susan and I left it when we moved to Oxford. We had it cleaned regularly and had the yard taken care of. When we first moved to Oxford, we returned once a month for a weekend stay in Sunshine. With the passage of time, those weekends had grown fewer and farther between. At some point, I knew I had to sell it, which was not going to be easy emotionally or practically. I had three generations of memories tied up in the house. And, it was worth a lot more than the few buyers who might be interested would be willing to pay.

Sitting at the old pine kitchen table in the house, I worried about how much of my family's net worth would be consumed in defending myself against the United States Justice Department. Most of my assets I inherited from frugal parents. My father was low-key, but made a solid business decision in starting the Sunshine Bank with Jimmy's father. My grandfather bought the farm land and passed it on to my dad. My mother acquired the antiques, some of them museum quality. I confess that I'm not a self-made man. I made a good living practicing law and being District Attorney, but what wealth I possessed I owed to inheritance and the fact that I was the only child of Katherine and Monroe Banks. I began to steel myself for what seemed to be the inevitable. A top flight white collar criminal defense lawyer would cost big money.

I called Susan and told her briefly about the scene at Mr. Fite's fishing camp. I told her I was going to spend the night in our house in Sunshine. She urged me to be careful. I had asked Jimmy Gray on my drive over to have his loan officer check again with his sister at the hospital. Jimmy reported back that our secret agent nurse said she heard through the hospital grapevine that Buddy had been moved out of the ICU in the morning as scheduled.

Jimmy picked me up at 5:30 p.m. in his bright red Navigator. I waited for him on the porch with two twenty ounce Styrofoam cups, mine filled with Tito's, tonic, and lime; Jimmy's filled with Maker's Mark and one-third water. The plan was to ride our customary circuit out in the county to inspect the crops and farmland, much of which our Sunshine Bank financed. We had done this together for almost thirty years. Before we left the city limits, I told Jimmy about Leopold Whitman coming to Sunshine the following Monday to take Walton's deposition.

"While he's here you want me to have him whacked?" he asked.

"Not yet."

"I would have hired Metzger to take Whitman out, but now that sorry no good s.o.b. don't have a leg to stand on."

I winced.

"He has one," I said.

"Probably a little too raw at this point to be joked about," Jimmy said.

"Let's let it settle a while. Even Metzger had a mother somewhere who loved him." I paused. "Or maybe not."

"The Shannon place is half cotton, half corn this year," Jimmy said as we drove through Shannon Farms, a ten thousand acre operation owned by a Memphis family.

"I want to ask you something," I said. "Have you ever been seduced by an older woman?"

"Martha. But she's only a couple of months older than me."

"I'm serious. Answer me."

"Super total confidential?"

"I didn't think we had any secrets."

"We don't but I didn't want to take a chance. There've been a couple of older ladies, customers of the bank, both widows, who came on to me. I think."

"What do you mean 'you think'?"

"You know what I mean. At the time, it was clear what they were hinting. More than hinting. It's hard to describe it exactly."

"Were you tempted?"

"Hell, no. But the way they were flirting and looking at me, it sure got my attention. And it really got Tiny's attention. Like I told you before, the two most powerful forces in the world are pussy and compound interest."

"You learned that in banking school?" I said, laughing. "But seriously, you thought about what it would be like, I mean as an abstract principle?"

"Exactly," Jimmy said. "Not that I would do it, but it's something when they turn it on, I don't care how old they are. Stronger than gravity."

"Were they good-looking?"

"Damn right. It was weird. That's the best way I could describe it. I was feeling this attraction that was...."

"Instinctual. Something deep in your makeup, at the cellular level."

Jimmy looked me like I had said something odd.

"What I was going to say," Jimmy said, "is that some of that stuff is as strong as an acre of garlic. Make a monkey eat pepper."

"Those are technical, scientific terms?"

"Why are you bringing up this shit? What happened?"

I described my encounter with Cissy Breedlove.

"Damn," Jimmy said, "that is a fine-looking woman, I don't care how old she is. It's like she hasn't aged like a normal person."

"I'm telling you, her breasts, her legs, she could be in her fifties."

"You felt a stirring in your loins, did you?"

"I certainly did, and she knew it. And let me tell you this. She liked the fact that she was turning me on. I could tell she was enjoying it."

"So you did what I would have done—you ran."

"Damned right. Intellectually, I had no interest. But at the physical level, it was like my body was on auto-pilot."

"It made you quit thinking about the Xerox of the photograph and who killed Russell Fratelli," Jimmy said and paused. "Maybe that's just what she intended."

CHAPTER FORTY-SIX

I woke up early Saturday, locked up our Sunshine house, and returned to the Fite camp. A new deputy blocked the dirt and gravel road where it intersected the county road. I didn't recognize him, but I introduced myself and told him I had been with Walton and Sheriff Jones at the scene the day before. He moved his patrol unit and I drove toward the camp. I passed soybeans on one side and milo on the other, then the junk trees and the curves through the bald cypress brake.

When I came through the tree line to the opening for the camp house, I mumbled, "What a perfect place for a murder." From the county road you could see no sign of a fishing camp. Not an inhabited dwelling in probably a three mile radius. Smitty's and Delroy's vehicle was parked across the cypress bridge from the house, easily accessed by the killers in the early morning darkness. Then all that remained was the wait in the trees for the deputies and Metzger to get in the car, flip the switch, and BOOM.

I drove to within fifty feet of the upside-down car. Almost all of the vehicles at the scene the day before had gone—the crime lab van, the coroner's wagon, the MBI and National Guard vehicles, and the half-dozen Yaloquena Sheriff's office units. Only Lee's Tahoe and one of his patrol units remained. I parked, spotted Lee in his Tahoe, and climbed in.

"You been here the whole time?" I asked.

"Un-huh," he said.

"You ought to get some sleep."

"I took a nap a while ago. I'm going to stay until the wrecker comes to haul off Smitty's and Delroy's unit."

"Who else is here?"

"I've got two men looking in the trees."

"Your men didn't find anything yesterday?"

"No. These two probably won't today, either."

We sat in silence a moment. The ambient early morning sounds of the Delta wetlands came through the Tahoe's open windows—frogs, bugs, screech owls, a pileated woodpecker working on a hollow cypress. I looked at the black stains on either side of the bombed-out car where the bodies had lain, the blood having soaked through the dirt and gravel into the earth.

"The National Guardsmen found it," Lee said, "the tracking device on the underside of my Tahoe. Crime lab people took it with them. Said it was something you could buy online. They're going to see if the purchase can be traced. They said probably not."

"It's not your fault, Lee."

"I should have paid more attention. It was stupid of me not to check. It seems so obvious now."

"Did Robbie Cedars tell you anything? Or the MBI?"

"The shots to the head were small caliber. They think .22 or .25. No exit wounds. They think the bomb was some kind of plastic explosive, they think maybe Semtex because of the smell around the car. They said Semtex has been manufactured with a detection taggant since the nineties. My men spent a lot of time combing the area around the car but didn't find any brass. Might have been a revolver or the shooters picked them up. I don't think forensics are going to be much help. These people knew what they were doing. Semtex is hard to come by."

"I'm going to drive back to Oxford," I said. "I'll check in with Walton later on today."

I waved at the young deputy and turned onto the county road. Buddy Richardson was conveniently in the hospital when the bombing took place. As a result of the mayhem, Buddy was no longer likely to be convicted of anything. Metzger was the key to the case. Without his testimony, Buddy would get away with the murder of his grandson-in-law. No doubt he paid someone to kill Metzger and the deputies, but it would probably require a lengthy, multi-state investigation to prove it. The chances of finding the professionals who planted the tracking device under Lee's Tahoe and the Semtex bomb under the deputies' vehicle were very slim.

The violent death of Smitty and Delroy in the line of duty put my investigation of the shooting of Russell Fratelli in 1962 into perspective. What Walton was dealing with now, the murderous Buddy Richardson killing his way to an acquittal, was serious business with long-lasting repercussions. Because he had deep pockets, Buddy could buy his way to freedom, especially since he had no compunctions about killing as many people as it took. It made a mockery of the criminal justice system in Sunshine and north Mississippi. And it was the type of thing Buddy had been doing all his life.

Cissy admitted she was in the picture against the tree with Russell. Given the shock effect of the fishing camp massacre, it took me a while to get my head back to the point in the Fratelli investigation where I thought the identity of the brunette with Russell was significant. But, James Butler was interested enough in the original photo to remove it from the archives. And now Butler was dead, murdered by someone who tried to make it look like a suicide. I wondered if Butler's death would turn out to be a bigger mystery than the killing of Fratelli in the Grove. It was certainly more recent.

I spoke to Susan as I neared Oxford. I suggested that we start seriously considering selling the house in Sunshine. She said all right, but neither of us had our heart in it.

Instead of exiting north on Old Taylor, on the spur of the moment I continued on Highway 6 to the Lamar exit and drove south. I parked in the Baptist Hospital lot, which was nearly full, and asked the receptionist for the Buddy Richardson's new room number.

"He's been moved into two-twelve," she said, tapping something into her keyboard.

I walked to the elevators and pushed the button.

"Wait," the woman said. "My computer just updated registration. Mr. Richardson must have left this morning."

"Are you sure?"

"That's what it says on my screen, but it's not always right. You might want to double-check just in case."

I exited on the second floor, found room two-twelve, and pushed open the door. The bed had been stripped. I checked at the nurses' station.

"He left about an hour ago with Dr. Finstermayer," she said. "Dr. Grillette tried to stop him, but Mr. Buddy caused a little scene. He made Dr. Grillette admit he couldn't make him stay, and walked out whistling."

CHAPTER FORTY-SEVEN

As soon as I closed the door and cranked my truck, I phoned Walton and left him a voice message to call me right away. Halfway between the hospital and the condo my phone buzzed. I told Walton about Buddy walking out of Baptist Hospital.

"That figures," he said. "I just got off the phone with Helmet Head. He's withdrawing as counsel."

"He tell you why?"

"No. He kept it vague. But I could tell he was irritated. He said he had phoned Judge Williams to let her know. Why don't you call him? You know him a lot better than I do."

"When I get home." I paused. "Walton, one more thing. I meant it when I said just tell the truth when Whitman takes your statement Monday. You'll be under oath, and you know the Justice Department likes to pursue perjury charges if a witness doesn't testify like they want. Truth is your friend."

"I know what the truth is, Willie Mitchell. I've watched you select grand juries since I graduated from law school. The truth is your friend, too. I'm certain of it."

"I hope you're right. I'll talk to you later."

I parked in the garage and walked inside. Over an early lunch of chicken salad, I told Susan what happened at the fishing camp. When she had heard enough, she changed the subject to the status of our house in Sunshine. Fifteen minutes later I closed my office door, and checked my e-mails. I clicked on one from newspaperman Jack Ray Weldon and downloaded the attachment. I glanced at the image of Buddy Richardson lifted from a fifty-five-year-old article in the Sunshine Courier, hit print, and called Helmet Head.

"Walton told me you've withdrawn," I said. "You know Buddy left the hospital this morning over Dr. Grillette's objections."

"Doesn't surprise me," J.D. Silver said.

"Why'd you get out of the case?"

A long silence on the other end. I waited.

"I'm not after anything privileged," I said.

"Since it's you, Willie Mitchell, I'll speak hypothetically about the incentives I build in to my representation agreement in a major case. If I achieve any one of several positive outcomes for a client, there is a bonus payment due immediately."

"And with a well-heeled client, I'm sure it's substantial."

"High risk, high reward," he said. "Sometimes a client fails to honor the specific commitment he or she was eager to promise at the outset to get me to handle their case. When it happens, I withdraw because I have every intention of enforcing the agreement. It may come down to suing my client to collect if I believe the client has the assets to pay me but just refuses. In such events, I can no longer represent the client without a conflict."

I let his explanation *sauté* a moment.

"Achieving a mistrial was one of the positive outcomes," I said, "and Buddy said he wasn't paying because he got the mistrial, not you."

"You are a very smart attorney," he said, "and let's just leave it at that. Besides, I got tired of the old s.o.b. talking to me like the hired help, refusing to follow instructions or even consider my suggestions."

"I'd like to think resignation had something to with the fact that Lynn Metzger and two Yaloquena deputies were blown to bits yesterday morning."

"I won't comment on that tragedy."

"Did you know he was going to leave the hospital?"

"I think it's best that we go no further down this road, Willie Mitchell. I regret any inconvenience that my withdrawing will cause Walton, but I had no choice. I will miss trying cases with you in the future because of your retirement. You were always a worthy foe."

"You never know, J.D.," I said. "Not sure what I'm going to do."

"Well, whatever you decide, best of luck," Helmet Head said and paused. "And Willie Mitchell, you tell Walton to be careful dealing with my former client. You and Sheriff Jones should continue to watch his back."

"Has Buddy made any threats?"

"Not to me. But I've been around many a dangerous fellow in my line of work. This old man may be the worst."

After the call I thought about Buddy Richardson. I removed the grainy *Sunshine Courier* photograph from my printer tray and studied it. It was slightly blurred, but a full-on head shot of Buddy as he appeared in 1960, speaking to the Yaloquena Citizens' Council. I turned to study the face on my computer screen to see if it were any clearer. I looked back at the printed version, and something clicked.

I had seen the image before.

In my mind's eye I tried to reconstruct the memory. Had I seen it in the *Oxford Eagle* archives? Or during the two visits to the records room at *The Daily Mississippian*? I studied the printed image, then on my monitor. Though not perfect, it was clear enough to convey the intensity in Buddy's dark eyes staring into the camera, and the clarity of his malevolent vision.

Susan tapped on my office door and walked in.

"I forgot to tell you. Mrs. Butler called this morning. She wants you to phone her when you get a chance."

"How did she sound?"

"Pretty shaky. Said she would be home most of the day."

I looked up the number and phoned Naomi Butler.

"You asked me on Wednesday if James had any old photographs from his work here at the house," Naomi said, her voice quavering. "I told you he didn't. But I started cleaning out his closet yesterday, then again this morning, and found a manila envelope with some old black and white pictures. I don't know what they're for or how long they've been here."

"Would you mind if I took a look?"

"That's why I called you. You are welcome to come see them. There are only a few."

"How about right now?"

In less than ten minutes I was in the Butlers' driveway. Naomi guided me to the kitchen table where the envelope lay. She said she had just made a fresh pot of coffee. I didn't want any coffee, but I said a half a mug would be great. I opened the envelope and spread the photographs on the table. Naomi placed an Ole Miss mug on the table and I took a sip.

Six photographs of the crowd gathered in front of the Lyceum—each shot from a different perspective. Four appeared to have been taken in the afternoon, the other two at dusk. The focus of the photographer was the crowd. There were no shots of the U.S. Marshals, the Mississippi Highway Patrol, or the officials on the Lyceum porch.

"Do you mind if I sit here a while to look at these?" I asked, taking another sip of coffee. "Am I keeping you from something?"

"Take all the time you want," she said and dabbed her eyes with a Kleenex. "I'll be in the back."

I studied the faces in the crowd. In the four shots taken in the afternoon, most of the onlookers were students. The two photos taken at dusk reflected the change in the makeup of the group gathered in front of the Lyceum as the day grew later. The coeds had left, leaving only men. All of them were well beyond student age. I asked Naomi if she had a magnifying glass. She reached into a cabinet drawer under the counter near the phone, placed a hand lens on the table and returned to the back of the house.

Without using the glass, I had detected the same young man who seemed to be the focus of each of the six photographs. He wore dark slacks and a long-sleeved white shirt. His hair was longer than the other men, some of whom wore crew cuts. Five of the pictures caught him in profile, but one taken at dusk captured his entire face. In fact, it seemed he was angry at the photographer, looking straight at him.

I studied the face with the magnifying glass until I was certain I was right. I had seen this young man's image twenty minutes earlier on my computer, addressing the Yaloquena Citizens' Council meeting in 1960.

It was Buddy Richardson. He was at the riot—in the middle of it.

When I looked up from the photograph, Naomi returned to the kitchen table. I handed her the magnifying glass and thanked her for letting me use it.

"Have you been able to sleep?" I asked.

"Not much," she said. "I take the sleeping pills but after two or three hours I'm awake again, thinking about James."

"Would you mind if I asked you a few questions about him?"

"Anything to pass the time," she said. "What would you like to know?"

"Have you heard of Buddy Richardson, the young man in these pictures?" I asked, pointing to Buddy in the photos on the table.

She studied the pictures and shook her head. She asked if they were taken at the time of the Meredith riot, and I told her yes.

"I've never heard the name Buddy Richardson."

"Do you know if Mr. Butler knew him?"

"He never mentioned him to me. I'm pretty sure of that."

"Did Mr. Butler ever discuss the shooting death of a young man named Russell Fratelli that happened on the night of the riot."

"Not that I recall. Not with me. I didn't meet James until he was out of college."

"Do you know who Cissy Breedlove is?"

"Yes," she said, smiling for the first time. "She was almost another Miss America for Mississippi, but ended up coming in third. She was a state senator and moved up here a few years back. I think she and her husband live in one of the townhomes off Jackson on the other side of the Square. I've seen her around town. She is still a lovely lady and seems nice, but I don't really know her, just who she is."

"Do you know if Mr. Butler knew Mrs. Breedlove?" I asked.

"Oh, yes. He knew her in college. I think she was a couple of years older. He followed her political career and helped welcome her to Oxford when she and her husband moved here after she retired from the state senate. There for a while I teased him because he talked about her so much. I accused him of having a crush on her, but I was just being silly."

"Would you mind if I borrowed these photographs?"

"I guess you can. I don't know why I would ever need them. I didn't even know they were in James's closet."

"I'll take good care of them," I said, gathering the six pictures and sticking them back into the envelope. "Thank you, Mrs. Butler."

On the way home, I stopped at a light. I picked up the manila envelope from the passenger seat. I looked at the edge of the flap—sharp enough to inflict a nasty cut. The envelope was stiff, no wrinkles or blemishes. The glue on the flap was fresh. Without a doubt, the envelope was new. It had not been in the closet long.

Why would James Butler have squirreled away six photographs featuring Buddy Richardson at the 1962 riot?

Chapter Forty-Eight

At five the next morning, I was wide awake. How I could have missed something so obvious? At the time it occurred, the Meredith standoff was the most significant event in Mississippi's civil rights' history of the 1960s. It jump-started the federal assault on Jim Crow in the South, and the forced integration of Mississippi's schools and other public institutions. Buddy Richardson was a moving force in the Yaloquena Citizens' Council, a committed segregationist. Violent opponents of Meredith's admission flocked to the Grove from every southern state. Buddy lived only a couple of hours from the Ole Miss campus. By the time of the riot, he had been fighting integration tooth and nail for several years. The battle in the Grove on September 30, 1962 was almost on his doorstep. Buddy would not have missed the historic confrontation for the world. He would have been on the front line.

James Butler covered the riot. He saw Buddy there; probably took the six pictures himself. But why hadn't he left them in the archives of the college newspaper with all the others? The evidence I had gathered indicated Butler also removed the picture of Russell Fratelli and Cissy together against the tree, but that photo was still missing. Why wasn't it hidden in Butler's closet in the manila folder with the other six pictures?

The riot was a public event, angry people streaming into Oxford from every direction. Other people were taking pictures, too, including the unfortunate reporter for the French paper who was fatally shot in the back. Surely there were photographs of Buddy Richardson at the riot in a number of collections, private and public.

I got out of bed quietly and ten minutes later was downstairs in my office drinking coffee and going through the computer files I had populated with notes and questions about the murder of Francis Fratelli. An hour of sitting behind my desk and reading the files was all I could stand. I tiptoed upstairs and dressed quietly, trying not to wake Susan. I started my truck and drove east to the new McDonald's on University Avenue. I bought a medium cup of black coffee, then went up the ramp to Highway 7 and exited onto the Highway 6 four lane. I put my cruise control on fifty-five and drove east in the right lane toward Tupelo. I do my best thinking on an early morning drive.

Thirty minutes later I turned around and headed back to Oxford. I called Sheriff Lee Jones first, then Jimmy Gray. Back at the condo, I showered and changed, put on jeans and boots, and a sport coat to conceal my .38 Chief's Special holstered in the small of my back.

Ninety minutes later I pulled into the gravel parking lot of Eddie's Bar-B-Q on Dundee County Road 343 at its intersection with Highway 8. I stopped next to Jimmy's big red Navigator, locked my truck and climbed into Jimmy's back seat. I shook hands with Lee in the passenger seat and patted Jimmy on the shoulder.

"'Bout time you got here," Jimmy said, struggling to buckle the seat belt around his big belly.

"I had a longer drive. If you're through flapping your gums let's go. I want to be there before he wakes up."

"He'll be laid up most of the morning," Lee said. "A hundred bucks says he spent Saturday night at some honky-tonk drinking and dancing with that girlfriend of his and is still sleeping it off."

"You sure you can get us there?" Jimmy asked Lee.

"Just drive. I know where Cheatwood lives."

"You bring Big D?" I asked Jimmy.

"I never go to Dundee County without it."

We drove for thirty minutes on county roads with crumbling asphalt at the edges, leaving the Delta flatlands for the hills of Dundee where crystal meth labs were a growth industry. I looked out of the window at the depressing landscape—dead-end hollows where blue smoke curled from crooked brick chimneys and sheet metal vents atop weathered frame houses and rusted-out trailers. We could have easily been in the foothills of Appalachia.

"Be on the lookout for a big-headed bald guy sitting on a bridge. He's got little-bitty eyes and plays a mean banjo," Jimmy Gray said.

"This is as sad as the Delta," Lee said. "How does anyone escape from this kind of poverty?"

"Speaking of escape," Jimmy said, "I hope Cheatwood doesn't shoot us."

"He'll be too hungover," I said. "We'll catch him off guard at home. That's the whole point."

"Slow down and turn into that drive right there," Lee said, pointing.

Jimmy stopped at the steel pipe gate twenty feet off the county right-of-way. Lee hopped out and removed the chain looped over the fence post, pushed the swinging gate open, then draped the chain back over the post after Jimmy drove through.

"Surprised he doesn't lock it," I said when Lee got back in.

"This is the second time I've been out here to his house," Lee said. "The gate wasn't locked the first time, either."

"And you lived to tell about it," Jimmy said.

"First trip was a regional Sheriff's meeting. Cheatwood had a big catfish fry for about twenty of us. I was surprised he invited me. Guess he had to."

I had been with Lee in Sheriff Cheatwood's office in the Dundee Courthouse in Kilbride three years earlier in connection with the fallout from my prosecution of Sunshine panhandler Mule Gardner. Mule had been involved in the shooting death of a Muslim commune recruiter in the parking lot of a convenience store in Sunshine. The Brewer clan of Dundee County was involved in the case because one of their own, through no fault of his own, was caught in the crossfire, got shot, and returned fire. Sheriff Cheatwood was unwilling to help Lee and me that day in his office, saying his constituents, the Brewers, had every right to refuse to cooperate with us. Cheatwood made it clear from his comments and attitude he didn't think much of African-Americans in general, and the African-American Sheriff Lee Jones of Yaloquena County in particular.

"The first time I came out here I was with some MBI investigators and federal ATF agents," Lee said, "wanting Cheatwood's help rounding up a particular moonshiner."

"Moonshine?" Jimmy Gray said. "Talk about living in the past. Why would the federal government even give a damn about illegal whiskey-making these days. There's more important things to waste our tax dollars on."

"I don't know, but Cheatwood claimed he didn't know the person."

"That was a lie," I said. "He knows everyone in these hills."

A fourth-of-a-mile off the highway we came to a three-or-four acre lake. The dirt road skirted the lake and led to a relatively new mobile home on cinder blocks in a copse of big red oak trees on a rise overlooking the water. We climbed out of the Navigator and Lee tapped lightly on the trailer door. I walked a few feet to check out Cheatwood's concrete patio and look down at his pond. A redwood picnic table with matching benches anchored the middle of the patio. The table was littered with empty beer bottles and cans. Crushed and nicotine-stained cigarette butts overflowed from a lime green plastic ash tray.

"Nice," I thought as I caught a whiff of stale beer and cigarettes.

I turned when the trailer door opened. Sheriff Bob Cheatwood stood resplendent in the door. A yellowed tee shirt stretched across his pot belly. Brown chewing tobacco dribbles stained the front of his tee shirt and his khaki work pants. His greasy yellow-gray hair was filthy. White stubble added to his grizzled appearance, along with his gnarled, yellow and gray toenails. "Nasty" was the word that came to mind. Looking at the condition of his feet and toes, I wondered how the man wore shoes. He squinted painfully into the morning light, shielding his eyes with his hand.

"Goddamn," he muttered. "It's Sunday."

"Sorry, Sheriff, but we wouldn't have bothered you if it weren't urgent," Lee said. "These things come up at inconvenient times."

"What do you want?"

"We need to talk to you. I had a bombing over the line in Yaloquena County Friday morning. Killed two of my men."

"I heard tell about it," Cheatwood said.

While we stood there, looking up at him leaning against the open door, his girlfriend appeared behind him, an unlit cigarette dangling from the side of her mouth. Her gray and bleached blonde hair was a frightful mess, her eyes caked with black mascara, smeared across her wrinkled, ashy skin. She squinted at us and rested her forehead against the Sheriff's shoulder. It was hard to judge, but I thought she might be in her fifties, and the Sheriff in his early seventies.

"Go have a seat at the table on the deck," he told us and closed the door.

We heard him growl something at his sweetheart inside the mobile home as we sauntered to the edge of the concrete patio. The three of us stood there looking down over Cheatwood's lake.

"Ain't that gal a mighty pretty little thing?" Jimmy Gray said.

"That's what they make alcohol for," I said, "for people like the Sheriff and her to get together."

"She's rougher looking than he is," Lee said quietly.

"I just hope he brushes his teeth before he comes out," I said.

"Shouldn't take long," Jimmy said. "He's only got a few."

We heard the trailer door slam shut and turned to see Sheriff Cheatwood ambling our way in rubber flip-flops, his big toenails rising up from the quick like putrescent stalagmites. He had thrown on an old Dundee County Sheriff's shirt but left it unbuttoned so we could continue to admire the stains on the front of his tee shirt. He wore a faded cap with the U.S. Marshal's logo on the front pulled down over his forehead, his wild, dirty hair escaping on the sides. Since I left my small bottle of extra-strength anti-bacterial wash in my truck at Eddie's Bar-B-Q, I was relieved that Cheatwood failed to offer his hand in greeting. We gathered at the end of the picnic table with the fewest beer bottles. It would have been a pleasant morning overlooking the pond but for the smell of beer and butts, and the fetid presence of The Right Honorable Bob Cheatwood, duly elected High Sheriff of Dundee County.

"You know Mr. Fite's fishing camp on the Tallahatchie west of here?" Lee said. "That's where it happened."

"I know the place," Cheatwood said. "He's supposed to be some rich fellow out of Sunshine. I've seen it from the river."

"We think Buddy Richardson had something to do with it," I said.

"You the Yaloquena DA, ain't you?"

"I was. And this is my friend Jimmy Gray from Sunshine."

Jimmy nodded at Cheatwood.

"What makes you think Buddy was involved?" Cheatwood asked.

"My two men who died were protecting the third man who was killed, Lynn Metzger," Lee said. "He was a witness in our case against Buddy for the contract killing of his grandson-in-law at his farm in Yaloquena County. Metzger is from over here in Dundee."

"I know Metzger," Cheatwood said. "Been telling lies since he was old enough to talk. I guess it's too bad he's dead and all, but he ain't never been nothing but a criminal his whole life. Known him since he was a boy. If you was depending on him to testify against Buddy Richardson, you didn't have much of a case anyway."

"You're probably right," Lee said, "but common sense says the person with the motive to kill Metzger was Buddy Richardson."

"Maybe so," Cheatwood said, "but there's lots of other people who'd want to kill Lynn Metzger, a long list in fact."

"We'd like your help in investigating Buddy Richardson," Lee said. "He's a Dundee County resident and we figured you've had dealings with him."

"I know Buddy, for sure, but not all that well. I'd be glad to help but you say the bombing was in Yaloquena County so I suspect I ain't got any jurisdiction over any investigation of it."

"If we need to talk to him and he won't come in," Lee said, "we'd like your help in bringing him in."

"Like I said, it ain't none of my business what happened in your county."

Lee nodded as if he fully understood Cheatwood's situation.

"I see where you're coming from," Lee said. "We've been contacted by investigators with the MBI, and also the FBI. For some reason they have a lot of interest in Buddy Richardson, and not just for the bombing last week."

"Hmm," Cheatwood said. "That's news to me. I ain't never heard of anything Buddy's involved in except being a good taxpaying citizen. He's a damned fine businessman, they say."

"I guess he must have a good cattle business," I said. "I talked to a fellow last week who sold some livestock to Mr. Richardson a few years back. Said Buddy was an honest man in his cattle dealings. The man's name is Boyland Burr. Lives over in Oxford, retired U.S. Marshal. You know him?"

"Can't say as I do."

"I thought he might have given you that cap you're wearing," I said.

Cheatwood pulled his cap off and glanced at the U.S. Marshal logo. He tried his best to seem puzzled.

"I guess I got this at some law enforcement meeting. Can't remember when."

"Well, all right," Sheriff," Lee said as he stood up. "I guess we'll be going. If you don't mind, keep this all under your hat for now. I'll be back in touch."

We drove away from the Cheatwood estate.

"Sheriff Cheatwood," I said, "apparently thinks his job is to side with Dundee County residents against any outside law enforcement that comes into his county, no matter what."

"That's why he keeps getting re-elected," Lee said.

We followed the drive around the lake and back to the county road. Lee wondered aloud how long it would take for Sheriff Cheatwood to call Buddy Richardson to tell him about our visit.

"I bet he's calling now," Jimmy said.

"Nope," I said. "I could tell from the look in his eyes he was in a hurry to get back to that fallen angel inside. After he and his honey make a little love he'll give Buddy a call, just like we figured he would."

"I wonder where he gets his toes done?" Jimmy said.

CHAPTER FORTY-NINE

It had warmed up considerably by the time Jimmy pulled in next to my truck at Eddie's Bar-B-Q. Jimmy put the Navigator in park and turned around as far as his large body would permit. He asked me if had considered why James Butler's "suicide" was staged on the road to my duck camp.

"I haven't had much time to think about it," I said.

"Well, Lee and I were talking on the drive over here before you showed up. Seems obvious to us someone is sending you a message. A threat, in fact."

"I'd say that's pretty obvious," I said.

"The message being you better back off or you could end up like James Butler with a hole in your head," Jimmy said.

"Walton and I agree," Lee said, turning to me, "Buddy Richardson's behind it."

"It's his m.o. all right," I said. "But since Lynn Metzger was blown to pieces last Friday morning, Buddy would no longer have a motive to take a shot at me or Walton."

"You're probably right," Lee said. "Odds of Walton re-trying Buddy without Metzger's testimony are pretty long."

"Crime pays," Jimmy said.

"And if there's no forensic evidence from the bombing that links it to Buddy Richardson, he's going to skate on that, too," I said. "It was a professional job by people who knew what they were doing. And they weren't from around here. Not many Dixie Mafia types know how to get ahold of Semtex, much less arm and detonate it."

"Just be careful numb nuts," Jimmy Gray said. "That's all we're saying."

I drove back to Oxford in time for the Geezer Group one o'clock Sunday tee time. Susan encouraged me to play, saying it would be therapeutic. She was right. I needed to get my mind off things a while, clear my head. I played well, had a beer at the turn and two at the nineteenth hole settling the bet. For supper that night, Susan had the thin fried catfish filets and I had a tender, delicious filet at Taylor Grocery, eight miles south of Oxford in an old country store in the center of the tiny village of Taylor.

We turned in early and I got plenty of sleep. I hoped the morning would start a less deadly, more productive week for me. Retirement from the DA's office had not been quite as peaceful as I expected.

I began running at six-thirty and finished at a decent pace; a decent pace for me, that is. I cleaned up and checked my e-mails on the desktop computer in my office. The only two of any consequence were from Cheryl Diamond and Robbie Cedars. Both had been sent around seven-thirty a.m., and both wanted me to call. I phoned Cheryl first.

"Good morning," Cheryl warbled when she answered. "I'm so glad you called. How are you doing?"

"Busy," I said. "Kind of like the old days."

"I know you've been making progress on the Russell Fratelli death."

"Not really."

"You are mistaken, Willie Mitchell. I went back over some of the articles you sent me on the 1962 disturbance last night before I went to bed."

"And you had a dream?"

"It's something between a dream and a vision, but I can't really describe it adequately. Anyway, I saw Russell in the Grove, and for the first time he was smiling. Do you know why?"

"No idea."

"Well, I'm not certain, but this is my feeling about it. Russell knows you're going to get to the bottom of it after all these years."

"I wish I shared his optimism," I said.

"Russell must believe you're doing better than you think."

"Good. I'm going to send you a photograph attached to an e-mail of Russell Fratelli and a co-ed named Cissy Summers taken in the Grove. Tell me what you think about it."

"I will. And one other thing before you go," she said. "And this is not so happy. You were in the Grove last night, too."

"What was I doing?"

"Standing there, looking at Russell. The dark force I mentioned the other day, the same one approaching Russell," she said quietly, "it was moving in your direction."

I thought about Cheryl Diamond after we ended the call. I usually share with Susan whatever Cheryl tells me, but I decided I would keep this to myself. Before I met Cheryl, I vaguely believed in the existence of some kind of communication between people existing outside the senses, messages that come to receptive people through a spiritual ether. Non-believers chalk it up to coincidence. On more occasions than I can count, I thought of someone from the distant past and a day or two later received a call or e-mail from them, or from someone conveying news about them. I have never doubted the sincerity of mothers who say "I bolted upright in bed in the middle of the night and knew something had happened to" a son or daughter. I think this spiritual ether binds all humanity, past and present. Obviously, there's no way to prove it.

When Cheryl contacted me out of the blue during the prosecution of Ross Bullard I was skeptical. She was persistent and eventually led me to the body of seven-year-old Danny Thurman in the most remote and primitive part of the county, an area previously combed over thoroughly by a dozen experienced woodsmen on foot and on four-wheelers. The day I saw Danny's body in the cave hidden under an overhang in that dry creek bed, my vague belief in psychic transmissions became concrete. I became a believer.

I made another cup of coffee and called Robbie Cedars. Talk about the yin and the yang. Cheryl dealt in the spiritual realm. Robbie dealt exclusively with the physical—analyzing the evidence found at a crime scene.

"I thought you might find this interesting," Robbie said.

"You're up and at it early today," I said.

"Always. Anyway, the gun that was found on the floorboard at the victim's feet, the .38 Chief's Special, I researched the serial number. It was manufactured in 1955."

"That revolver's sixty years old."

"Smith and Wesson came up with the design on a new frame after World War II, and began manufacturing them in 1950. They introduced it at an international Chiefs of Police convention. These things are workhorses and last forever with just a little care."

"I don't guess guns were registered in the fifties."

"There was no registration required for any types of pistols."

"Did you have a chance to do a comparison with the bullet taken from James Butler's brain?"

"Definite match. No surprise there."

I entered Robbie's information in my computer files and did a search in the U.S. Marshal's website to get the contact information on the head man in the Oxford office. I hoped he was old enough to remember Boyland Burr.

CHAPTER FIFTY

Two hours later, I walked into the Federal Building on the corner of Jackson and North 9th for my ten o'clock appointment with Oather Madison, the chief of the U.S. Marshal's office in Oxford. I had called Billy Shelby, my friend in the Oxford FBI office and asked him to call Madison to give the chief some background on me and help me get a meeting.

When I met Oather Madison, I recognized him. We had never been introduced, but I had seen him in the Oxford federal building at different times when I was DA. He was five or six years older than I, with salt-and-pepper hair and heavy jowls. His skin was a deep black, the same tone as Everett Johnson, Mayor of Sunshine. The chief asked me to call him Oather and invited me to have a seat.

"I followed your career as a prosecutor, Willie Mitchell," Oather said. "You won some important cases."

"Appreciate it," I said.

"Eleanor Bernstein speaks highly of you," he said.

"She's an excellent lawyer. Glad she's on the right side now."

"Eleanor's doing a fine job for us."

"Thanks for seeing me on short notice."

"Not hard to get an appointment with me. At my age they just have me doing ceremonial stuff. Be putting me out to pasture soon."

"I don't know if you followed the trial that got derailed in the Oxford Circuit Courtroom last Wednesday."

"I looked in for a moment during jury selection just to have a gander at that old gangster you were trying."

"You know Buddy Richardson?"

"Known of him for many years. Never met him. He has operated on the fringes of criminality for decades. I didn't know he was still alive."

"Why in particular were y'all interested in him?"

"I was a young man in the Jackson office, green behind the ears, in the days when the Dixie Mafia was at its peak. Buddy's name was always popping up, but he was too smart to ever get caught at anything. In the lonely hearts scam centered in Angola Prison in Louisiana we had to do some witness protection. Those were some bad actors. Judge Sherry and his wife got killed in their home in Biloxi over it. Buddy was somehow connected to the fellow in the prison running the con. When all that hit the fan Buddy just faded into those Dundee County hills and kept a low profile until it blew over. We looked at him for some heavy equipment theft, but he had kept himself insulated. Too many layers between him and the people on the ground for us to do anything to him. He's a shrewd old cuss."

"I met a guy about ten days ago who used to work in your office here. Big heavy fellow, lives on...."

"Boyland Burr," Oather said. "He's a real piece of work."

"So you knew him?"

"More than I wanted to. He and I never got along too well."

"A week or so after I met him I passed by his house and saw him on the porch talking and laughing with Buddy Richardson."

"Birds of a feather. He used to drive Buddy around when he was off duty. I tried to get him fired over it but the bosses in Washington said no. They started talking about freedom of association and his rights and worrying about a lawsuit, so I just backed off. I did pressure him into retiring when he had maxed out his pension."

"Burr was at the Meredith riot in 1962."

"Yeah? Which side was he on?"

I laughed. "He was supposed to be guarding the Lyceum."

"I bet he would have burned it himself if he could have gotten away with it. He's an old Klukker, if you ask me. I don't know if he was ever an official member, but he sure drank the Kool-Aid."

"Buddy Richardson was in the Grove that night, too."

"That figures. Glad I wasn't. James Meredith was a brave man."

"How long was Burr a driver for Buddy?"

"I don't know. A long time. And I don't know if he got paid or if he just liked hanging out with Richardson. They had the same view on race relations, I know that."

I stood up and shook hands, thanked Oather for the information.

"I don't know what you're working on, Willie Mitchell, but if those two are involved, let me and Billy Shelby know if you need some help. Buddy is dangerous. Boyland Burr looks like the Pillsbury Doughboy, but he's mean."

"It's nothing concrete. Just nosing around a cold case."

"Take my advice. Watch your back."

CHAPTER FIFTY-ONE

Walton called me in the afternoon to tell me how his deposition went with Leopold Whitman. I had been trying to suppress my worry, but the Justice Department investigation constantly nagged at me. I knew I had done nothing improper in grand jury selection and had no reason to discriminate in the selection of foreman. In my twenty-four years as the elected DA, my black grand jurors were just as cooperative and attentive as my white grand jurors. The grand jury is a charging body. It's often criticized as being a rubber stamp for the prosecutor, but structurally, it can do little else. The standard of proof for the grand jury to bind a defendant over for a petit jury trial is minimal.

All the DA has to establish is "probable cause," which can usually be accomplished through the primary investigating law enforcement officer. Hearsay is admissible, so instead of calling the coroner to testify, for example, the investigator can testify to the contents of the coroner's written report. The defendant is not present and no defenses are presented. There's no cross-examination. The prosecutor presents just enough of the facts for the grand jury to decide this question: IS THERE ENOUGH EVIDENCE FOR THE DEFENDANT TO BE TRIED FOR THE CRIME? It's an antiquated process that should be eliminated in all but capital offenses and major felonies. But that's my opinion, not the law in most states.

Walton was circumspect about the details of his statement, but said the questioning was what we had expected. Whitman focused on the process Zelda and I used to ask one of the jurors to serve as foreman. I asked Walton about Whitman's attitude.

"The guy's a worm, Willie Mitchell. He'll always be a whiny, vindictive, undersized worm. When he asks his questions there's an arrogant sneer on his face. He has no concept or appreciation of what we do. He thinks everyone outside the Beltway is a dumbass."

"But other than that you got along fine," I said.

Walton laughed. I asked him if he had talked to Robbie Cedars about the sixty-year-old .38 Chief's Special used in the Butler murder.

"Yes. It's an interesting fact, but not much help. It could have changed hands ten times since it was manufactured."

"What's the plan on re-trying Buddy?" I asked.

"I have no idea. Zelda sent out a notice that Buddy has fifteen days to hire new counsel and have him enroll. Robbie said it will be weeks before they have anything for us on the bombing at Fite's camp."

"Keep me posted," I said and we ended the call.

I had a sinking spell. I turned on the Golf Channel and melted into my easy chair, the routine I followed when I needed a ten-minute nap. For me, nothing matched watching a few holes on an Asian Tour event as a soporific.

I woke up to my phone buzzing in my pocket. I didn't recognize the number. Thinking it was a misdial, I let it go to voice mail. The caller hung up after the third ring, probably realizing he or she had called the wrong number. I put the phone back in my pocket and watched a nineteen-year-old Korean sink a forty-foot putt.

My phone pinged—I had a text.

"PLS CALL THIS NUMBER. IMPORTANT."

I did as requested, wondering who it might be.

"This is Lisa Sanders," she said. "Do you know who I am?"

"Yes. I saw you in the courtroom."

"We need to meet."

"If it's about the case you should call Walton Donaldson."

"No," she said, urgency in her voice. "I need to see you. Alone."

"When?"

"Right now. In the Lafayette County library. I'll be in the audiobook section. Do you know where that is?"

"Sure. I'll be there."

"Don't drive. Walk."

"Why?"

"Humor me. Tell me you'll walk."

"All right. It'll take me twenty-five minutes."

She hung up. I stared at my phone a moment. She didn't sound scared, just very intense. I looked at the time. It was 2:45 p.m. I changed from my boots to an older pair of running shoes, and left the condo.

I walked into the library audiobook section. Lisa was there, looking at the titles. I extended my hand.

"Lisa," I said. "I'm...."

"I know who you are, Willie Mitchell. You were the DA in Yaloquena my entire adult life. You're famous."

"Don't know about that, but nice to meet you. Is your son with you?"

"Robbie's in story time," she said, pointing to a gathering of small kids sitting around a woman reading to them in the corner of the main floor.

She led me to the other side of the audiobook shelves. More privacy from the patrons.

"I want to know what you're willing to do about Buddy," she said.

"He's got fifteen days to get another lawyer, then...."

"You don't get it. He's never going back to trial. He murdered the key witness against him, that worthless Lynn Metzger, and had no problem killing the two deputies along with him."

"We can't prove that yet. The crime lab...."

"But of course you know he did it. He's done things like this all his life. He needs someone out of the way, he contracts out the murder. No one else had anything to do with the bombing. Tell me you believe that. And don't give me any legalese. What's your gut say?"

"You're right," I said after a moment. "I'm sure Buddy did it. But we've got to come up with the evidence to prove it."

Lisa jabbed her finger at me as she spoke. She was one forceful woman. Her dark eyes bored through me like her grandfather's. She wore jeans and a sweater set, her blonde hair straight, parted in the middle. No makeup except for lipstick and a light touch of mascara. She was an outdoorsy type, tanned and pretty, lean and strong-looking.

"Nobody knows what he's really like except me," she said. "Robbie and I are the sole survivors of his reign of terror."

"Why did you insist I walk down here?"

"Because he's got eyes everywhere. There's probably someone watching your truck all the time. I know it sounds crazy, because it is. He's not just mean anymore, he's become a madman. He has plenty of money to pay for what he wants done, and the connections to make it happen. He's the devil, and has nothing to lose. Your legal system can't stop him. You guys play by the rules. Buddy thinks the rules are for suckers. And losers."

I took a deep breath.

"What are you willing to do?" she asked again.

Her eyes burned with intensity, locking on mine.

"He killed my husband," she said. "The one man who changed my life, gave me hope again. Buddy had him put down like a dog all because of his twisted vision of Robbie taking his place someday at High Hope."

For the first time, her voice cracked. She turned away from me for a moment, wiped her eyes and cleared her throat.

"I need your help," she said. "We have to stop him, or he'll kill again."

CHAPTER FIFTY-TWO

The next morning at eleven Jimmy Gray and I walked into the lobby of the First National Bank of Dundee. The big building was old and stately, built when banks were designed to give the impression of strength and integrity. One customer waited at a teller's window in the spacious, high-ceilinged lobby.

"We're here to see Mr. Poleman," Jimmy said to the receptionist.

She pushed a button on her phone and spoke quietly, then pointed to the office in the corner.

"Mr. Poleman said for you to go right in."

Niles Poleman met us at the door. He was our age, maybe slightly older, with dark hair graying at the temples, a pleasant smile and retiring demeanor.

"How've you been, Niles?" Jimmy said.

"Good, Jimmy. Things are quiet around here, just the way I like it. How's your new branch in Oxford doing?"

"Going gangbusters, just like the town."

"Glad there's prosperity somewhere," Niles said. "I don't think we've had a new business startup in Kilbride in the last year."

Jimmy had told me his banker friend Niles Poleman was one of only a handful of men in Dundee County who could keep a confidence, and had first-hand knowledge of the Richardson family. Niles had lived in Kilbride all his life and ran the only bank in the county.

"I'll tell you all I know," he said quietly, "but you have to promise me you won't let on where you got the information. I don't want to cross Buddy."

"We were never here," Jimmy said.

"Buddy had only one child," Niles said. "Buddy Junior. He was a major disappointment to Buddy. The boy never really had a chance. He was nothing like Buddy—reserved and shy. Buddy pushed him to farm, built him his own house on High Hope, tried to get him interested in the cattle operation. Buddy Junior should have been an architect. He was good at designing and building, skills Buddy had no use for."

"How long's Buddy's wife been dead?" Jimmy asked.

"Long time. She died when they were in their fifties. Cancer. He never remarried. I guess he had no need to. After the wife passed away, seems like Buddy got even harder on his boy. Buddy Junior tried to drink himself to death after his Mama died. He finally ended it all, put a shotgun under his throat and pulled the trigger. Did it in the big barn he had designed and built on the place.

"Buddy Junior's wife Ellen had some problems when Lisa was born, female-type problems, and they never had any more, which angered Buddy because he wanted a male heir to run High Hope after he was gone. He kept on Buddy Junior to leave Ellen but he wouldn't.

"Lisa was fifteen when Buddy Junior killed himself. I don't know why Ellen didn't take Lisa and leave after that, but she didn't. Now this next thing, I don't know if it's true or not. Word in the county was that Buddy forced himself on Ellen out there at High Hope, started having his way with her whenever he wanted. Finally she just up and ran away one night, leaving Lisa to fend for herself at High Hope. Buddy raised Lisa after that, moving her into the big house. I read in the *Clarion Ledger* obits that Ellen died last year. I guess she would have been fifty-seven or fifty-eight."

"What a sorry mess," Jimmy said.

"Oh, it gets worse," Niles said. "Buddy hand-picked Lisa's husband, Ernest Bailey from over at Cleveland. Big farming family. Ernest was good-looking and a fast talker, but I figured him for a gold digger from the get go. Lisa said she didn't want kids, but eventually I guess Ernest talked her into it and they had little Robbie about six years ago. Lisa ran Ernest off after Robbie was born, and I guess Buddy was all right with that, because it gave him the opportunity to raise the boy like he wanted at High Hope. He would finally have the kind of male heir he wanted, groom him to take over the place. After Lisa divorced Ernest, Buddy had lawyer Hutchinson re-draw his will.

He's leaving everything he owns to Robbie, lock, stock, and barrel, with Lisa as Trustee."

"Primogeniture," I said. "Only males inherit."

"I guess," Niles said. "I like Lisa a lot, especially since she had the strength to go against Buddy's wishes and marry Carl Sanders last year. She's always been feisty. Lisa was in and out of trouble when she was a teenager and on into college, wild as a March hare. She was still a hellcat around here while she was married to Ernest Bailey. But Carl Sanders turned her around. Carl was a good, hard-working farmer with his own money and land. He loved Lisa and treated her with respect, and adopted Robbie as his own. He moved them over to Yaloquena to his farm and I think they were doing real well as a family until Buddy had Carl shot to death on his own place."

"What is Buddy worth?" Jimmy asked. "You have any idea?"

"He doesn't bank with me except for a farm account they use to pay bills. I would guess his net worth is in the tens of millions, not counting High Hope and his other land. That video poker truck stop was a gold mine and he rigged his books so he didn't pay tax on a lot of it. Friend of mine told me Buddy netted three million the first six months he was open, and that was after everything was paid for."

"Thank you for this background on the family," I said.

"Well," Niles said, "you got your hands full, Willie Mitchell, if you're going to try to send Buddy to prison. He's a resourceful man, and he's bankrolled a lot of these meth cooks in the hills around here, and some of them just as soon shoot you as look at you.

"And something else, no matter what crookedness he's into, somehow there's women involved. He's the most licentious man I've ever seen; been a hound all his adult life, before his wife died and after. I could tell you some stories about Buddy and women that would curl your hair. He's cut a wide swath, and never cared who he hurt along the way."

"Damn," I said in Jimmy's Navigator as we drove back to Oxford. "Buddy is a piece of work."

"A real family man. What are you going to do?"

"That's what Lisa kept asking me at the library. Only she said 'willing to do? What was I willing to do'?"

"Well?"

"I don't know. She gave me her number. A pre-paid cell. She said to call her when I knew the answer."

CHAPTER FIFTY-THREE

Back in Oxford after meeting with Dundee County banker Niles Poleman, I waited until 4:30 that afternoon to knock on Cissy Breedlove's door. I wanted to surprise her, so I didn't call ahead. I knocked. Knocked again, then a third time. No answer. I drove on the side street and saw her empty garage on the back of the house. In a window above the garage on the back of the townhome, I saw the curtain move.

I drove through the Square to Boyland Burr's house on South 11th, parked on Hayes and walked up on the porch. I knocked on the door. I peered through a window on the porch and saw the front room cleared of all the newspapers, but devoid of furniture. I could see his battered La-Z-Boy in the next room, but no Boyland luxuriating in it.

Back at the condo, I fixed VTs for Susan and me. She asked me what the Kilbride banker said, and I related the Richardson family's sordid history. I told her about going to see Cissy Breedlove and Boyland Burr and finding neither of them home.

"I hardly slept last night," Susan said, "thinking about your meeting at the library with the Richardson woman."

"Lisa."

"Lisa. Walking there so your truck wouldn't be followed, meeting her in the stacks and whispering—you do realize you're not DA anymore, don't you?"

"I know."

"And you know Buddy Richardson is capable of doing anything. He killed three men last week, or had them killed. You don't think he'd do the same to you? He wouldn't think twice."

"Somebody's got to do something."

"The Marshal gave you good advice. Get Billy Shelby and the FBI involved. They ought to be doing this, not you."

"Lisa was right when she said the legal system can't stop Buddy. He's shown that time and time again."

"When did you decide to become a vigilante? This is so not like you."

I patched our drinks in the kitchen. I tried to explain to Susan what I didn't quite understand myself.

"When Lisa asked me what I was willing to do, it jarred me. Look at what Buddy did to postpone his trial, all perfectly within the rules, orchestrated by a very capable, high-priced lawyer."

"Faking a stroke is not within the rules."

"But the way he's played it, there's nothing Walton or Zelda can do. Dr. Grillette is not one of Buddy's henchmen, but he's bound by the rules of his profession and the threat of litigation, which is always there. If he says Buddy did not have a stroke and he has one later, his reputation, maybe his license, is on the line. And Richardson knows all of this. He's gaming the system."

"Even if all that is true," Susan said, raising her voice slightly, "why do you have to be the one to take him on? Why is it your job?"

I didn't have a good answer because I didn't fully understand it myself. My phone buzzed and a number came up. It took a second for me to realize it was Lisa Richardson's burner phone. I answered and Lisa started a monologue, telling me what she had done that morning. She wasn't asking my opinion, merely telling me what she was doing. She ended the call abruptly.

"Lisa," I said to Susan. "She's moved back into High Hope with her son."

"Why on earth?"

"She said she's going to be my eyes and ears out there. Said she'll call when she can to report what Buddy's doing, who he's meeting with."

Susan didn't get angry often, but Lisa's call set her off.

"You are going to get yourself killed," she said, tears filling her eyes. "You don't even know this woman. How do you know she's not working with Buddy to set you up? You always say the apple doesn't fall far from the tree."

She walked out of the room and quickly up the stairs. I picked up the remote and turned on the evening news. I listened to the anchor relate the day's events, but none of it registered. It was just background noise.

I didn't know the complete answer to Lisa's question about what I was willing to do. But I did have a partial answer—if she had the guts to move back in with her murderous grandfather, the least I could do was take her calls.

CHAPTER FIFTY-FOUR

Susan did not speak to me the rest of the evening, and I didn't sleep because of it. We had promised each other decades ago not to go to bed angry with one another, but that Tuesday night she broke the rule. I didn't blame her for being upset with me.

Walton had called me earlier in the evening, after Susan stomped up the stairs. He said Leopold Whitman had taken sworn statements from Circuit Clerk Winston Moore and Deputy Clerk Eddie Bordelon Monday afternoon, and spent Tuesday talking to a random selection of grand jurors who served during my years as District Attorney. Walton said that Whitman came by his office in the courthouse late in the afternoon Tuesday to say he was flying back to D.C. from Jackson that night but would be back in touch soon.

I was fed up with tossing and turning and got out of bed at four a.m. I crept downstairs in the darkness, trying not to wake Susan. At the bottom of the steps, before I turned on the hood light over the stove, I thought I heard something in my garage. I stood without moving for a minute or so in the darkness. I heard a bump at the back door, like someone pushing it against the door jamb.

I tiptoed into my office, opened my top desk drawer, and pulled out my .45 caliber pistol. I chambered a round as quietly as I could and walked through the kitchen down the hallway to the back door. I switched the pistol to my left hand, and placed my left index finger on the light switch for the garage. With my right hand, I felt for the dead bolt and the door knob. I kept my right hand on the dead bolt, my left on the light switch, and took a deep breath.

I flipped the light switch and the dead bolt at the same time, twisted the door knob and opened the door, quickly squatting and shifting my pistol to my right hand. No one in front of me, or between my truck and Susan's Lexus, but the automatic garage door was open. I tried to remember.

Had I left it open? I always closed both bays as part of my nightly routine, but I had no specific recollection of doing the night before. I stood in the doorway for a moment, listening for any movement.

After a while, I held my pistol in front of me with both hands, ready to fire. I walked around the Lexus first, then my truck. The garage was clear. I stole a glance into the lighted concrete driveway behind the condos that lead to South 8th, but no one was there. I closed the garage door behind my truck and walked to the back door. It was slightly ajar. With my gun in my right hand, I noticed something stuck on the doorknob. At first I thought it was a big wad of chewing gum. On closer inspection, it looked like an orange ball of Silly Putty the size of a large marble.

I froze when I realized what it was. I backed away without touching it, reopened the garage door and walked out onto the concrete driveway in my pajamas, my gun ready. I was a sitting duck in the light, but I had no choice. I made it around to University Avenue and opened our front gate. I felt under a brick ledge and removed our secret key, opened the front door and called Oxford Police Chief Mike Columbus on his cell.

I apologized for waking him and told him I was pretty sure someone had placed a ball of Semtex on my back door knob.

Three patrol units were at my condo in ten minutes and Chief Columbus arrived a few minutes later with a detective he said had some training with his military bomb unit. I showed the detective to the back door. He looked at the orange wad a moment, then sniffed it.

"It's Semtex all right," he said, "but there's no detonator fuse or wiring. It's harmless without some kind of mechanism to set it off. You want me to remove it?"

"No," I said. "Let's call the crime lab. The technicians who examined the explosion that killed the witness and the two deputies last week can compare this to the explosive residue they picked up at the fishing camp. Maybe they can pull a print off it."

I told the Chief I would call Robbie Cedars at the State Crime Lab and ask him to send up a man or two to take possession of the Semtex. Chief Columbus assigned two of his men to stay at the condo to wait for the crime lab technicians.

I walked inside and up the stairs. Susan was sitting on the edge of our bed facing the wall. She had been downstairs earlier when the patrol cars arrived. I told her what was going on. On the floor was her favorite suitcase, partially packed with clothes and her makeup kit.

"I'm going to my parents' home until this is over," she said angrily, still staring at the wall, refusing to look at me. "Ask Jimmy Gray to call me and let me know when they kill you."

CHAPTER FIFTY-FIVE

It wasn't the first time Susan left me. But this time was different. She was angry. When she headed west eight years ago, she was disconsolate, telling me she needed time alone. She went first to her parents' home in Louisiana, then set off on a journey of "self-discovery" that lasted three years. Three very bad years for me.

We spoke regularly during those years. She would call to tell me she was safe and making progress. She said she still loved me. Susan stayed in close contact with our two sons during her absence and later told me that her "empty nest" in Sunshine accounted for some of her unhappiness. But the main source of her depression was our relationship and her life.

I say depression, but Susan maintained it wasn't the clinical sort that is cured by SSRIs and counseling. She said it was more of a dissatisfaction with herself and what she had done with her life, a mid-life *ennui*. When I would point out that her departure happened to coincide with the onset of menopause, she would acknowledge the fact but deny it as a cause. During her time away, she remained faithful to our marriage. I wish I could say the same for me.

I was drinking too much. Way too much. I always attributed her leaving in part to my alcohol consumption and my obsessive wallowing in self-examination of my career as a small town, small-time lawyer and politician. In my mind, I could have been a contender, but I chose to stay in Yaloquena County. I probably told Susan a thousand times that I set my career goals too low. She got tired of hearing it, I'm sure.

In retrospect, I was an easy target for Mary Margaret Anderson, a married woman with a long-term plan to eliminate her wealthy husband and use me as an insurance policy against the legal ramifications of her plot. Susan finally came home and helped rescue me from myself. The last five years had been the happiest in our marriage. We had weathered the Mary Margaret disaster, an attempt on my life that left me with seizures and pain, a slew of high-profile murder cases, a tumultuous re-election campaign, and last year's move to Oxford.

That Wednesday morning in early May, five hours after I discovered the Semtex globule on our back door, Susan left for Louisiana in her Lexus. She had cooled down a bit, but was still upset with me for getting involved so deeply in the pursuit of Buddy Richardson. I admitted to her it was a mistake, but that I was so far into it I could not back off. I could not let Buddy Richardson get away with the murders. It had become personal.

Like James Butler's murder on the road to my duck camp, the Semtex was intended to be a warning. But for me, it was more of a wake-up call. I had assumed Buddy Richardson had brought in professionals from out of state to kill Metzger. Now it looked like whoever planted the Semtex bomb at the fishing camp might still be in Oxford.

The crime lab crew and the OPD detectives had come and gone. I spent an hour in my office on the phone with Jimmy Gray, Lee Jones, and Walton. I also spoke to my son Scott. I wanted them to know the stakes had been raised, and it was time to force the action—go on offense for a change.

I sent a text to Lisa asking her to call me when she could. I had to get a better handle on what she could do from High Hope to help bring down her grandfather. Susan was right. I did not know Lisa. She might have been playing me just as Buddy had. But I had a gut feeling Lisa was exactly as she appeared to be that day in the library—a forceful woman angry at the man who murdered her husband, willing to risk her own safety to help bring him down.

By mid-afternoon I hadn't heard from Lisa. Instead, I received a call from my son Scott and his boss Skeeter Sumrall. They were on a speaker phone in the Senator's office.

"We've gotten to the bottom of this grand jury thing," Skeeter said.

"It's not what we suspected," Scott said. "It turns out the pressure for the Justice Department to target you did not come from Whitman after all."

"I'm listening," I said.

"Our friend Patrick Dunwoody called that little peckerwood Whitman into his office on some administrative matter yesterday morning," Skeeter said. "After they finished discussing it, Patrick started probing for information about Whitman's focus on you. Whitman told him the department had collected the grand jury selection data over a year ago and didn't see any smoking guns in any of the Mississippi counties they looked at."

"So what happened to change their mind?" I asked.

"Senator Chad Breedlove happened," Scott said.

"Whitman told Dunwoody that it was Breedlove who initiated the meeting in Breedlove's office. During the meeting, Breedlove specifically asked Whitman about Yaloquena County's data. Whitman said the Senator told him that his office had some complaints from minorities in Yaloquena about discrimination in grand jury foreman selection. Breedlove said the complainants specifically mentioned you and said you had a method of making sure no blacks served as foreman on your grand juries. That it was intentional."

"That's bullshit," I said.

"We know it is," Skeeter said. "After Dunwoody called us to fill us in on what Whitman told him, I made a surprise visit to the junior Senator's office. I bluffed my way past his staffers and went right into his inner sanctum. By the way, the son-of-a-bitch was reading *Sports Illustrated* when I barged in on him. I asked him point blank why he was pressuring the Justice Department to proceed against you on what we all know is a bunch of baloney."

"What did he say?"

"He stuck by his story about some constituents complaining. I asked who they were and he said he had to protect their privacy, some bullshit about the Whistleblower Act. I've played enough poker to know when someone's claiming they got something when they don't. Breedlove knew he was caught red-handed. He never admitted it, and never answered my question when I asked him what he had against you. But he knows we're on to him now, so I did some good anyway."

"Did Dunwoody say what effect this would have on the case against me?"

"The news isn't as good on that front," Scott said. "Mr. Dunwoody said once these things get started they take on a life of their own. He said he was going to talk to Whitman's supervisor and try to slow the process down, see if they won't take another look at it. He said he couldn't promise anything."

"Some of these government agencies," Skeeter said, "when they get pressure from a Senator they fold like a cheap suit. It's all about protecting their funding, you know. But I think Dunwoody can do us some good now that he knows that Senator Breedlove is the source of the pressure on the Justice Department."

I thanked Skeeter and Scott and opened my computer files on the Fratelli investigation. I stared at the monitor wondering why Cissy Summers Breedlove would have her son sic the Justice Department on me.

I left a message on Eleanor Bernstein's cell phone, asking her to call me. I didn't know if she could do anything to help me with the Justice Department at this point, but it couldn't hurt to ask.

Because the physical threat to me was more pressing than the Justice Department's attack on my professional and financial well-being, I decided I needed to learn a lot more in a hurry about the Breedloves. Given the fast-moving nature of the Buddy Richardson mess I was in, I didn't have much time to dig into the background of the Breedlove family. But since I knew a little bit about elections and Mississippi politics, I knew the best way to do it.

CHAPTER FIFTY-SIX

State Senator Jeffrey Simmons said in our phone conversation that he'd be glad to meet with me after five. It was only a two-hour drive from Oxford to his office in Wyattville, so I left the condo and drove east on Highway 6.

I called Jimmy Gray on the drive and related what Senator Sumrall and Scott had said about Chad Breedlove being the impetus for the Justice Department investigation. I told him I was headed to see State Senator Simmons to talk to him about the Breedloves. Jimmy knew Simmons. He said the Senator had a thriving private law practice in a renovated brick building near the Chickawamba County Courthouse on the main drag downtown.

It was after six when I walked in the front door of the building. The receptionist was gone, but a young attorney walking past the front desk saw me and escorted me into Jeffrey Simmons's private office. Simmons was about fifty, with short, gray hair and a quick smile. His only memorable feature was a pair of prominent ears.

"You mind my asking why you're looking for information on Cissy Breedlove?" the Senator asked.

"I guess I must be crossways with them," I said, "because Senator Breedlove has asked the Justice Department to look into some of my office's practices when I was District Attorney in Yaloquena. I wanted to learn something about how the Breedloves operate, and I figured the last candidate to lose to Cissy before she retired would have the opposition research from the campaign still relatively fresh in his mind."

"I'll tell you what I know, but I'd appreciate your keeping it confidential. I tangled with them one time and I don't want to ever do it again."

"Was the election close?"

"It was at first, then they pulled out to a big lead halfway through. I closed the gap pretty good but she held on. Cissy ended up with fifty-five percent. She ran strong around Tupelo, where she and her husband are from, and I couldn't overcome it in the other counties."

"You must have run a good campaign. It's hard to get forty-five percent against an incumbent unless there's been a scandal of some kind."

"I kept it clean, because I had that in the back of my mind. I knew it was probably going to be her last term. Besides, it's hard to make anyone believe anything bad about a former Miss Mississippi."

"And third-runner-up Miss America."

"But she didn't keep it clean," Simmons said. "Or at least her campaign staff and her husband didn't. They put out some flyers in the black sections saying I would set back civil rights gains for women and blacks, and some other vague crap like that. Stuff you can rebut but it only brings more attention to the original slander."

"How was she on the stump?" I asked.

"She's a beautiful woman, as you know, and she was always very lady-like in her speeches. But her platform was full of generalizations, nothing specific about what she had done in Jackson and why they ought to return her to office. I had some very specific proposals, but she would not engage me on them. She would never agree to a debate."

"Typical incumbent strategy. Don't give free exposure to the challenger."

"Yeah, and it worked. I never had a problem with Cissy during the race, but that husband of hers, he was the king of dirty tricks."

"What kind?"

"Juvenile stuff. Stealing our yard signs. Grafitti on our billboards. They did some robo-calling at three in the morning, waking people up and telling them they were calling for my campaign. Shit like that."

"There are some people that think she might have been governor if Gavin had been a more presentable husband."

"Don't count me in that camp," Simmons said. "She's not smart enough. She's plenty ambitious and highly competitive, but she's not quick enough on her feet and couldn't hide from a debate like she did against me if she ran for governor. She became a senator because of her popularity as a beauty queen, and her looks and personality. And because her husband was willing to do anything to win. I'm sorry they're coming after you, because they are a formidable team. If it hadn't been for Gavin getting sick, they'd have beaten me a lot worse."

"What kind of sickness?"

"Cancer," Simmons said. "He had a radical prostatectomy in the middle of the campaign, put him out for weeks."

"I didn't know that," I said.

"A urologist friend of mine who supported me in the race found out through the hospital grapevine that they removed everything—the entire gland, nerves, and surrounding tissue. Then he got some kind of infection down there after the election, had to have more surgery. My doctor friend had a good source for information on Gavin. Whatever infections or surgeries he had, I don't know, but my friend said Gavin had crossed Dead Pecker Creek, if you know what I mean. None of the ED pills, Viagra, Cialis, and the like, would work for him. Neither would any kind of prosthetic because of some kind of damage to his penis." Simmons shuddered. "Now don't get me wrong, I hate Gavin Breedlove. He's a no-good s.o.b. But I wouldn't wish that on any man, even him."

"That's pretty bad all right. Do you know how the two of them got together in the first place?"

"They're both from around Tupelo. Gavin was a few years older. They say he was always in love with her. When he came back from Vietnam he enrolled in Ole Miss on the G.I. bill just to be in the same town with her."

"Vietnam? When was he there?"

"He was among the first military people the U.S. sent over there. The government said they weren't soldiers, just "advisors," but the truth was they were there to train the South Vietnamese army and fight alongside them. A lot of the advisors had special forces training. I heard Gavin did for sure. They say he's always been a tough bastard, hurt you bad in a fight."

I thanked Senator Simmons and reaffirmed that I would keep our conversation private. I asked him to do the same. I let myself out and stood a moment on the sidewalk, checking out downtown Wyattville. It was six-thirty and the place was deserted.

Driving back to Oxford, I remembered James Butler in his kitchen saying Gavin was enrolled at Ole Miss the summer before the riot, adding he was "fresh out of the military." But it never crossed my mind that Gavin had been a specially trained "advisor" in Vietnam. Fifty-four years later, Gavin was thin, wiry, and slightly stooped, but I learned long ago not to judge a book by its cover.

CHAPTER FIFTY-SEVEN

It was dark when I pulled into Oxford. I had talked to Susan on the ride home. She made it safely to the Woodforks' home near Mansfield in DeSoto Parish, and her anger had transitioned to fear for my safety. I assured her I was being careful, and I was not going to put myself in harm's way. Not intentionally, anyway.

Before going home to the condo I drove past two places, the Breedlove townhome and Boyland Burr's house. Neither showed any sign of someone there. No lights on at Boyland Burr's house on South 11th. At the Breedloves, a central hall light burned, the light you would leave on to give the impression someone was home.

When I arrived on University Avenue, I drove slowly past the front of the condo. I did the same on South 8th. Everything looked normal, but I had my .45 resting in my lap. I stopped on the floodlit concrete drive behind the condo and used the remote to open both bays of the garage. Nothing. I moved slowly into the garage, glancing at my rear view and side mirrors to make certain no one followed me in. My pistol in hand, I closed the garage doors and waited a moment.

I flipped the inside light switch and unlocked the back door. I pushed it open and stared inside. I saw no one and heard nothing. I locked the back door behind me and moved from room to room, checking every conceivable hiding place. I walked up the steps to our bedroom, locked the door behind me, breathed a sigh of relief, and dressed for bed.

I picked up *Blood Meridian,* removed my bookmark and began reading. In the middle of the first paragraph, my mind drifted from the Mexican border back to the Breedloves. After ten minutes, I grabbed my .45 Springfield and walked quietly down the stairs, checked the front and back doors again, then booted up my computer in my office. I went over my notes, adding the information about the Breedloves from Senator Jeffrey Simmons in Wyattville.

I checked my phone. Still no response from Lisa at High Hope. I turned off the computer, picked up my pistol, checked the doors again and locked myself in my bedroom.

I had just gotten back into bed when my cell phone buzzed. Eleanor Bernstein's name came up on the screen.

"Hello, Eleanor."

"Hi, Willie Mitchell. I got your message. Is it too late to talk?"

"No, not at all. I appreciate your calling back."

"I've checked with people in the local office. No one here knows anything about the investigation into grand jury foreman selection in Sunshine. Apparently it's all being handled out of D.C."

"Leopold Whitman was in Sunshine two days ago."

"This past Monday?"

"Yes. He took sworn statements from Walton, Winston, and Eddie. Court reporter and everything. Do you remember him?"

"Sure I do. He was a thorn in your side when he was the U.S. Attorney in the Jackson office. You and he fought over jurisdiction in the drug cartel case involving El Moro."

"Right. He's head of OIG inside Justice. Senator Chad Breedlove called him in for a meeting at the Senate Office Building and said his office had gotten wind of some complaints about my handling of the grand juries."

"That is such baloney," she said. "This whole thing is such a waste of time and money."

"I agree."

"I wish I could do something to help, Willie Mitchell, but I've been with Justice less than two years and I don't know anyone in Washington."

"I know, Eleanor. I don't think there's anything you can do from the Oxford office to help. And it has to be by the book, all above board."

"Certainly. I understood that from the beginning."

"I don't want you to do anything that would jeopardize your position."

"I'll keep my ear to the ground," she said, "and if I hear anything, and can talk to you about it without violating any office policies, I'll call you."

"Thanks, Eleanor. Good night."

I dozed off after ten minutes with *Blood Meridian*. The next morning I slept later than usual, and ran for almost an hour, paying more attention than usual to cars approaching me from any direction. I tried to come up with a game plan for the day. In the pursuit of Buddy Richardson, I planned to call Walton to see if the crime lab investigators had come up with anything on the bombing. Then I'd send another text to Lisa to find out what was going on at High Hope. I decided I was more productive concentrating on one investigation at a time.

Russell Fratelli's case would have to take a back seat. As soon as I had time, I planned on confronting the Breedloves to find out why the United States Senator would pressure the Justice Department to come after me. I was certain that Cissy and Gavin put their son up to it to divert me from asking more questions about Russell Fratelli. From my point of view, it was an encouraging development. There must be something there if the Breedloves were trying to put a road block in my way.

Back from the run, I checked my phone. Lisa had finally responded. MEET ME CYPRESS BEND PARK. NOON. TAKE BACK ROAD, HIGHWAY 321. I showered and dressed as quickly as possible, filled a Styrofoam cup with fresh coffee from my Keurig, and drove west. I had looked at the park on Google Earth and figured out the best way to get there, jotting down the numbers of the state and county roads I had to take.

I headed south on I-55 at Batesville and drove thirty minutes before exiting west. The state highway meandered through the Yalobusha River watershed. At times borrow pits lined both sides of the built-up road bed. I glanced at the notes I made. Highway 321 did not get me all the way to the park, so I was going to have to take County Road 112 to get to it. I had never been to Cypress Bend Park, and Lisa did not say where we were to meet once I got there. I assumed it was one of the small state parks in or on the edge of the Delta with wooden walkways through a primitive cypress swamp. Several such parks were spread throughout the Delta for tourists. If Cypress Bend were like the others, it had one small parking area and not a single tourist or local in the entire facility.

I phoned Jimmy Gray and left him a message telling him what I was doing. I looked at the phone and noticed I had lost service. I hoped the message got through, but couldn't be sure. Jimmy got irritated with me when I didn't keep him up to speed.

I thought these nature parks were a waste of tax money. Locals lived among cypress brakes and sloughs, so they didn't visit. They could see the same thing in bayous in their back yards or neighborhoods. The parks were remote and served by highways too small to comfortably accommodate large tourist buses, which needed a lot of room to turn around. The cypress brake parks were isolated and unattended, requiring very little cost to maintain. The initial outlay to construct the gravel parking lots and the wooden walkways was negligible. Thereafter the parks were on their own, and mostly vacant.

I turned at the Cypress Bend Park sign on County Road 112. Looking at Google Earth, I had estimated the distance at only a couple of miles. The road was paved for a mile, then turned to gravel. As I neared the park entrance, I groaned when I saw a bulldozer and front-end loader blocking the road. I slowed to a crawl and stopped ten feet from a large road worker in a khaki uniform shirt and pants holding a STOP sign. He had his back to me and never turned around. With his free hand he used a large, red rag to wipe sweat from his forehead. I put the truck in neutral and stepped out to ask him if I could get by. The man didn't look at me. He said something to the bulldozer operator.

"Excuse me, sir," I said to the big man's back, "I'm wondering if you fellows would pull off the road long enough for me to get into the park."

The road worker turned around to face me, the stop sign in one hand, a long-barreled revolver in the other. He pointed the pistol at my chest.

"Well, hello, Willie Mitchell," Boyland Burr said. "What are the chances of running into you out here?"

CHAPTER FIFTY-EIGHT

I would like to report that I disarmed Boyland Burr with a dramatic, lightning-fast defensive move, or that I drew my pistol and shot the gun out of his hand, but that's not what happened. My .45 was safely on the seat in the truck, and as I raised my hands, my aura sequence began. With both hands in the air, I knelt down on the gravel road. Keeping my hands raised, I moved clumsily to a sitting position, and finally on my back. Then I lost consciousness. I do remember the last thing Boyland said.

"Well, lookie here, Mr. Breedlove. This is going to be easier than we thought."

When I came to, I was by myself in the back seat of the extended cab of a large truck, my hands zip-tied behind my back, my feet shackled with a pair of old-fashioned, heavy steel cuffs. I was a bit dizzy, but managed to sit up in time to see Gavin Breedlove on the bulldozer push my F-150 off the road and into the roadside borrow pit. To my surprise, the water in the pit was deep. I watched my truck float awhile, then gradually sink below the surface. I felt a twinge of sadness—it had been a really good truck. As the black water closed over it, large bubbles surfaced, then subsided, leaving no visible trace. It was if my truck and I had never been at Cypress Bend Park.

"We threw your phone in there, too," Boyland said when he opened the door. "But I kept your pistol as a souvenir," he said, admiring my well-oiled .45 caliber Springfield 1911, holding it up and turning it for me to see. "Soon as we get the equipment loaded we'll be on our way."

I turned around as far as my bindings would allow. Out of the rear window I saw Gavin Breedlove drive the bulldozer up steel ramps onto the long flatbed trailer hooked to the big truck. The front-end loader was already on the trailer. A few minutes later, Gavin climbed into the driver's seat and Boyland wedged his big frame into the passenger seat in front of me.

"Thank you for being so accommodating back there," Boyland said. "Mr. Buddy told us you had some kind of problem with your brain."

"Where are you taking me?" I asked.

"Where do you think?" Boyland said, his Andy Devine voice cracking.

"I suspect we're going to High Hope," I said. "Buddy Richardson wants to get in on the fun."

"I told you he was smart," Boyland said to Gavin.

"Shut up," Breedlove growled as he drove. "Both of you."

I had plenty of time to observe Gavin in the silence of the forty-five minute trip. He was nothing like he appeared to be the first time I saw him. Working in the small yard behind their townhouse while Cissy and I had coffee, he was concentrating on fertilizing the beds, and seemed submissive, perhaps atoning for being the alcoholic he was reputed to be. But my initial observation of him at his home was tainted by rumors I had heard, and way off base.

The Gavin Breedlove driving the truck was an intense, dominant presence, in total control of the situation. Ten minutes into the trip, Boyland opened his mouth to ask a question. Gavin turned and snarled, and Boyland shut up midway through the question. Breedlove was not a big man, but he had a big presence. Incredibly forceful and overtly venomous.

Breedlove turned off the county road onto a private gravel drive. He waited while Boyland waddled out of the truck to open the aluminum gate and lock it back after he drove through. I guessed this was the rear entrance to High Hope. A stylized HH in wrought iron was affixed to the gate. The drive bisected a long hill in front of us. Cattle munched grass on either side of the gravel road, which was dotted with large black, layered discs of manure. The cattle were black and, I think, of the Simmental breed. I was not about to ask.

The top of the long hill provided a panoramic view of High Hope. I had to admire what I saw spread before me— thousands of acres of green, rolling hills with a scattering of oak trees left throughout to provide shade for the herd in the summer heat. The black cattle had the run of the place, except for about twenty fenced acres around the plantation home on the next rise. High Hope was a working farm, with two large barns down the hill from the house outside the fence. Buddy had built a huge metal equipment shed consisting of a metal roof supported by steel beams but no walls, housing tractors, hay balers, and other heavy equipment needed to run a place of this size. I figured it was where Breedlove would drop off the bulldozer, front-end loader, cab and trailer after he dumped me off at the big house.

I cannot say I wasn't scared, but my curiosity crowded out some of the fear. What in the hell did Buddy think he was doing? I was no longer a public official, but his rubbing me out would generate a good bit of interest. Then I remembered he didn't hesitate to kill two deputies with Lynn Metzger. And I recalled postulating that at his age, maybe Buddy felt he had nothing to lose. If my speculation were right, I would not come out of this alive.

We stopped in front of the house, a Louisiana-style raised Acadian Colonial house with a wide gallery around the front and sides. It didn't appear to be very old, and was the only house of its style I had seen in north Mississippi. Since he owed much of his fortune to a Louisiana video poker truck stop, the architecture was entirely appropriate. Breedlove ordered Boyland to check my zip tie and my shackles, and the two of them went inside.

Alone in the back seat of the truck, I thought about Lisa Richardson Sanders. If she had set this up, she was a great actress, selling me at the library on her need to avenge her husband's death and protect her son Robbie. But, she had Buddy's DNA, so I guess I shouldn't have been surprised at the betrayal. I was disappointed in myself for being so gullible. Susan had been right. I hardly knew the woman.

I looked up at the two dormers on the high-pitched roof. The main floor of the wooden house was raised ten feet on brick pillars. The central portion of the ground floor was bricked in, surrounded by open space among brick pillars. The open area at ground level matched the wrap-around porch on the main floor. A wooden staircase in the front, twenty feet wide, with steps and handrail painted battleship gray and the bannisters and risers white, made for a dramatic entrance to the main floor.

Gavin Breedlove and Boyland Burr walked out of French doors on the ground level toward the truck. Boyland carried a large, black cloth of some kind. As Breedlove opened the back door, I saw Buddy standing at the top of the stairs on his porch, looking down on the festivities.

"We can do this the easy way," Breedlove said, "or you can resist and go the hard way. It's up to you."

"What do you want me to do?" I asked.

"The Marshall's going to open the door on the other side, and we're going to spread this out and wrap you up in it. Then we're going to carry you inside the house. If you cooperate, you won't get hurt."

"Okay," I said, scooting up on the seat while they spread the black blanket.

I lay down on the seat in the blanket. They wrapped it around me. Breedlove pulled me out the door feet first. Boyland caught me by the shoulders before my head hit the ground. They carried me for about fifteen seconds, then up the steps. I heard a wooden door open, then close behind me. They carried me inside for another ten seconds, then stopped. I heard a motor or some kind of machine engage. Seconds later, they carried me a few steps further. I felt the floor drop a bit, then heard the motor start up again. When I felt movement, it confirmed what I guessed moments before. I was in an elevator. A slow elevator.

It stopped after about twenty seconds. I heard the door open and felt myself being carried out. Ten seconds later, I heard the sound of creaking metal in need of oil. They let go of me and my back hit the floor first, absorbing most of the force. They removed my shackles and the zip tie. I remained motionless and heard metal striking metal. A moment later, someone peeled back the black blanket from my face.

CHAPTER FIFTY-NINE

Lisa Richardson's face loomed above me.

"Sorry," she said. "Buddy sent you the text. He knew about our meeting at the library."

I looked around. It was a jail cell of some kind. I had put plenty of people in a room like this, but it was a first for me. Three walls surrounding us were brick, the fourth made of heavy steel bars with a door just like the Yaloquena jail. The floor was concrete. A metal toilet and sink graced one corner. Bunk beds were pushed against a wall, two folding metal chairs along the other. I unfolded the chairs for us. I told her what happened at Cypress Bend Park.

"This is nice," I said, admiring the cell. "How did Buddy find out about the meeting at the library?"

"I have no idea. Had me followed, I guess. It turns out he didn't quite believe that I had come to my senses so quickly when I told him I was returning to High Hope with Robbie to live with him. As soon as we got settled in Tuesday, Buddy put Robbie on the new mini four-wheeler he bought him. While Robbie was out riding the hills, Buddy and Boyland put me in here, took my phone. He's always been one step ahead of me."

"Where's Robbie?"

"He's in six-year-old heaven, either on his four-wheeler or riding the horse Buddy gave him. They've been shooting Robbie's new .22 rifle Buddy had custom made for him."

"How do you know all this?"

"Buddy comes down to check on me. He tells me what a good time they're having. He said he told Robbie I had gone to Jackson to visit friends."

"What's he got planned for us?" I asked as I rubbed my wrists where the zip tie had cut into them.

"I have no idea," she said. "He's been down here high as a kite a couple of times. I hear people walking above us on the main floor. I don't know how many people are up there."

"Boyland Burr and Gavin Breedlove for sure," I said. "You know them?"

"Been knowing Boyland since I was a little girl. He's got an I.Q. of about fifty, does anything Buddy asks. He thinks Buddy's a rock star; always looked up to him for some reason. Follows him around like a puppy. Sometimes Buddy is downright mean to him, but it doesn't seem to bother him. He'll do whatever Buddy tells him."

"What about Gavin Breedlove?"

"I don't really know him. He scares me, though. He was here Tuesday when Robbie and I moved in. Helped carry some things. His wife's with him, too. Buddy's girl friend."

"A tall woman? Dark hair, really pretty?"

"Cissy," Lisa said. "She was here Tuesday and Buddy told me last night she and Gavin are staying a while. He was wired up on crank, bragging about how she was a Miss America and she couldn't get enough of him. Said he had been seeing her for years."

"And Gavin knows?"

"He'd have to unless he's deaf and blind. Buddy said Gavin's done odd jobs for him going back a long way. Says Gavin is a very resourceful fellow. Knows how to do a lot of things."

"Like handle explosives," I said.

"You think he killed Metzger and the deputies for Buddy?"

"Breedlove was in South Vietnam before Americans knew we were over there. He was what our government called a military advisor. They were actually well-trained operatives who fought alongside the ARVN against the North Vietnamese before we had a large presence in the country. I'm sure he knows tactics, weapons, demolition, anything to do with fighting a war."

"I never knew."

"How does Buddy think he's going to get away with all this?"

"I don't know. He's no longer in his right mind."

"You've spent two nights down here?"

"Sure have."

"Does anyone know you're here?"

"Not that I know of. What about you?"

"I'm not sure," I said. "I made a call but not certain it went through."

"What time is it?" she asked. "No natural light gets in here."

"I got to the park at noon. I guess it's about two." I paused, looking at the light bulb in the ceiling. "Did you know this cell was down here?"

"No. This house is only a few years old. He tore down the old house, the one I grew up in. Tore down the barn where my Daddy killed himself. Tore down the house where my parents lived, and my first husband and I lived. He stayed in a trailer on the place while this house was under construction. He got some jake-leg rednecks to build it. It looks all right from the outside, but it's real shoddy construction."

"Why the elevator?"

"Buddy said it was for when he got old and couldn't climb the stairs anymore."

"Old?" I said. "He had to be eighty-one or two when he started building this place."

"He thinks he's going to live forever," Lisa said. "Last night he sat in a rocking chair outside this cell and told me all about his big plans for Robbie. It's like he's obsessed with him. His pupils were wide open—made his eyes look solid black. Like a shark. I heard people stomping around upstairs all night."

"Is it only Buddy doing the crystal meth? Anyone else?"

"I have no idea."

I looked at the brick walls and the steel door, then eyed the bunk beds.

"You in the upper or lower?" I asked.

CHAPTER SIXTY

It was a very long afternoon. I don't want to go into the details of the privacy issue in connection with the bare toilet in the corner. It's enough to say Lisa and I worked out the least embarrassing system we could. I asked her questions about growing up around Buddy. She wanted to know about my family and what it was like being District Attorney. It's difficult to describe the atmosphere in our cell—tension and fear mitigated by boredom.

I told Lisa I didn't think Buddy would harm his own flesh and blood. On the other hand, I felt Buddy was so far into his crime spree that he would have no problem putting an end to me. Lisa said Buddy's focus was Robbie, and anything or anyone who stood in his way was in jeopardy. She said we were both in the expendable category.

Lisa added an observation that chilled my bones. She said Buddy had killed or caused the death of everyone she ever loved, except for Robbie, and that she always expected Buddy would come for her at some point if she ever stood between him and her son.

"I guess my time has come," Lisa said.

"We're not done yet," I said. "We're going to figure out some way to get out of this."

Gavin and Boyland appeared outside the cell door. Gavin held out two pairs of heavy steel shackles in his left hand. In his right hand he trained a semi-automatic pistol on us through the steel bars.

"The Marshal's going to put these around your ankles," Gavin said. "Buddy says to leave your hands free. I told him I didn't think that was a good idea. I said if either of you made any kind of false move I would shoot you."

"What did he say to that?" I asked.

"Shut up," Gavin said, glaring at me. "I don't need much of an excuse to put a hole in you, you meddlin' son-of-a-bitch."

I took the man at his word and watched silently as Boyland secured the shackles around my ankles. The Marshal smelled awful, a disgusting mix of sweat, fat old man b.o., garlic, and stale liquor.

I could not imagine a more bizarre situation. I was a prisoner in Buddy Richardson's house. Gavin Breedlove was mad at me for "meddlin" in his business, which I took to mean investigating his wife's connection with the murder of Russell Fratelli. The two initiatives that I undertook only a month earlier, helping Walton with the Richardson trial, and looking into François Fratelli's brother's death, had merged into one unholy mess, which in turn coalesced with the Justice Department's plan to charge me with a criminal civil rights violation in connection with grand jury selection. Buddy Richardson and the Breedloves, including Senator Chad, were now inextricably intertwined. In the hallowed words of Jimmy Gray, the whole situation was "one gigantic cluster fuck." I did not understand exactly how the three pieces all fit together, but I knew I was getting close. I hoped I lived long enough to find out the answers.

The four of us rode up silently in the elevator. Lisa and I pressed against one side. Breedlove was against the other wall, his gun pointed at my chest. A sneering Boyland Burr stood next to Gavin with his big arms crossed against his chest. Gavin gestured with his pistol when the door opened on the main floor, and we shuffled out into the wide hallway.

"This way," Buddy called out. We followed his voice to the first room off the hall, where he was seated at the head of a long dining room table set for dinner. "You sit over here, Willie Mitchell," Buddy said, "and Lisa, you sit across from him. Cissy will be opposite me at the other end of the table. Gavin, why don't you sit next to Lisa so you can keep a sharp eye on the DA."

"You eat here often?" I asked Boyland when he plopped next to me.

"Shut up," Gavin said.

"Now," Buddy said, "let's be civil."

"Where's Robbie?" Lisa said, anger in her voice.

"He's upstairs watching a DVD in his pajamas," Buddy said. "He ate supper earlier and is worn out from all the fun he had today. He's going to love living out here. I gave him some Benadryl, so he's probably already asleep. And don't worry about waking him, either. From his room you can't hear anything that goes on down here. The Benadryl will keep him knocked out."

"You gave him Benadryl?" Lisa shrieked. "You shouldn't be giving him anything. Especially when you're loaded on that shit you shoot up."

"Calm down, Lisa," Buddy said. "Everything's going to be fine."

Cissy Breedlove walked out of the kitchen holding a tray of steaks in front of her. She placed the tray in front of Buddy. He put a steak on the top plate of a stack of six dinner plates and passed it. Cissy re-emerged from the kitchen with baked potatoes wrapped in aluminum foil and placed one on each of our plates.

"Boyland grilled the steaks," she said with a smile.

It was the most unnatural, lugubrious smile I had ever seen. For the first time, Cissy looked close to her age. Gray roots showed in the part in her hair. Her makeup was uneven, lipstick smeared on her upper lip. When she placed the steak on my plate, I looked into her eyes, which were dilated and glazed. Cissy was loaded, courtesy of Buddy's meth stash—the aged beauty queen as Stepford wife.

"There's butter and sour cream," Cissy said, her eyes not quite focused.

"Open that nice bottle of wine I set out, Boyland," Buddy said.

Boyland pushed away from the table, tripped and fell in his rush to get to the kitchen. He hit the wooden floor hard, shaking everything on the table.

"Well, I'll be," Buddy laughed as Boyland got up. "Be careful, Marshal. This house ain't none too sturdy as it is." He looked around the room then directly at me with a stupid grin. "Kind of wish this big old house would burn down, if you want to know the truth, Willie Mitchell. It ain't built worth a damn and I got plenty of insurance on it. Insurance don't pay if it falls down on its own."

"I'd be glad to sue your contractor for you," I said.

Buddy slapped the table and laughed.

"You a funny man, Mr. D.A."

Boyland returned with the wine, and Buddy told him to serve the ladies first. After pouring Lisa and Cissy a glass, he filled Buddy's and his own. Gavin grunted and shook his head, placing his hand over his wine glass. Boyland walked to me, standing much too close for comfort, enveloping me in his rancid stench. He looked at Buddy for guidance, holding the cheap Merlot over my glass.

"Pour the DA some wine," Buddy said. "Let him enjoy his last meal."

Buddy tossed back his wine, wiped his mouth on his sleeve, reached into his shirt pocket and pulled out another syringe full of liquid. He held it up for Cissy.

"Want a little toot, Sweetie?" he said.

Cissy closed her eyes and shook her head from side to side. Her movement was exaggerated, and poignantly helpless. I was certain she was not a regular user of the drug, but had been injected by Buddy to enhance his enjoyment of Cissy's predicament.

Buddy Richardson—what a vile human being.

CHAPTER SIXTY-ONE

I was certain it was the most macabre dinner party since Ed Wood Jr. dined by himself in Hollywood. Only half of the attendees actually ate anything. No doubt accustomed to cold SpaghettiOs out of a can, Boyland tore into his steak and potato. Gavin ate heartily, and so did I. Even though it may have been my last meal, I was hungry. Lisa pushed her plate away without eating. She glared off and on at her grandfather. Cissy drank her second glass of wine in gulps, but never touched her food. She stared into the mid-distance, loaded to the gills on crank and an undistinguished Merlot. Buddy ate only two bites of steak, and no potato. He spent most of the meal orating loudly, jumping from one uninspiring topic to another, evoking a repugnant sense of redneck *noblesse oblige*. Midway through a rambling, nonsensical discourse on the unconstitutionality of the federal income tax, he paused to remove a pre-loaded syringe from his shirt pocket and inject more crystal meth into a vein in the crook of his arm.

I tried not to be obvious, but I kept glancing at Gavin's semi-automatic pistol on the table next to his plate. It would definitely be a high risk move, but I viewed his pistol as one possible solution to our captivity. Gavin was somber and surly during the dinner, still angry at me. I didn't want to give him an excuse to shoot me. But the path I was on would not have a happy ending, so I decided to shake things up.

"Is that a Baretta?" I asked Gavin, gesturing to the pistol. "Where's your TT-30? Do you still have it?"

"Keep your mouth shut," Gavin said.

"What's a TT-30?" Boyland slurred.

"A Russian semi-automatic pistol," Buddy said, proud to demonstrate his intellect, "used all over Asia in the first half of the 19th Century."

"Robbie Cedars at the State Crime Lab told me a couple of weeks ago," I said, "that Russell Fratelli was killed in the Grove with a TT-30. Shot in the back of the neck. Bullet lodged in his brain." I paused a moment. "You were in Vietnam in the late fifties, Gavin. TT-30s were available all over Southeast Asia in the fifties and sixties."

"That's enough," Gavin said, picking up his pistol and aiming it at my face. "Let me end this now, Buddy."

"Naw," Buddy said, "we havin' too much fun. Ain't we, Cissy?"

I looked at the end of the table. Except for tears running down her cheeks, Cissy seemed paralyzed. Finally she moved, dabbing her eyes with her napkin. In a high-pitched, stressed-out voice that barely escaped her throat, she asked Buddy if he minded if she went to her room.

"Not yet, sweet thing," Buddy said.

Lisa looked across the table at me. She knew what I was doing and decided to help.

"Who was Russell Fratelli?" Lisa asked Buddy.

"Ask Gavin," Buddy said. "Or Cissy."

Lisa turned to Cissy, who was in no shape to comment, then to Gavin, whose face was red, contorted.

"Do you know, Mr. Breedlove?" Lisa asked, playing innocent.

Gavin grabbed his pistol and stood up, stuffing it in his belt. He took Cissy's hand and helped her up. Standing with his wife, Gavin glared at Buddy.

"There's no cause for this," Gavin said.

"Aw, simmer down," Buddy said. "Bring Cissy down here to me."

Gavin walked her slowly to Buddy's end of the table. Buddy pushed out his chair and patted his lap, gesturing for Cissy to sit. Standing there holding Gavin's hand, Cissy was in a daze. She didn't move.

"Come on, baby," Buddy said. "Sit in your big daddy's lap and gimme one of those sweet kisses of yours. Lay some of that good Miss America lovin' on me."

It happened so fast I could hardly believe what I saw. Gavin went for the pistol in his belt but Buddy was quicker. He reached under the table, pulled out a revolver and stuck it against Gavin's chest, firing twice before Gavin could clear his pistol. Gavin grabbed his chest and fell to his knees. Lightning fast, Buddy grabbed the semi-automatic from Gavin's belt and pushed him away. Gavin clung to Buddy's arm rest with one hand for a moment, then crumpled onto the floor. Before I could move, Buddy aimed the revolver at me.

"Don't think about it, Willie Mitchell." He gestured to Boyland. "Marshal, if you ain't too drunk, get a couple of zip ties and for Lisa and the DA then put'em back in the cell downstairs. Leave their feet shackled. Get moving."

Watching his co-worker get killed must have sobered Boyland somewhat. He walked to the kitchen, came back and zip tied our hands behind our backs, then frogmarched Lisa and me to the elevator. Waiting for the door to open, I saw Buddy leading the stupefied former Miss Mississippi toward the master bedroom. She looked down at her dead husband on the floor as she passed.

CHAPTER SIXTY-TWO

Boyland closed the cell door behind us, shaking it to make sure it locked.

"Give me your hands," he said to us.

Lisa and I stepped to the door. Through the steel bars, Boyland removed Lisa's zip tie, then mine.

"You know, Marshal," I said, "I couldn't imagine why after all these years you picked last week to hire someone to haul off those newspapers. Then I figured it out. Buddy put you back on the payroll when he came to town. He gave you a wad of cash, didn't he?"

"So what?" he said, his voice cracking. "Sleep tight."

Boyland turned off the light and rode the elevator upstairs, leaving us in the dark.

"My God," Lisa said. "We're as good as dead."

Lisa was not crying or hysterical. Instead, she was angry. Lisa was one tough woman. I kept waiting for my eyes to adjust to the darkness. Maybe they did, but I didn't notice. No ambient light of any kind reached us. We weren't in a cellar, but the brick structure that housed our cell had the feel of a cellar. French doors provided access from outside to the ground floor, but no hint of light made it to our cell. Pitch black is a good description; so dark it was disorienting.

"Maybe not," I said. "Let's listen, see if we can tell what's going on."

After a few minutes the silence became palpable. It was as if I could actually hear the absence of sound. Then, heavy footsteps above us.

"That's Boyland," I said. "Has to be."

The footsteps concentrated in one spot above us, then faded as they moved away. I heard clomping down the front steps.

"He's removing Breedlove's body," I said. "I wonder where he's taking it?"

"No telling. A million places to bury it out here."

"The good news is the best-trained killer is dead," I said. "That leaves Buddy and the Marshal. But I guess they're still plenty enough to handle us because they've got the guns. And Buddy is quick on the draw."

I thought I heard a woman scream.

"Did you hear that?" I asked Lisa.

"No."

"Probably my imagination."

We listened for any sound that might be a clue to what was in store for us. We heard nothing for what seemed like an eternity.

"Tell me about Russell Fratelli," Lisa said after a while.

I told her what I had learned in the last month.

"Jesus Christ," she said. "Did Buddy have anything to do with it? I mean, he was there in the Grove. And if Breedlove did shoot the boy in the back of the head, why'd he do it?"

"I don't know."

"Did you see Cissy's eyes?" Lisa said. "She's high as a kite."

"That's Buddy's doing. She's no meth head. He's injecting her."

After what might have been another hour of sitting in the metal chair, I began to get sleepy. The huge surge of adrenaline at the dinner table had subsided, leaving me drained. I felt my way to the bunk beds and climbed onto the top one.

"If you hear anything, wake me."

"I don't see how you could possibly sleep," Lisa said.

I closed my eyes. Buddy's deadly quick-draw performance at the dinner table played over and over in my head. I don't know how long I lay there, and I'm not sure I was asleep when I heard it, but the sound of the elevator motor engaging jarred me out of the bunk.

"Where are you?" I whispered to Lisa.

"Here," she said, and I moved toward her voice.

I reached out and felt her back.

"Get ready," I said as the elevator slowly reached ground level. "It's almost here."

"To do what?" she said.

"Hell, I don't know. Just get ready."

We heard the elevator door open. In a few seconds the overhead light came on, blinding us. I heard someone walking toward the cell. Squinting, I recognized the big, smelly form of Boyland Burr. He wasn't alone.

"Stand back from the door," he growled, pointing my own pistol at me.

Cissy Breedlove was next to him, leaning against the steel bars. Lisa and I backed against the wall opposite the door. Boyland stuck the key in the door and opened it. He kept his eyes and the gun on me, grabbed Cissy by the arm and flung her into the cell. I moved to catch her, and kept her from hitting the floor. The Marshal locked the cell door and started walking away.

"Boyland," I said, "where are you going?"

"Mr. Buddy and the boy are in the elevator. We're headed out."

"You can't just leave us in here," Lisa yelled.

"You won't have to stay long," he said.

"What does that mean?" Lisa said.

"Just be grateful your boy is going with us," Boyland said to Lisa. "He'll have a better life than you could give him."

"You fat bastard!" Lisa screamed at Boyland's back.

"Listen," I said to Lisa as I heard the elevator door close.

The motor started moving the elevator. I turned my head to make sure I was actually hearing what I thought I was.

"The elevator is going down," I said. "Is there an underground floor?"

"I don't know," Lisa said.

We listened until the motor stopped. We heard the door open. After a moment it closed below us. We waited in silence, but the motor did not re-engage.

CHAPTER SIXTY-THREE

Cissy sat hard in the metal chair. Lisa tore off a piece of the bunk bed cover and wet it in the metal sink. I stepped back as Lisa cleaned Cissy's face.

Cissy was a wreck. Slumped in the chair, her hair and makeup ruined, the buttons ripped off her silk blouse, she was a far cry from the elegant lady in the slinky black dress and pearls at the St. Jude's benefit a year earlier.

I was sorry she was drug-addled and possibly injured, but I needed information. I was certain we didn't have much time. I patted her cheek with my open hand. Her eyes remained closed. I patted harder. No response. Lisa pushed me aside. She slapped Cissy hard. Cissy groaned. Lisa slapped her again, this time harder. Cissy's eyes opened. She shook her head from side to side and raised her arms in defense. Lisa grabbed Cissy by the shoulders and shook her as hard as she could.

"Stop," Cissy said. "Leave me alone."

"We don't have that luxury," I said, moving Lisa aside. "Listen to me. What did Buddy say they were going to do with us? Where did they go?"

Cissy's head dropped against her chest. Lisa turned on the water in the sink and cupped her hands, then threw the water in Cissy's face.

"What?" Cissy said, sputtering.

"Where are they going?" I said, grabbing Cissy by her shoulders.

"He didn't say," she said, and started crying.

"What are they going to do to us?"

"I don't know," she sobbed. "I don't know."

Lisa rubbed the wet cloth across her face again. Cissy took a deep breath and blinked her eyes. She focused on my face, perhaps recognizing me for the first time in her confused state.

"What are they going to do to us?" I said again.

"I don't know, Willie Mitchell. I would tell you if I did."

I walked away from her to lean against the steel bars.

"How did Robbie look?" Lisa asked, desperation in her voice.

"He's all right," Cissy said. "He doesn't know what's going on. Buddy's not going to hurt him."

I caught a whiff of something. I prayed to God I was wrong. I winded like a dog, my nose in the air. There it was again.

Smoke.

"Smoke," Lisa said. "You smell it?"

"I do," I said. "There's our answer."

I couldn't see the smoke, but it was there. Lisa and I smelled it at the same time. Buddy had started a fire to burn down his house with us in it. I had never felt so helpless. My feet were shackled. We were locked in a cell with brick walls and thick steel bars. I checked the door, trying to rattle the steel lock. Little or no give. It was solid and locked tightly.

"Is that smoke?" Cissy asked, as if she hadn't heard a word we said.

"Yes," I said. "Your boyfriend Buddy's going to burn it down around us. If we don't die of smoke inhalation or get burned to death, the house above us is going to fall on top of us and crush us."

"No," Cissy said, "you're wrong. Buddy wouldn't do that."

I watched Cissy as the smell of smoke grew stronger. With each breath, she became more aware she was wrong about Buddy's intentions. I half-expected her to shriek or cry, but instead, she appeared resigned to her fate. I watched her take a deep breath. With an audible exhale, her entire being seemed to let go of any tension or pain. A sense of peace came over her. I could sense the change.

"Are you all right?" I asked her.

"Yes," she said. "It's finally over."

"What is?" Lisa asked.

"Everything. No more lying; no more deceit. I am so tired of it all."

"Maybe you're satisfied," I said, "but I'm not. If I'm going to die down here in this cell I'd like to know why. I want the whole story."

"Where do you want me to start?"

"Tell me about Russell Fratelli," I said. "You did love him, didn't you?"

The light in the cell began to flicker. Right before it went out, plunging us into total darkness again, I saw one tear course down Cissy's cheek.

"It was the best summer of my life," Cissy said.

CHAPTER SIXTY-FOUR

"I was in love for the first time," Cissy said.

The blackness was absolute. The smell of smoke was growing stronger. I heard Lisa reach her chair and sit. I felt my way over to the bottom bunk.

"I had never met anyone like Russell. He was handsome, funny, with no pretensions. He was nothing like the fraternity boys I had dated in school. Russell was already a man, mature and ready to make something of himself. And he would have, too."

She sobbed. After a moment, she cleared her throat.

"At the end of May, after finals, we partied a lot. I had too much to drink one night, and, well, Russell was my first. It was in his apartment on North 11th. He was so gentle and sweet about it. I stayed for summer school because I knew Russell would be in Oxford working. We spent some wonderful hours in his apartment that summer. It was the first time I felt like a real woman instead of a Barbie doll. I went home after summer school and by mid-September, I realized I was pregnant. My family doctor in Tupelo told me I was about two months along."

"Russell wanted to marry you," I said.

"He begged me, and I wanted to. But I had been in beauty pageants since junior high, working my way up. Most Beautiful in high school, then I began to compete in Miss Mississippi. My senior year at Ole Miss was the year I had been working up to all that time. It was my time. I couldn't get married and have a baby and lose all of that."

"Good God, woman," Lisa said.

"I know. I know. I was shallow and stupid. You don't know how I have regretted my selfish, heartless decision."

"Russell tried to talk you out of an abortion," I said.

"He was a strong Catholic and wanted our baby. He said it would be murder but I didn't care. We argued about it every day when I came back to campus from Tupelo. But my mind was made up. I was going to be Miss America and Russell wasn't going to stop me.

"But then, he did something that changed everything. He said if I didn't marry him right away he was going to tell my parents, his parents, friends at school, everyone."

"What did you do?" I asked.

"I panicked. I had no one I could talk to. Except for Gavin Breedlove. We grew up together in Tupelo. Gavin was two years older and always wanted to date me. We went to the same schools and I liked him as a friend, but that was all. He was in Oxford for summer school and was staying there for fall semester. He was just back from Vietnam.

"I confided in Gavin, and he took my side. Russell told me the Saturday before the riot that on the following Monday he was calling my folks. Gavin had been at the Grove Sunday afternoon, and knew there was going to be trouble that night. He had me call Russell to meet me in the Grove by the bridge. Gavin told me he was going to be there when Russell showed up, and talk him out of calling my parents. Gavin said if Russell didn't agree to back off, Gavin was going to beat the hell out of him, beat some sense into him. Gavin said even if Russell told the cops about the beating, Gavin could deny it and say Russell got in a fight during the riot. Gavin had me make the call from a pay phone."

"You made the call," I said. "Russell showed up and Gavin shot him."

"He was only supposed to beat him up," Cissy said and started to cry. "I didn't know Gavin was going to kill him. I swear I didn't. I didn't know Gavin was like that. I didn't even know Gavin had killed him until Russell's body was found that following Thursday. Gavin just told me he had taken care of it. I thought he had talked Russell into letting it go.

"When I found out on Thursday that Russell had been shot and killed the night of the riot, I didn't believe it. I found Gavin and made him tell me the truth. He admitted he shot him to shut him up. Said he used a special gun he brought back from Vietnam they could never trace back to him. I went crazy, crying and yelling at Gavin. It was then I learned how cold-blooded he was.

"Gavin said he would drive me to Texas to get the abortion. No one would know but us. He said I would get over Russell, and I could be in the pageants like I planned. I said no, I was going to tell the police. Gavin said if I did he would tell them I planned it and tried to get him to do it but he wouldn't kill him for me. He said he would tell the police I must have found someone else to kill Russell, because Gavin wouldn't do it. He said he would tell them about the pregnancy being the motive. He said I could forget about Miss America forever."

"So you went along with Gavin's plan?" I said.

"You went to Houston," Lisa said. "And competed in the beauty contests?"

"He gave me no choice about anything. After the pageants were over, he said I was going to marry him or he'd turn me in for Russell's death."

"You've been married to him all this time?" Lisa said. "Fifty-three years?"

"And I never loved him," Cissy said, and began crying again. "When Chad was born, it made things better. I had Chad to love. And Gavin never mistreated me."

"Other than killing your lover and threatening you with prison," Lisa said. "A solid foundation for a marriage." She paused a moment. "You deserved to be used by Buddy."

The smell of smoke in the cell was getting stronger. In the blackness I could not see the smoke or feel the heat, but I knew it was coming for us. Being at ground level, surrounded by brick and steel, it would take some time to get to us. But, I was sure it would. The three of us would be among the last things to burn in the raised Acadian mansion at High Hope Plantation.

CHAPTER SIXTY-FIVE

"Speaking of being used by Buddy," I said, "how in the world did you and Gavin get tied into Buddy Richardson?" I asked.

"Bad luck," Cissy said. "Buddy saw Gavin that night in the Grove forcing Russell toward the ravine. Buddy had seen Gavin earlier on Sunday and somehow found out who he was. Buddy's got a criminal mind. He put two and two together after Russell's body was found. He knew people from Clarksdale who knew Russell. Then he found out about me, nosed around Tupelo, then conned Gavin into filling in the blanks for him. About the pregnancy, I mean.

"From then on Buddy blackmailed Gavin into doing jobs for him. It started small. He had Gavin help him pistol whip the bar owners in the Delta if Buddy thought they were cheating him on the slot machines. As time went on the jobs got more serious. Gavin would be gone for weeks at times. He paid off some people in Baton Rouge for Buddy on the video poker thing, probably threatened some as well. I'm sure he burned things down, maybe killed people for Buddy."

"When did you and Buddy start your affair?"

"Affair?" Cissy said. "That's not what it was. It was the same thing he did to Gavin. Made him do those things or else he would expose us. After I was elected to the Senate Buddy threatened to tell everyone unless I gave in to him. Gavin had his surgery after the cancer, and in some perverse way, I guess Gavin could live with Buddy having me since Gavin was no longer able. I know it sounds really sick, because it was.

"Buddy got a place in Jackson. I had to meet him whenever he wanted. And do whatever he wanted. It was like being a prisoner. When I retired and we moved to Oxford, Buddy left me alone for a while, then out of the blue he started up again after he got indicted for killing his grandson-in-law."

"No good bastard," Lisa said, and coughed from the smoke, which was getting denser in the cell.

"Buddy had Gavin trash Walton's apartment on the Square during jury selection to shake him up I guess," I said.

"I didn't know about that until afterward," Cissy said. "Gavin told me."

"Why kill James Butler?" I asked. "That makes no sense."

Cissy tried to answer but her voice broke. She began crying again.

"That was all my fault. James had always liked me when we were in school. When I got into politics he helped in my campaigns, used his newspaper connections. After you came to the house the first time, I called James to tell him you were trying to link me with Russell's death."

"That's why he said it wasn't you with Russell in the photograph," I said.

"He was protecting me. He even took the original from the archives after you saw it."

"Who stole the six pictures of Buddy at the riot?" I asked.

"James took those, too."

"Why?"

"I mentioned to Buddy what you were doing and he asked me to have James remove his pictures, too. Buddy is paranoid about being photographed. He doesn't want anyone having his picture."

"Pillow talk," Lisa said, an edge in her voice.

"You still haven't told me who killed James Butler," I said.

"Gavin."

"Why?"

"It's obvious, Willie Mitchell," Lisa said. "She slept with Butler, too."

"No," I said.

A barely audible whimper floated from the darkness in Cissy's direction.

"Breedlove killed James Butler because he was sleeping with his wife," Lisa said. "Cissy is no better than Buddy."

Lisa and I were silent in the darkness as we considered the monumentally perverse behavior of Cissy Summers Breedlove.

"I'm sorry," Cissy whispered and began to sob again.

After a moment I asked Cissy why her husband picked the road to my duck camp as the venue for the murder of James Butler. I had figured out the answer, but I wanted to hear Cissy say it.

"Gavin thought it would get him in good with Buddy. Scare you and Walton into backing down in the case against Buddy."

"And then you asked your son to put pressure on the Justice Department to come after me when I started looking into Russell's death."

"Chad did that for me, but he doesn't know anything about any of this. I told him it was political. At that point I would have done anything to stop you. I had kept the secret for over half a century. But when you talked to me about it the first time, I had this feeling it was all going to come out."

After a delayed reaction, it hit me like a ton of bricks. I was partly responsible for James Butler's death. If I hadn't talked to Cissy Breedlove, she wouldn't have slept with Butler to get his help in the cover-up. If Cissy hadn't slept with Butler, he'd be alive. After putting up with Buddy bedding Cissy all those years, I guess finding out about James Butler doing the same sent Gavin over the edge. It was the final straw.

Lisa and I lay face down on the floor to breathe what little clean air remained. Cissy said she didn't care if she died. I dragged her out of the chair and made sure she was face down on the concrete.

My nose and throat burned from the smoke. I began to feel heat on my back radiating from the ceiling.

I heard Lisa praying between coughs. Cissy lay between us in silence. She was ready to die, but Lisa and I weren't. I felt something shake the foundation, as if the roof and upstairs had fallen onto the main floor. It would be only a matter of time before the main floor joists burned through and what was left of the house would fall on top of us. I had prosecuted several arson deaths. In their reports, the coroners would invariably say that the victims suffocated to death before their bodies were burned in the fire. I hoped what they said was true.

I reverted to my Catholic upbringing. I said the Act of Contrition, shocked that I remembered it word for word. I said prayers to God in my own words, asking him to forgive my sins, receive my soul, care for Susan and my boys.

At the end, I struggled mightily to get oxygen in my lungs. Lisa coughed and wheezed, fighting for air. Cissy was quiet. I inched closer to her, found her face. She had already quit breathing.

The dark force Cheryl Diamond saw coming for me in the Grove had overtaken me.

I felt myself losing consciousness. I opened my eyes one last time. They burned like hell. It was still pitch black in the cell.

As dark as I imagined my coffin would be.

CHAPTER SIXTY-SIX

My eyes continued to burn when I opened them again. I saw a billion stars above me. I thought I might be in the next world until I started coughing into the plastic oxygen mask covering my nose and mouth. There are no oxygen masks in heaven.

Jimmy Gray's big face appeared over me, grinning.

"Quit lollygagging," he said. "We got work to do."

I coughed harder, turned on my side, ripped off the mask and threw up.

"Lisa?" I croaked.

"She's up and walking around. That girl's tough. She's no pansy like you." He paused a moment. "Cissy didn't make it."

On my back again, Lee Jones and Walton came into view.

"That was close," the Sheriff said.

I tried to get my bearings. A hundred yards away, the big house continued to burn. I was on a stretcher of some kind.

"Jimmy Gray got part of your voice message," Walton said. "It stopped halfway through. He called Lee, who got the MBI involved. We retraced your route and tried to figure out what happened. By the time the deputies and the MBI got here, the roof had already fallen in."

"How'd you find us?"

"Jimmy and Lee had the deputies bust in those French doors and look around the ground floor, because it was the only part of the house left where you might still be alive. The MBI had an armored vehicle with a huge winch they used to pull the cell door down."

"We went to a lot of trouble to save your skinny ass," Jimmy Gray said.

I stood up and hugged my 312 pound friend.

"I'm going to try to be nice to you from now on," I said to Jimmy, and hugged Lee and Walton. "You don't know how great it is to see you guys."

"Lisa already gave us the play-by-play," Lee said. "We've got an APB out for Buddy and Boyland, an Amber Alert for Robbie."

"The cell was on the ground floor. The elevator took Buddy, Boyland, and the boy down to the next level," I said. "Any idea what's down there?"

"As soon as we have enough daylight we're going to use some of Buddy's equipment to dig out behind the house," Lee said.

I felt a hand on my arm and turned to see Lisa, who wrapped her arms around me.

"Way to hang tough," I said.

"I've always been a badass," she said. "I'm going to find Robbie."

"You'll have plenty of help," I said.

By late-morning High Hope was a beehive of activity. MBI had scores of investigators and Highway Patrol officers combing the place. The State Crime Lab brought two vans and a half-dozen technicians. The Dundee County coroner was on hand, as was the Honorable Sheriff Cheatwood with three deputies. Cheatwood and his men were onlookers, watching the law enforcement activity from a distance and spitting tobacco juice, ceding the investigation to the state people.

A Highway Patrolman who knew how to operate heavy equipment used Buddy's bulldozer to uncover a concrete tunnel leading from under the house to an opening 150 feet away.

Several hundred yards from me, a Highway Patrol checkpoint controlled access to High Hope. I watched the officers stop and question the driver of a white crossover vehicle, then wave it through. As it neared the top of the hill where I stood with Jimmy, Lee, and Walton, I realized it was Susan's Lexus.

Thirty minutes later, Susan and I left for Oxford. Riding in the passenger seat, in between catnaps, I told Susan the entire sordid story. We pulled into our garage around two p.m. I showered and got in bed, exhausted.

Susan woke me up at dinner time and fed me. I got back into bed and read two paragraphs of *Blood Meridian* before the book hit me in the face. I turned off my bedside lamp and slept.

CHAPTER SIXTY-SEVEN

I was drinking my second cup of Caffé Verona in front of the condo when Sheriff Lee Jones called me on our land line. I had just spoken to the Kowalskis, the older couple walking my favorite Chinese Pug, J. Edgar, on the sidewalk. It was Saturday morning and University Avenue was quiet.

"Louisiana State Police found Boyland Burr's body floating in Lake Pontchartrain next to the I-10 bridge just east of the La Place exit," Lee said. "They said some fisherman called it in, saying it looked like a beached whale."

I winced at the mental image of Boyland's bloated white mass.

"I guess Buddy no longer needed the Marshal's services," I said.

"They're concentrating the search for Buddy and the boy on the New Orleans area."

"Keep me posted," I said.

I placed the portable kitchen phone on the wrought iron table, walked inside to heat my coffee in the microwave, and resumed my University Avenue watch on the front patio. I stopped bouncing in the new chair long enough to sip my coffee, and thought about the miserable life and times of Boyland Burr.

"How'd you get my land line number?" I asked Robbie Cedars when I answered the portable phone again.

"You're in the book," he said. "Something must be wrong with your cell phone. You ought to get it checked."

I pictured my phone nestled in the mud next to my deceased F-150 in the borrow pit near Cypress Bend Park.

"The reason I'm calling," Robbie said, "I've got the ballistics done. I have the answer to your question."

"What did you find out?"

"The .38 caliber Chief's Special that was used to kill James Butler on the road to your duck camp did not fire the bullet that killed Paul Leslie Guihard on September 30, 1962."

"Damn," I said. "You sure?"

"No question. Very different lands and grooves. But it was a nice theory."

"Anyway, I'm glad the bullet that killed Guihard is still available in your evidence vault. Maybe someday...."

"Don't count on it," Robbie said.

It would have provided perfect symmetry to have learned that photo-phobic Buddy Richardson had shot the British reporter working for the French news agency after Guihard unwittingly took Buddy's picture that night in the Grove. I theorized that Buddy had given the same Chief's Special to Gavin Breedlove to use in the execution of James Butler. But, I guess it was too much to ask from the gods of serendipity. At least it would have provided some sort of bizarre motive for the thirty-year-old reporter's senseless, tragic death that night on the Ole Miss campus. He was executed, just like James Butler, just like Russell Fratelli. I just knew the bullets would match. But I was wrong.

I would have also loved to have reported that I joined in the massive manhunt in New Orleans, and through deft detective work, I single-handedly found Buddy Richardson in his historic *pied à terre* in the French Quarter. I notified the authorities and the entire Quarter was cordoned off. A three-day standoff finally ended with an agreed-upon quick-draw gunfight on Bourbon Street where I outdrew Buddy and shot him down like the mad dog he was. Little Robbie ran and jumped into Lisa's arms after she broke away from the NOPD officers holding her back.

But that's not what happened.

Being the well-prepared, shrewd gangster that he was, Buddy Richardson had a Plan B in case he had to flee after he had me kidnapped and held in the cell at High Hope. The morning before I was taken at Cedar Bend Park by Boyland and Gavin, Buddy had picked up a new batch of liquid crystal meth from the young entrepreneur who had previously provided Buddy with preemo crank. This was the same young businessman who had been beaten nearly to death by Buddy's goons after the young man objected to Buddy changing the terms of their deal, and whose young girl friend had been subjected by Buddy to a night of Viagra and meth-fueled sexual humiliation and beatings.

In retribution for Buddy's rudeness, the young chemist mixed in more than enough battery acid to render Buddy's going away batch of methamphetamine highly poisonous. Buddy checked into the Hilton New Orleans Riverside with Robbie, using a credit card and identification he had obtained using his dead grandson-in-law Carl Sanders's identity. Perhaps to reward himself after a successful escape, he injected himself to celebrate. The toxic meth killed him in his lovely room overlooking the Mississippi River.

Proving that resourcefulness ran in the Richardson family, on finding his great-grandfather stone cold dead with a needle in his arm, six-year-old Robbie used Buddy's cell phone to call his mother. Within twenty minutes the NOPD had secured the hotel room. They kept the sole heir to Buddy's land and fortune, six-year-old Robert Edward Lee Bailey, safe and sound until Lisa, who was already in the New Orleans area to aid in the search for her son, arrived to take him back to the home in Yaloquena County they shared with her late husband Carl.

Buddy Richardson's life-long reign of terror was finally over.

CHAPTER SIXTY-EIGHT

I had coffee with François Fratelli the following Monday morning at High Point on North Lamar. I told him the facts surrounding his brother's death. François sipped his coffee, never reacting to any detail. I asked him if he wanted the media to know about Cissy Summers Breedlove's carrying Russell's child, and Gavin's murdering Russell to keep it quiet.

The press and television coverage had been focused only on Buddy Richardson, attributing the bombing death of Metzger and the "odd couple" deputies, Smitty and Delroy, to Buddy's attempt to short-circuit the case against him for the contract murder of his grandson-in-law, Carl Sanders. A rumored love triangle involving Cissy, Gavin, and Buddy was the press's explanation for the Breedloves' presence at High Hope the night it burned. The death of Russell Fratelli fifty-three years earlier was not mentioned.

"Nah," François said. "No reason to. It'll dredge up the Ole Miss riot and remind people of the way things used to be in the South. Mississippi's come a long way. Those old days are gone forever."

He thanked me for solving the mystery of Russell's death and stood up to leave the coffee shop.

"You playing today?" he asked.

"Course is closed," I said.

"That won't stop me. I'll be out there. I have a key to the cart shed. I got a good report from the oncologist last week. I'm playing every day from here on out."

"Good for you," I said. "I'll be out there Wednesday."

"Bring plenty of money," François said. "I've been hitting the ball better."

I watched him shuffle off, out the door. I sipped what remained of my coffee and looked around. The place was busy. I didn't know anyone there.

Later that week, I got a call from Patrick Dunwoody IV, Senator Skeeter Sumrall, and my son Scott. They were on a speaker phone on the other end.

"We got some good news for you, Willie Mitchell," Skeeter said.

"I could use some," I said.

"I'll let the Assistant Attorney General tell you," Skeeter said.

"Justice Department has closed its case against you relating to the grand jury foreman selection process in Yaloquena County," Dunwoody said. "It's over."

"That *is* good news," I said. "What happened?"

"We convened a special meeting in our offices in D.C. yesterday," Dunwoody said, "and some Yaloquena citizens gave Mr. Leopold Whitman and the Justice Department prosecutors he had working on your case some information they weren't aware of."

"Who were these citizens?" I said.

"Sheriff Lee Jones and Judge Zelda Williams," my son Scott said, "along with Mayor Everett Johnson, Congresswoman Rose Jackson, and the person who put it all together and requested the meeting."

"Who was that?" I asked.

"Eleanor Bernstein," Scott said.

I tried to speak but my throat closed. They must have heard me trying to gather myself on the other end of the call. Scott said he would call Susan and me later to give us more details.

Well, there it is. My story of the fifty-three-year-old homicide on the campus of Ole Miss the night of September 30, 1962. I've told you exactly how the investigation unfolded. I left out only the boring stuff.

You might think this story is gruesome, a tale of humanity at its worst. There's that element, for sure. But I like to think of it as a story about the power of love, too. Different kinds of love. Destructive, like Gavin's obsessive love for Cissy and Buddy's infatuation with Robbie, his only male heir. And redemptive, exhilarating love—the love of Russell Fratelli for Cissy Breedlove; Lisa's powerful maternal love for Robbie; the love Susan and I share; my love for Jimmy Gray, the brother I never had.

And by the way, if you tell this story to someone who lives in another part of this great country, be sure to elaborate on François' comments about Mississippi. Susan and I have traveled enough to realize, much to our disappointment, that people in this country associate Mississippi with segregation, opposition to civil rights, lynchings, and the bloody fight to keep James Meredith out of Ole Miss.

It's disheartening to me, because most of the southern states have pasts just as shameful as ours, but people don't come down on those states as hard as they do Mississippi. The media and some popular writers would have you believe there's a Klukker lynch mob behind every tree in Mississippi. I guess that perception sells papers and books. But it's not true.

When Susan and I travel, we can sense people shudder internally when we say we're from Mississippi. We tell them Mississippians are the kindest, most generous people in the U.S. and the dark days of our racial history are many, many decades in the past. We're not perfect in our race relations, but neither is any other state.

My complaint about this misperception will probably fall on a lot of deaf ears, but I wanted to get it off my chest.

I've enjoyed visiting with you, telling you this story. Let's stay in touch.

Acknowledgements:

Much thanks to readers and sounding boards: Mike Hourin, Dickie Scruggs, Angelita Morris, June Goza, Dave Curry, Archie Manning, Kaye Bryant, and Cattie Case.

Thanks to David Fite for urging the return of Willie Mitchell; to Curtis Wilkie for his valuable store of first-hand knowledge of the events of 1962; to Sam Haskell for his efforts on my behalf; and to Christine Maynard, one of the most creative minds I know.

Author Biography

Michael Henry graduated from Tulane University and University of Virginia Law School. MURDER in THE GROVE is his eighth novel. He currently resides and writes in Oxford, Mississippi.

Made in the USA
San Bernardino, CA
18 March 2016